Siobhán MacDonald was bor̶ ̶ ̶ ̶ ̶ ̶ ̶ ̶ of Ireland. She was raised in Cork where ̶ ̶ ̶ ̶ ̶ ̶ ̶ te, and in Limerick where she ̶ ̶ ̶ ̶ ̶ ̶ ing a writer.

Siobhán studied engineering at National University of Ireland, Galway, and had a successful career writing for the technology sector in Scotland and the south of France before returning to Ireland.

Growing up in a large family, there was a premium attached to being able to spin a good yarn. Siobhán published her first novel, *Twisted River*, in 2016. She followed this up with her second novel, *The Blue Pool. Twisted River* won an AudioFile Earphones award in 2016 and *The Blue Pool* has been a top ten bestseller in the Kindle charts. *Guilty* was her first novel for Constable, Little, Brown. *The Bride Collector* is her second.

Siobhán is married with two sons and lives in Limerick.

Instagram: siobhan.m.macdonald

Facebook: Siobhan MacDonald

Twitter: @SiobhanMMacD

Also by Siobhán MacDonald

Twisted River
The Blue Pool
Guilty

THE
BRIDE
COLLECTOR

SIOBHÁN
MACDONALD

CONSTABLE

CONSTABLE

First published in Great Britain in 2021 by Constable

1 3 5 7 9 10 8 6 4 2

A CIP catalogue record for this book is
available from the British Library.

ISBN: 978-1-47213-415-8

Typeset in Caslon Pro by SX Composing DTP, Rayleigh, Essex, SS6 7EF
Printed and bound in Great Britain by Clays Ltd, Elcograf S.p.A.

Papers used by Constable are from well-managed forests
and other responsible sources.

Constable
An imprint of
Little, Brown Book Group
Carmelite House
50 Victoria Embankment
London EC4Y 0DZ

An Hachette UK Company
www.hachette.co.uk

www.littlebrown.co.uk

For Neil, Jamie and Alasdair.
And for my brothers and sisters, always on my storyboard.

1

Myrtle Crescent, 21 January

Isolde Hanly lay fast asleep in her large double bed in Myrtle Crescent. Moonlight seeped through the landing window, down the dark stairs and across the empty hallway. She was not the only person in the house.

Halfway up the staircase was a hooded figure, creeping up the steps. Someone dressed in black. On the landing, the figure paused and listened at the bedroom door.

The handle turned, the door opened and the figure stood in the doorway. *Tick tock. Tick tock.* It was loud for a bedside clock. Its hands glowed a sickly green in the dark.

The hooded figure slipped inside and took a step, a floorboard creaked, a few steps more. A shaft of light came through a gap in the curtains. The figure moved to peer outside. The street was still and empty. The figure set a backpack down.

Clothes lay in puddles over the floor, more were over the back of a chair. Among them was a bolero cardigan and a dressing gown. The intruder lifted the gown, pressed it against a cheek and inhaled the fragrance in the folds.

The intruder sat down, produced a flashlight and a notebook, and directed the flashlight from the notebook to the woman in the bed. The beam of light went up and down, over her bare arms, her face. Down and up. It was a time to savour, a precious time. The intruder set aside the notebook and the flashlight, and stroked the dressing gown as if it were a cat.

It was time.

The intruder made towards the woman. Her bedclothes rose and fell. In sleep her breath was shallow, her hair spread out, knotted and uncombed across the pillow. A cushion was held high above her head. It made no noise as it cut through the air, coming down over her face. She made moaning sounds. She flailed. She kicked. Her assailant whispered:

'*Something old, something new, something—*'

Isolde's hands shot out, blindly seeking her assailant. They locked on to her assailant's wrists like claws.

'*Something old, something new,*' the whispering continued, '*something borrowed, something blue.*'

Care was needed. That perfect nose, those lovely cheekbones.

'*Ssshhh. Ssshh now.*'

Isolde's moans became a whimper. Her grip released, her fingers loosened. Drained of life, her hands surrendered, slipping to the sides.

Five seconds.

Eight seconds.

Ten.

The killer strained to hear. There was nothing in the silence, not a stirring, not a sigh. Nothing in the room but the ticking of the clock. Lifting the cushion, the killer blinked and leaned over. It was done. It had taken a bare two minutes.

The dead woman looked strangely surprised, her mouth and eyes wide open. *Tick tock* went the bedside clock. The killer stood, thinking. *Tick tock, tick tock.* Closing Isolde's mouth and eyes, the killer sank to kneeling at the bedside.

A suitcase was dragged out and opened. The layers of white tissue made a rustling noise as they were peeled apart. The killer removed a dress, draped it over the chair and traced a fingertip over the satin buttons. It was a garment to be admired, a garment to be caressed. Closing the gap in the curtains, the killer switched on a bedside lamp.

A dull light was cast on to the high-ceilinged room as a low-energy bulb warmed up. A cobweb dangled from a cornice. A number of paperbacks sat on a bedside locker, along with a magazine, a hairbrush, hand cream and a small brown pill container. The killer cleared a space and set out the contents of the backpack.

First the nightdress.

Unsheathing a pair of scissors, the killer cut a line from the hem to the neck. The body of Isolde Hanly was levered on to one side, then the other, and the nightdress was pulled free.

Next the bridal dress.

The long white garment had lots of buttons. One, two, three unfastened. Four unfastened.

Wait.

The killer edged towards the window. Down in the street, a man dragged a wheelie bin to the kerb.

The killer returned to work. The dress was ruched and the dead woman's feet put through, then the dress was tugged up over her thighs, her hips, as far as her neck. Turning Isolde face down, each of the buttons was refastened. The task was slow and painstaking and when complete it was disappointing. She'd lost weight. Taking a pin, the loose folds were grabbed in a fist, gathered at the waist, tightened and secured in place, then the body was rolled on to its back once again.

Hold-up stockings – something new. Expensive too. Her legs were oddly heavy. Inside the suitcase was a box, and inside that box was a pair of shoes. White, size five, with small white bows. They slipped on nicely over Isolde's feet. The killer settled the dress by straightening the underskirt, allowing the lace to sit smoothly on the top.

Time for hair and make-up. Taking the brush from the bedside locker, the killer pulled it through the tangles and arranged the hair in sections. Each section was rolled with a Velcro and finished off with a spritz of hairspray.

Eyebrows. The strays were tweezed.

Complexion. A primer first. Apricot, to neutralise dark circles. It was spread evenly over the dead woman's forehead, over her nose, her cheeks and under her eyes and chin. A dewy foundation followed. A mid-brown pencil defined the brows.

Lipstick. Pink, perhaps. Something tasteful. Nothing garish. A slick on top, a slick on the bottom.

A touch of blusher? Maybe not. Slightly clown-like, that wouldn't do. A dusting of powder it would be.

The make-up kit was slipped back into the backpack, the Velcro rollers too. 'Clean as you go,' said the killer, arranging the dead woman's hair across the pillow.

A drawer in the bedside locker revealed a small velvet ring box. A bit of coaxing and the ring slipped on.

Time for flowers. The corpse's cooling fingers were wrapped around a blue, dried posy from the bottom of the suitcase. Berried viburnum, eryngium and freesia.

The killer checked the notebook. Something borrowed. *The Complete Poems of John Keats*, on loan from the library. The book was opened at 'Ode to a Nightingale' and set face-down over the dead woman's midriff.

It was done. She was centre stage and she was beautiful.

The killer listened.

There was rumbling . . . a wheelie bin, like before. Tomorrow was bin day in Myrtle Crescent.

The killer stooped.

Wait.

No kiss.

No DNA.

It was time to say goodbye to Isolde. Time to leave her private chamber, to exit by the back door, over the wall and into the laneway beyond. The killer picked up the butchered nightdress, gathered the kit and switched off the lamp.

House lights down.

All was quiet.

The man of the house would be back soon.

He'd find her.

2

7 March

'I'm not imagining things!'

'I think you are, Marina. Admit it. You've been looking over your shoulder all night long checking for weirdos.'

'You would too . . . if you were m-me,' the woman slurred. 'I'm telling you that guy was gawping straight at me. OK, I've had some cocktails but I'm not stupid, I'm not totally paranoid. It's fine for you two – neither of you is getting married.'

Marina's friend stuck out her lip. 'Three times a bridesmaid, never a bride.' In her long black gloves and a bunny-girl headband, she clutched on to a pink, inflatable willy. Ellie itched to burst it.

She'd deliberated about picking the women up outside McSweeny's in the dank, dark night. Learner Bride had been tottering about in stiletto heels and wasn't exactly the blushing bride, despite the 'Learner' plate around her neck. Her two friends were equally intoxicated. Ellie was determined to drop them off before any of them threw up. She didn't fancy cleaning vomit from the inside of her new black Škoda.

Ellie loathed hen parties with a passion. She couldn't see the point. Gaggles of vodka-fuelled women dressed up as tarts (although it was getting harder to tell these days), traipsing around the town with their stupid, blow-up willies.

The council frowned on hens and stags. Not the image they wanted for the heritage town of Kylebeggan, they said. And proper order too. Not that Ellie had one scintilla of fondness for the council. Not after all the hassle they gave her in applying for her taxi licence. That said, hens and stags were the devil's work. Worse than New Year's Eve. Tacky, crass and unnecessary. But she couldn't afford to be too sniffy. This was her new life now.

'We get that you're freaked, Marina,' slurred the friend with flashing willy earrings. 'I didn't notice anyone in McSweeny's pub gawking at you. I swear—'

'Of course you didn't, Rose. You were busy making doe eyes at those Neanderthals. I thought you were supposed to be looking out for me.'

'I am,' she protested. 'We are.'

'Oh, please come, Marina. Pleeease . . .' Three-Times-a-Bridesmaid rowed in. 'Everyone will be at Godiva's. It's only eleven. The night's just started. It's way too early to go home, on your hen night too.

'Jen's right,' Willy Ears agreed. 'You can show off all your *Strictly* moves.'

'No.' Learner Bride was firm. 'I didn't want to go out in the first place. I'm feeling a tad too old for all this lark. And now I'm going home.'

Ellie glanced in the rear-view mirror. Learner Bride was gnawing at the side of a thumbnail.

'That weirdo played it twice. "I can't take my eyes off of you." *Twice* on the jukebox. All the while he's looking at me, all drool and crazy-eyed.'

With a giggle, Three-Times-a-Bridesmaid broke into a rendition of the offending song.

'Not funny,' snapped Learner Bride. 'I don't want to end up like that poor woman over in Myrtle Crescent back in January, or like Imelda Gannon, laid out like an altar above in her bed. I *knew* Imelda. We used to be in the same German class in school.'

'We know that, Marina,' soothed Three-Times-a-Bridesmaid. 'Why not try to forget all that for just one night?'

'A tall order with that lot out there, trawling around for stories.'

As they drove past Brosnan's pub, a guy poked a microphone into a party of women sucking on cigarettes, hugging themselves and shivering. Another wild-haired man hoisted a camera on to his shoulder.

'It's hard for me as well, remember.' Three-Times-a-Bridesmaid was subdued. 'I was to be Imelda's bridesmaid too.'

For the first time since she'd picked the women up, all three of Ellie's passengers fell mercifully silent. The taxi stopped at a red light, and the only sound was the clicking of the indicator. Checking the mirror, Ellie observed Marina look over her shoulder to the rear windscreen.

'Maybe . . . maybe what happened was a freaky coincidence,' Willy Ears piped up.

'*Two* women found dead in their homes within *two* months, laid out on their beds in their bridal gowns?' Learner Bride was scathing. 'Coincidence? *I* don't think so. And neither does the state pathologist.'

'How do you know?' Three-Times-a-Bridesmaid said sharply. Ellie's ears pricked up.

'Some buddies in the force, down at the district court last week.'

'My brother's pal is a detective in Coleman Street,' Willy Ears joined in. 'He told Dara at football training that he couldn't go into any d-details like' – she hiccupped – 'but according to the detective, there were similarities between the two cases. Big similarities.'

'You don't say?' Learner Bride was quick. 'Two women laid out in their wedding dresses and a detective says that there are similarities? No shit, Sherlock.'

Unperturbed, Willy Ears continued. 'I think the similarities go beyond the dresses. The big guns are down all the way from Dublin to help the gardaí in Kylebeggan. The Dublin guys are calling the killer "The Bride Collector".'

'Fuck's sake,' wailed Learner Bride. 'And that's supposed to make me feel any better?'

'Right. Sorry, Mar. But listen, the guy is bound to be gone by now. They suspect it could have been a tourist. You know, maybe someone passing through. They're going through the guest list at Shanaglish, and all the other hotels and guesthouses too.'

This was news to Ellie. Shanaglish Mountain Lodge was a resort hotel built adjacent to monastic ruins, with a golf course designed around a spring-fed lake. According to guests she'd dropped there, the course was considered one of the more challenging ones in Kerry, with its narrow fairways, long grass and tricky greens.

Marina snorted. 'You're telling me the geniuses at Coleman Street reckon some tourist played a snappy nine holes, then nipped out to kill a bride or two while he was passing through? I hardly think so.'

Ellie cut in. 'I take it you're giving Godiva's a miss tonight, ladies?' she asked over her shoulder.

'Yes.' Marina was firm. 'Straight to Arbutus Road, please. Number nine.'

'Right you are.'

Wise girl, heading home.

When Ellie reached the tourist office, she took a left and

proceeded up Barrack Hill, heading for the tree-lined suburb of Arbutus Road. She was chuffed she didn't need the sat nav. As the months went by, she was becoming even more familiar with the Kerry town and surrounding area that was home to 19,000 residents or thereabouts.

A blue flashing light appeared over the brow of the hill. It barrelled towards them. The garda car was closely followed by an ambulance. Neither vehicle sounded a siren. Ellie sensed heads turning in the rear of her taxi, tracking the speeding vehicles as they went by.

'I wonder what that's about?' Learner Bride said with a wobble.

'Listen, Mar, if you're that freaked out, you could always call the wedding off,' Three-Times-a-Bridesmaid suggested.

'Jen, are you completely mad? My dress cost a whole month's salary. It's hanging up ready to go. Dunseally Castle is paid for. Anyway, I couldn't do that to Dylan.'

'Ah . . . the future Mrs Coyle.' Willy Ears gave something between a snort and a snigger.

'What's so funny, Rose?'

'It's nothing. Nothing really . . .'

'Clearly something is causing you amusement. Go on then, tell us.' Marina paused. 'Oh God, it's not that stupid Marina Coyle thing again, is it? I thought you were done laughing at that.'

'If you're cool being named after a contraceptive—' Rose collapsed into giggles.

'You should keep your own name, Marina.' Jen was indignant. 'Why are you going all *Handmaid's Tale*? Why should you change? You're a qualified solicitor in your own right.'

Learner Bride was a solicitor, was she? Ellie wondered what she specialised in. And, more importantly, how much she charged.

'Look, girls, we've already discussed the whole surname thing. It's what Dylan wants. I've already agreed. Can we *not* talk about it any more, please?'

Imagine that. An educated woman.

When Ellie checked the mirror again, she noticed that Marina was gripping the neck of her faux-fur jacket, white faced. Despite the woman's friends persisting in poking her with the silly, pink inflatable for the remainder of the journey, Marina didn't laugh. Not once.

Ellie made it to Arbutus Road as quickly as she could, but she was careful not to break any speed limits. It was darker now, the moon behind the clouds. Out on the road, bare-branched trees cast shadows in the streetlight. As she pulled up outside number 9, she cast her eyes about. Very nice. Very nice indeed. Whatever Marina's future surname, she'd done well for herself.

The mid-terrace Edwardian house had a long front garden with a path winding through various shrubs. With a house like that, Learner Bride would know how to charge. An elegant white light was visible through the fanlight above the door. It bounced off the crystal beads of a large chandelier. This home was several notches above ones that Ellie had called to earlier in the night. Both sides of number 9 were in darkness. Across the street the small private nursery school lay in darkness. Now, Arbutus Road wasn't Pottershill by any stretch, but it was respectable nonetheless, like most of Kylebeggan.

The town boasted a wealth of amenities and breath-taking scenery. So said the Kerry tourist guides. The Black Pins loomed over the town, protecting it from the worst of the weather, guarding its secrets. The sandstone and siltstone mountain range included some of the highest peaks and sharpest ridges in Ireland. Beyond the mountains with their deep gullies and sharp arêtes, and further west, crashed the waves of the wild Atlantic ocean.

Locals insisted Kylebeggan had a microclimate. Ellie enjoyed the area best in late spring when it exploded with rhododendrons. Later, in the autumn, it blazed with red and golden leaves. Little wonder brochures named Kylebeggan 'A jewel in the Garden Trails of Ireland'.

The town had a horse track, two championship golf courses and no fewer than three luxury hotels to cater for the Ring of Kerry tourists. Civil servants and the medical fraternity held conferences in Kylebeggan. With little to blight the landscape, retirees on generous pensions enjoyed the bowling greens, the golf and flat walks around the shores of Lough Avulla. Well served by hotels and country houses, the town was a popular venue for weddings. And for those whose pockets ran deep, the ancestral home of the Earls of Dunseally could be hired.

Any unpleasant aspects of the town's past were hidden or glossed over. Lisquinna Lodge, the notorious former industrial school for boys, was now a grade A hostel, earning it a place in the *Lonely Planet* guide. There was no mention of any vicious beatings meted out or the dark truths that lay within its walls. Apart from one or two run-down housing estates like Lowertown, everyone agreed that Kylebeggan was a wonderful place to live. Or they had, until now.

'Are you getting out, ladies?'

The three women looked at one another. They seemed uncertain.

'You two want to go on to Godiva's. I know you do,' said Marina. 'I'm sorry to spoil your night. I just can't relax and I realise I've been sarcastic and irritable, and I sincerely apologise. Go, go on . . . don't feel you have to stay with me.'

'You're sure?' Rose sounded doubtful.

'I'm certain. One of you come in with me first so I can check the place? Dylan's away on the stag, remember.'

'I'll come.' Three-Times-a-Bridesmaid had already opened her door. 'I won't be long.' She checked with Ellie. 'Then onwards to Godiva's, yeah?'

'Yes, madam.'

None of this 'love' or 'pet' business for Ellie.

She watched as the two tipsy women tottered their way to the front gate, flung it open, burst out laughing and sashayed their way through shrubbery up the path to the door.

'They've gone in.' Willy Ears' face was pressed against the window.

Ellie checked the dashboard. It was 23:16 p.m.

She sat back and waited.

3

'What do you make of it all?' Rose leaned towards her. 'Those poor women, I mean?'

'It's horrendous,' said Ellie.

She could hardly confess the shocking events were yielding unexpected fruit. Despite the increased garda presence on the streets, the women of Kylebeggan were loath to walk at night with a killer on the prowl. Ellie's takings were up five-fold on the month before.

'I didn't want to say anything in front of Marina,' Rose's voice dropped to a whisper, 'but my brother's pal, the lad that's the detective – he was saying there's talk in Coleman Street of some taxi driver called Joseph Liston. Have you come across him?'

Ellie stiffened. 'I can't help you there, I'm afraid.' She liked to keep to herself.

'No?' Rose sounded disappointed. 'The story is that he used to drive a taxi or a minibus back in the day . . . popular service with women, by all accounts.' She hiccupped. 'But then a couple of local women were attacked. They're saying he could be back on the scene.'

Ellie checked the central locking. 'As I say, I've never heard of him.'

'It's all *sooo* spooky. Marina isn't herself at all these days. She's really edgy about everything.' Rose shuddered, turning her attention to the house. 'Look, they're doing the shutters.'

One by one, the lights went on and off in each of the rooms as the women inside moved through the house.

'Marina's the first of the three of us to get married. My mother says I'll be left on the shelf.' Rose sounded wistful. 'Marina was the first of us to move away. Work abroad. Get a car. A boyfriend. A fancy house.' She sighed. 'I feel like I've worked for ever in the tourist office but I still can't imagine even affording a place of my own. Me and Jen are only trotting along behind.'

'Is that so?'

Ellie did her best to sound polite. It hadn't taken her long to grasp that there was a social contract between a driver and a fare. She was obliged to listen to all manner of disclosure and indiscretions. She often thought of herself as a confessional box on wheels.

Passengers would solicit her advice and seek her absolution. 'Three Our Fathers and one Hail Mary,' she once flippantly remarked to a departing fare when she was new on the job and working on her patter. 'Fuck you, lady. Mind your own fucking business and you can stick your prayers up your arse,' was all the obnoxious thanks she got for enduring a rant from a punter who'd just blown his kid's birthday money at the racetrack.

'I should have put a bit more work in at school but it's too late now.' Rose sighed. 'Marina was a right old swot. Did everything right. Got a scholarship to Trinity, you know. Left us behind and went up to Dublin. And she aced that too. She got a First in Law.'

'Good for her,' said Ellie.

'Yeah.' Rose remained wistful. 'Marina worked in London for a good few years, but then her mother got sick and she had to come home. She got a job at Coyle & Coyle, no problem. She hadn't seen

Dylan since Kylebeggan Comprehensive, and in the beginning I think he found her coolness amusing. But Marina didn't have too much time for a social life, looking after her mother. And anyway she wanted to keep her personal and business life separate.'

'Clever lady.'

'Dylan doesn't take no for an answer though.' Rose chuckled. 'He was used to women flinging themselves at him. After he and Marina dated for a while, his father got all heavy, saying it was high time he settled down. Of course, Marina was aware of Dylan's reputation, but she told us he had changed. She said she could handle him.' Rose tittered. 'I guess we'll see.'

'A leopard doesn't change his spots,' Ellie muttered.

'Are you married?' Rose enquired.

Ellie turned to answer. 'I'm beginning to think marriage is outdated. No longer fit for purpose.'

Rose eyed her suspiciously. 'Do you mind me asking how old you are?'

'I'm in my late thirties.' She could get away with that, couldn't she?

'You know what?' Rose looked her up and down. 'You don't really sound like a taxi driver. You don't look like one either.'

Ellie said nothing. Turning back, she pulled at the wrinkles that had formed on her sleeves.

She'd decided early on to wear the designer jackets. No point in letting good clothes hang unworn in the tiny wardrobe. The jackets made surprisingly good car coats. Not too short. Not too long. Purchased in the Via Condotti in Rome. The pastel shrugs came in handy too. Bought in Cannes, for sitting on the deck at night.

23:29 p.m.

The meter flashed red in the dark. A simple look-see around the house shouldn't take this long, should it? Ellie told herself to be patient. The meter was running, that's what mattered. It all added to the fund.

'Ah, this is becoming a joke! What's keeping her?' Rose squashed her nose up against the window.

A dog barked into the still night air. All along Arbutus Road, cars were parked at the kerbside. The road was quiet. Cloud spilled over the top of the Black Pins in the distance, dulling the light from a watery moon. Ellie edged forward in her seat, watching as a scrawny cat slinked out from underneath a parked BMW and skulked, low-bellied, across the road, disappearing under a gate. She eased back. The bells of St Malachy's tolled on the half-hour from the town.

23:32 p.m.

'I'm giving her one minute more and then I'm ringing her. Where's my mobile?' Rose rummaged in her handbag. 'What in the name of God are those two doing in there? Oh shit—'

Ellie heard the contents of her bag fall all over the floor. Rose huffed and hiccupped and cursed and thankfully stopped her talking as she busied herself retrieving stuff that had fallen. Over the sound of grumbles and moans came a low murmur from outside. A hum and the sound of a nearby engine kicking into life.

Angling her head, Ellie checked the side-view mirror, but she determined that the noise wasn't coming from behind. Ahead, she observed a vehicle pulling away. An unmarked van, a Renault, perhaps. No headlights. She tracked it as it crawled off up the road to the T-junction where it turned left and disappeared from view.

There was a sudden knocking on the door behind. Ellie jumped. She unlocked the doors. Distracted by the van, she hadn't spotted her passenger return.

'I'm so sorry' – Jen was breathless – 'Marina made me check everywhere.' She got into the back seat. 'Back to town, please.'

17

'Of course.'

Ellie flicked the indicator and, though the road was free of traffic, she pulled out cautiously. Remaining in a low gear, she passed the spot where the van had been.

'She made me look in all the walk-in wardrobes and under all the beds. I even had to go down to the wine cellar. Dylan's big into his wine, isn't he?'

'Big into himself, more like,' retorted Rose.

'Oh, I wouldn't go kicking Dylan out of bed for eating Taytos,' murmured Jen.

'You wouldn't kick anyone out of the bed for eating Taytos,' Rose scoffed. 'Sure you wouldn't kick anyone out of bed, full stop.' She lowered her voice. 'Tell me, you're not still—'

'None of your business, Rose.'

'What if—'

'I'm a big girl and as I said it's none of your business.' Jen shut her down.

'But if Marina—'

'Drop it, Rose. Now, what's way more interesting is Marina's house. You should see the size of their bed. Jeez, it's massive. A super king.'

'Just like Dylan.' Rose laughed.

'Seriously, Rose, you should see how organised Marina is. The place is cram full of wedding stuff. Dark umbrellas in case it rains. White umbrellas in case it's sunny. Boxes of fans. Flip-flops for after the church. No expense spared.'

'I wish I was a bit more like her, I really do.'

'Me too,' said Jen. 'Oh, Marina played her cards right there.'

Rose heaved a deep sigh. 'What's that in your hand?' she asked.

'A fifty. Marina insisted. Money for the taxi and a drink on her in Godiva's.'

'Aahh . . . isn't she a sweetheart?'

'That she is. Little Miss Perfect.'

A fine mist had started to appear on the windscreen as Ellie approached the centre of town. Two uniformed gardaí were patrolling Main Street. The closer she got to Godiva's nightclub, the more she anticipated a request to drive back to Arbutus Road. This was getting just a little bit tedious.

'You think she'll be OK in that big house on her own with a psycho on the loose?' Rose whispered. 'I feel pretty bad about leaving her now.'

'Marina will be fine.' Jen was firm. 'It's only for one night. Dylan's home from his stag tomorrow.'

'How do you know?'

'Well, I don't for sure . . . obviously.' Jen hesitated. 'But I assume that'll be the case. A stag is usually the one night, right?'

'But maybe he's gone for longer—'

'Oh, Rose, stop looking for trouble, please.'

When Ellie pulled up outside Godiva's the queue was all the way down Beggar Man's Lane. Gym-muscled men wore tight-fitting jeans and spray-on tops. Despite the cold, the female night-clubbers wore practically nothing. The very thought of putting herself out there like that made Ellie shudder.

Settling the fare, Rose and Jen clambered out, leaving a tip for all their messing about. Ellie was just about to pull off when she spotted something. She wound down her window, calling out after the women.

'Haven't you forgotten something?'

Jen looked at her sheepishly. She tottered back towards the taxi with one eye on the back seat.

'Oh . . . I don't really want that any more. Can I leave it with you?'

19

'I don't think so.' What was Ellie expected to do with a giant inflatable willy?

'Only, I feel a bit stupid with that thing now.'

And so she should.

Jen opened the door and reluctantly reached in.

Rose waited on the pavement. 'Look, Jen, this doesn't feel right,' she whined. 'Maybe we should go back to Marina's after all—'

Ellie wound up her window immediately, revved the engine and took off before she became embroiled in any more carry-on. It was time to go home. She was withered. It had been a long evening and not at all pleasant.

Every one of her passengers had quizzed her about the two women who'd been found murdered in Kylebeggan. Had Ellie ever heard the like of it before? Imagine, laid out cold like that, in their own homes, dressed in their bridal gowns.

They asked Ellie about her thoughts. They asked for her opinion. What did Ellie's other passengers think? they asked. Had she picked up any of the reporters that were in town? Did they have anything new? Did anyone know anything at all? Had anyone any theories? Any little titbit at all?

And all night long Ellie had trotted out the same response. One woman being found dead in such circumstances was strange enough. But a second, turning up in exactly the same way? Well, there was nothing else to say. It was downright freaky.

4

It was gone midnight when Ellie squeezed into the designated parking space across the cobbled road. The space was narrow. She edged the car as close as she could to the cut-stone wall that separated Botany Row from the convent school.

Ellie could see the convent gardens from her bedroom window. Benches dotted the lawn. There were statues and a fountain. It was where the posh girls went. Girls who went to university and then on to become solicitors and doctors. Like that solicitor woman she'd just dropped off. Women with fancy houses and walk-in wardrobes. Ellie missed her walk-in wardrobe.

Her mouth watered at the smell wafting around the car. She grabbed the carrier bag from the footwell, opened the door and stepped outside. It was damp and murky as she made her way across the road, taking care not to slip on the wet cobbles.

Leaving an outside light on made the little house in Botany Row more welcoming on nights she came in from late shifts. As she approached the house, she detected movement. A curtain twitching. Pauline Brennan next door checking up on her. God forbid she'd ever end up like Pauline. Spending her days checking local property prices and the death notices.

Turning the key, Ellie pushed the front door open and bent to pick up the newspaper that had been delivered. The house was chilly but it wouldn't take too long to warm up. It was one of the few benefits of the tiny living space. She switched on the little green lamp from the charity shop. She turned on the electric fire – a reasonable imitation of a French firewood stove. The fake flames were quite convincing after a glass of wine.

Popping her handbag on the settee, she went to the bank of drawers by the kitchen sink. She could eat out of the plastic cartons the Golden Chopsticks had provided. It was late, she was tired and she did not have company. But she had her standards.

Finding what she needed, she opened up the fold-out table. She doubled over the linen tablecloth and draped it on top. She laid out a napkin along with a single dinner plate from the Wedgwood dinner service. The full service was stored away under her bed. She placed a silver knife and fork on either side of the plate. The canteen of cutlery was also stowed under the bed upstairs. They were wedding gifts. Ellie didn't entertain and saw little point in cluttering up the compact kitchen.

Striking a match, she lit the candles on the shelf above the fire and moved the candlesticks to the table. Putting on the French café music she liked, she sat with a serving spoon and doled out General Tso's chicken. It wasn't lemon sole or sushi, but the general certainly knew how to bring comfort after a late-night shift.

Two mouthfuls in, there came a knocking through the wall. Bloody Mervyn. Ellie gave the wall two fingers. She could barely hear the music so she had no idea how Mervyn could. She turned it off. She couldn't risk the guy showing up in his skimpy dressing gown on her doorstep. She couldn't give him any excuse.

Ellie missed her old house. Not adjoining any other. However, Botany Row was what she could afford in rent. As she cast a jaundiced eye about, she thought it might aspire to be what the magazines called 'eclectic', if she ever finished painting the place. The colour she'd chosen was Elephant's Breath. The colour of her old sitting room. So far, she'd only painted the wall behind the small settee.

She got to her feet. There was half a bottle in the fridge. A cheap Sauvignon. She'd only have one glass. She was up in the morning with a long drive ahead. These days she scarcely drank at all, mindful that she was driving for a living. Before, they used to share a nice Chablis at dinner. And if they were on holiday, Ellie would follow with a gin and tonic. Sometimes, too, she'd have a glass of sherry beforehand.

This time last year they'd been on a cruise. They both enjoyed getting away from the sheeting rain and the aching cold, sitting on the deck, allowing the Mediterranean rays to soak their bones.

Ellie always enjoyed the port visits, the tours of museums and art galleries, meeting people from different countries. She enjoyed the shows on board at night and making up a four for bridge. As she sipped wine in her little house in Botany Row, she wrestled with a threatening gloom.

She should have furthered her education. She'd always meant to. She should have done the Open University. She could have had a degree. Maybe in the future, when she'd finished paying for the taxi and saving for more legal fees, she'd put something aside for a course.

Ellie didn't finish her meal. Saving the leftovers would have been thrifty and wise. Instead, she proceeded to the back door, unlocking it as gently as she could. She stepped into the concrete yard and waited.

Hermano appeared over a high wall as if he'd been on sentry duty. Ellie had no idea if the cat belonged to anybody, or even what his real name was, but she had named him Hermano.

'There you go,' she said softly. She set the container down.

The animal weaved a dance of thanks around her ankles. Bending to stroke him, Ellie heard a rustling sound. And breathing. Heavy breathing. She looked over her shoulder.

She bolted upright.

It was Mervyn. Ogling her over the eight-foot wall. A small man, he had clearly found something to stand on. How long had he been there like that, staring down at her rear end?

'Please don't do that.'

'Sorry, Ellie . . . I heard you coming in. Just wanted to check that you're OK. You know, with all that's going on—'

'I'm perfectly fine, thank you.'

Merv the Perv was the last person Ellie wanted looking out for her.

'What's the news around the town?'

'No news, Mervyn. You'd hear more than I would.'

Mervyn ran a tanning salon.

'Isn't it awful for Harry Kirby?' Mervyn was hell-bent on conversation.

'Indeed.' Ellie pulled her jacket close and backed up towards the door.

'People couldn't believe that he was getting hitched after so many years as a bachelor.' Mervyn's eyes looked piggy in the dark. 'He liked the women, you know.'

'I wouldn't know anything about that.' Ellie started to close the door.

'The story's all over this week's paper. They're saying—'

Mervyn was still talking when she shut the door.

Ellie had left *The Kylebeggan Echo* on the chest next to the settee. With the remains of her wine, she sat, curling her legs underneath her, and scanned the headlines.

HARRY'S DEAD VALENTINE, read one.

FEAR IN KYLEBEGGAN, read another.

MUCH-LOVED TEACHER WAS BRIDE-TO-BE, was another.

Ellie sipped from her glass and read.

HARRY'S DEAD VALENTINE

by Cormac Scully, Crime Correspondent

Former rugby star and publican Harry Kirby has been left reeling after the murder of his fiancée, Kylebeggan woman Imelda Gannon. Popular primary school teacher Imelda was found dead in her flat on Saturday 14 February, in Friary Lane, off Main Street. She had been murdered.

Imelda, 35, had been due to marry Harry, 37, on Saturday last in St Malachy's church. Harry and Imelda planned to celebrate their big day with family and friends at Cronin's Country House Hotel.

Both had shared a keen interest in sport, Harry involved with Kylebeggan Rugby Club and Imelda playing for the Ladies' Firsts at Kylebeggan Hockey Club. The couple were due to move into their newly built home at Ardeevin Cross, outside the town, during Imelda's school holidays.

Tragically, that will not be. Harry returned from his stag in Temple Bar, Dublin, dropping by his fiancée's flat on his way home to the Fiddler's Arms in Main Street, where he lives with his parents above the pub. Harry grew concerned when Imelda wasn't answering his texts or calls.

When his fiancée didn't answer the door, Harry contacted Coleman Street garda station. Gardaí arrived to the grim discovery of Imelda's body. Pathologist Constance Kiely confirmed that the death was suspicious, and it is being treated as a murder. The case bears much resemblance to the recent case on 21 January in Myrtle Crescent, but gardaí are disclosing very few details for operational reasons.

Ellie closed the paper, folded it and set it aside. The town had never had a crime correspondent before. She'd come across Cormac Scully's name on the news when the story had first broken about the murder at Myrtle Crescent. She was pretty sure Scully had also been on TV reporting on the second murder, that of Imelda Gannon at Friary Lane.

Of all the articles she'd come across on the Internet and in the press, this was the most informative. The other articles had been riddled with typos and poorly constructed clauses. This guy, Scully, could know even more than he was free to say, either on air or in print.

The sound of Mervyn coughing came through the walls. Ellie stiffened. Soon she'd have the pleasure of hearing him snore. She got to her feet, went to the kitchen, rinsed her glass and stood it to drain next to the dinner plate.

Just before heading upstairs, she stopped at the photo on the mantelpiece. There they were – the three of them. Ellie, Johnny and baby Owen. 'Good night, Johnny,' she said. ''Night, baby Owen.'

Upstairs, she drew the curtains in her bedroom. She undressed, hanging the cashmere sweater and the trousers in a wardrobe neatly recessed into the angled roof. A taller person would have difficulty walking around the room. Were people that much smaller two centuries ago, she wondered?

Climbing into bed, she breathed in the smell of the bed-linen that had dried outdoors. Ellie was careful what she chose to hang outside. Undergarments were dried on a frame indoors. The thought of Mervyn ogling her underwear was more than she could bear.

Before setting an alarm on her phone, she checked for texts. All was good. Every Sunday after lunch was the standing arrangement. She picked up the book she'd read many times before. It had been gifted to her, and these past few weeks it had been a friend to her. It felt like a time from another world, when it had first caught her eye on the shelves in the drawing room, an ash-scented fire hissing in the grate.

Tonight, her eyes were heavy. She set the book back on the bedside table. *Rebecca* and Manderley would have to wait. Ellie needed to be fresh in the morning. It was a two-and-a-half-hour drive to the prison.

5

'Good morning!'

Pauline was at her front door in slippers, wiping her hands on an apron.

'Morning.'

Ellie had left the house quietly, or so she'd thought. Obviously not quietly enough.

'I was up with the lark. Couldn't sleep a wink for thinking about those poor women. Thought I'd do some baking before I went to church. Would you like some scones?'

The early morning barrage was a ploy. Scones for information. 'No, thanks, Pauline. I'm off to work.'

Her neighbour's face fell. A retired schoolteacher, Pauline was still trying to get the measure of Ellie. While Ellie sensed an approval of her appearance and the way she spoke, she sensed a certain puzzlement at how she earned her living.

'You wouldn't like one or two for lunch? You should look after yourself more. You're always working.'

'Go on then. You're very kind.' It would be quicker all round not to argue. Ellie could give the scones to Johnny.

Pauline beamed. 'Just a tick.'

As Pauline hurried back indoors, Ellie gazed idly about the row.

Some houses had been upgraded and had modern grey window frames and plantation shutters. Others guarded their privacy with net curtains and china figurines. Most houses in Botany Row were plain on the outside. Not Mervyn's. His house had window boxes with plastic flowers. He also had a brass goblin-like creature as a doorknocker and a painted nameplate.

A grin crept up on Ellie. The guy would go nuts. Completely nuts. It had happened again. Someone had scuffed out the letter 'n', changing it for an 'l'. Mervyn's nameplate read *The Slug*.

Pauline reappeared, handing Ellie a tin-foil package. Ellie tilted her head. 'He'll blow a gasket,' she said, chuckling.

Pauline followed her gaze. 'Oh, sweet divine Jesus. You're right about that.' She thought a moment. 'I'm pretty sure it happens the nights he stays with his mother.'

According to Pauline, Mervyn was attentive to his ageing mother – staying over a few nights a week. It rankled with her, as Pauline's own family seemed to keep their distance. Ellie could understand it. The woman could be meddlesome and insisted on knowing everyone's business. Ellie didn't share with Pauline that Mervyn had in fact been in residence in Botany Row the previous night. Or in the early hours of the morning at least.

'He won't be one bit happy, I can tell you that for nothing.' Without taking a breath, Pauline turned to Ellie. 'Isn't it wicked about—'

'Thanks.' Ellie cut her short. 'I'd better not delay, I'm late already.'

She made immediately for her car, slipped in behind the wheel and drove out of the row, careful not to clip the wing mirrors of any parked cars. It irked Ellie that because she drove a taxi, people thought she must have inside knowledge of what had happened to the murdered women. That she was somehow privy to morsels of information from fares she picked up.

Stopping for petrol outside town, Ellie treated herself to a take-out Americano and, settling in for the drive, she tuned to her latest podcast – a true crime series. Episode four. Ellie loved the challenge of guessing who a villain might be, trying to figure out a villain's motives. She half fancied herself as a detective. Now there was a dream job.

The black Škoda climbed steadily out of the valley. Winter seemed slow to release its grip this year. Ellie was looking forward to spotting the tell-tale hue that would herald the arrival of blue-bells in between the hawthorn trees that lined the road.

She passed a ribbon of roadside guesthouses with signs swing-ing in the wind. A few like the popular Bluebell Lodge and Clashbeg Rectory advertised vacancies, but it was generally quieter in the early months of the year. Surprisingly, she was alone on the road and didn't have to dodge the usual pack of mountain-bike enthusiasts.

The sky had borrowed a deep grey mantle from the Black Pin mountains around the valley. The bright crisp days of spring were yet to come. She put on headlights as she approached a tunnel of trees. As she cleared the tunnel, she noted the solitary Scots pine standing apart from the rest. There was little to mark what had happened at the tail end of last year. There had been no mention of it in the local news or in the papers. And Ellie only knew what had happened there because of a fare she'd driven out this way. From time to time, she did hear things that were not made public.

A hard-working man, who'd farmed nearby all his life, had found himself disinherited by his uncle. The uncle had left the farm to the man's younger brother. Sorely disappointed, the forty-nine-year-old farmer had hanged himself on the tree.

The man had been left hanging on the Scots pine at the mercy of the crows. He'd be there yet, her fare had said, only for the

30

driver of a passing milk tanker noticed something strange in the low December light.

There was nothing nearby to remember what had happened. No ribbon. No decaying bunch of supermarket flowers. No plaque. Nothing but a council road sign a few metres further on.

YOU ARE NOW LEAVING THE HERITAGE TOWN OF KYLEBEGGAN
TWINNED WITH ANNÉCY IN FRANCE
SLÁN ABHAILE
SAFE HOME

Johnny was glad to see her. He grinned as she sat down. Ellie knew fine well he was putting on a show for her.

'And how is my posh sister today?'

Ellie pulled a face.

'Bake these yourself?' he asked.

The prison guards had been obliged to put the package of scones through the scanner. They'd jokingly threatened to eat them.

'What do you think?'

Her eyes were quickly drawn to his hand. It was wrapped in a bandage. 'What happened?' she asked. The prison housed some hard-core individuals.

'Accident with a circular saw.'

Ellie winced.

Johnny was doing a diploma in woodturning. She opened her mouth to enquire further but shut it just as quickly. She might as well accept his explanation. It would be the only one she would get.

'You're looking good,' she said. 'Apart from the hand, obviously.'

'Yeah . . . I'm working out in the gym. There's a bit of five-a-side as well. And I'm doing a stint in the kitchens.'

In his T-shirt, Johnny's arms bulged with muscle. One was

31

tattooed with *ELLIE* and the other with *OWEN*. She wished he hadn't done that. She was not a fan of tattoos.

'Tell me' – Johnny leaned across the table – 'what in the name of God is happening in Kylebeggan? I couldn't hardly believe when they found a second woman dead on her bed. Jaysus . . . Kylebeggan, of all places, flashing up like that on the telly. What do you make of it, Ellie? You're always good for a theory.'

Johnny was right. When people went missing or someone was murdered, she normally had a theory. With a Netflix mystery or thriller, she could generally figure out what was going on long before the end. But here and now, in real life, Ellie was flummoxed. More than flummoxed, she was fearful.

'I have no idea. Honestly, not a clue.' She shook her head. 'There's a weird air around the town. You can really feel it. The fear. Everyone looking over their shoulders. Everyone on edge. About the only thing I've come across is mention of some guy called Joseph Liston . . . used to drive a taxi, so they say. Or a minibus, maybe. Detectives in Coleman Street are looking into him.'

'You want me to do a little asking around?' Johnny sat back in his chair and swivelled his eyes about the visitor room.

'Would you?'

'Nothing but the most obliging sorts in here.' Johnny winked.

They spoke about the murdered women, then drifted on to Johnny's plans for an appeal. At the trial, Johnny had been entitled to legal aid. His lawyer had been a twitchy type, nervously spoken, with a sweaty pallor. Completely ineffective, as it turned out. Ellie couldn't blame the jury. There had been no defence worth speaking of.

She'd always known that Kearney and Dessie were bad news. Johnny should never have kept company with them. Some lads got sense and left behind their lives of petty crime. Kearney and Dessie were the kind that never grew up. The kind that would always go the extra mile. Fancied themselves on a par with the Brinks Allied robbers even in their thirties. No matter what she said, Johnny wouldn't listen.

When Kearney and Dessie had asked Johnny to collect them outside that casino in Cork, Johnny thought the request was no more than that. An innocent request to collect his two mates. Well, maybe not that innocent. Maybe he had an inkling that they'd done a spot of robbing. But there was no way Johnny knew they'd shot two staff inside. One died in hospital later. Johnny would never be party to something like that. But that's where his background went against him. It hadn't helped that he had a record.

Ellie had started saving for an appeal when she was living in Pottershill. She was still determined to save enough to get her brother a decent solicitor. Whatever happened, she was getting Johnny out of jail.

Like always, they moved on to talk about old times, with Johnny once more expressing concern for Ellie's safety.

'Now with this character Joseph Liston – whoever he is – on the scene, I'm more than a little uneasy.' He looked her in the eye.

'Don't worry, Johnny. You know I can handle myself.'

'There's handling yourself and handling yourself, Ellie. You're vulnerable driving a taxi. It's not exactly Pottershill and luxury cruises.'

'Who are you telling?' Ellie sighed. 'It's only until I get sorted out with something else.'

'You ever see them around?' he asked softly.

'Ken and Barbie?'

He nodded.

She looked up at the clock. 'I do my best to avoid them.'

'That house should be yours, you know.'

She shrugged. 'I got the Wedgwood and the silver.'

He drew a circle on the table with his finger. 'Ever consider talking to someone about what happened? You've been through a lot, Ellie.'

'I'm good.'

'But are you, though? You don't look so good.'

The bell suddenly sounded, signalling visiting time had come to a close. Ellie had her coat on in seconds.

'Something I said?' Johnny looked at her in amusement. He set a hand on her shoulder. 'Listen, I get that you don't like talking about Pottershill and all that went on—'

'Yeah, well . . .' She shrugged him off.

'OK, then. See you next week.' His face clouded over. 'It's baby Owen's birthday on Tuesday but I'm sure you remembered.'

'Of course.' She nodded. 'I put flowers on his grave.'

The March sun was veiled by a jagged cloud as Ellie left the building by the portcullis. She walked briskly by the outside walls of the prison. The forbidding stone walls were topped by spirals of barbed wire.

Her taxi was parked in a small housing estate a short walk away. Ellie wasn't wasting money on a parking meter. Pulling her shoulders back, she got into her stride. One day soon, she'd get Johnny out of prison. One day soon, he'd be coming back to Kylebeggan with her. He'd set up a woodturning studio. He'd have a place to showcase his work, maybe on Main Street, in between other craft shops and cafés. He could sell carved wooden pieces to tourists. Fruit bowls and the like. He could sell bigger pieces like giant chess to the hotels and municipal buildings. He could make wooden sculptures of local football stars and sell them to the council.

Once in the taxi, Ellie headed in the direction of the discount stores that had sprung up by the social housing on the edge of the city. She stocked up there every week. It was cheaper than shopping in Kylebeggan. The discount stores took her back to her childhood. To the smell of chips and vinegar. To the smell of poverty.

By the time she'd completed her shopping, the sky had turned to rain. She took the motorway, grappling with a banana as she drove. She followed signs for Kerry and the southwest. Stopping at the Half-Way service station, she dodged oily puddles as she ran in for another coffee. She'd often thought about packing a hot flask, but the journeys were grim enough without a treat to break them.

Back in the car, she returned to her podcast. It was becoming increasingly grisly. The presenter gave an account of ravens refusing the remains of some woman, killed and left mutilated by a disused railway track, at the same time as Ellie swerved to avoid something furry, matted with blood on the road. She turned the podcast off, turning to local radio instead.

Bilious grey clouds tumbled over the jagged peaks of the Black Pins on her approach to Kylebeggan. She switched her lights to full and reached to turn up the volume on the radio.

Now back to this afternoon's top story here at Skellig FM. Reports are coming in of what appears to be another suspicious death in the heritage town of Kylebeggan. The picturesque tourist town has found itself in the national and international spotlight for the strange and shocking deaths of two women in as many months. This afternoon, the town finds itself dealing with even more disturbing news. Over to reporter Cormac Scully at the scene:

'Yes, indeed, Teresa, I can safely confirm that the residents of this bustling tourist town are truly appalled at the latest discovery. As I speak, I stand outside a refurbished Edwardian house in leafy Arbutus Road. My sources say that shortly around lunch time today a distressed call was made to Coleman Street garda station, alerting them to the discovery of the body of a young woman. Gardaí are at the scene. We don't yet know if the body of the young woman was found in circumstances similar to those of the murdered woman in Myrtle Crescent in January and the murdered woman in Friary Lane in February. As the day goes on, we'll find out more about this tragic story. Back to you in the studio, Teresa.'

Ellie's knuckles whitened on the wheel. She pushed the pedal to the floor. She'd been looking forward to curling up on the settee with the Sunday papers. But she was heading to Botany Row no longer. She was heading into town. Straight to Coleman Street garda station.

6

When the tip-off had come through, reporter Cormac Scully had been at home in the kitchen. His stone cottage was at the end of a rough boreen, a few kilometres outside Kylebeggan in the shadow of the Black Pins.

With the phone between his ear and his shoulder, he checked the goose-fat roast potatoes. In hushed tones, his caller had told him something was going on in town. In Arbutus Road. Number 9 Arbutus Road, to be exact.

The caller hadn't been able to give many details, but Scully had his suspicions. Typing the address into a search engine revealed a planning permission notice for renovations to the property by the current owners. Scully recognised the name.

Cooking lunch with the girls was something he usually did on a Sunday but he had to forgo that now. He couldn't waste this lead. He'd have to tear a path into town before any big-name media crews descended and stole the story from him.

Scribbling instructions on how to joint the chicken, he left the girls under Jill's lethargic gaze. He jumped into the Land Rover Defender, bouncing and bumping down the boreen through an archway of knotted hazel until he reached the junction. He turned left, taking the fastest route to town. Branches of wet mountain ash slapped against the rusting car as he hugged the winding road.

At Darglin Drive he slowed, meeting a team of council workers and their vans. They were busy sweeping, filling flower baskets on poles and tending heather-filled tubs along the path. Damn them anyway. Couldn't they rest on a Sunday?

To make things worse, he had forgotten all about Sunday worship. The devout were spilling on to the pavement from lunchtime services at Holy Cross Church of Ireland and Kylebeggan's Catholic church. Scully was forced to stop as groups of women in fur hats and men in wax jackets sauntered across the road back to their cars, entirely unaware of the news that was about to break.

Someone who was taking his Sunday rest seriously was Paudie Jones, Scully's soundman from Skellig FM. He sounded none too pleased when Scully got him on the phone.

'Fuck sake!' exclaimed Scully.

'Scully, is that you?' Paudie cleared his throat.

'Yeah, sorry about that, Paudie. I'm not swearing at you. There's a crowd here and I'm in a hurry. They're coming out in their droves from church. Full of hymns and Jesus. Oh, great, now there's a pony and trap blocking the road ahead. Bloody town tours.' Drumming his fingers, Scully filled Paudie in on what his caller had told him.

Beyond Darglin Drive, the roads were quieter and Scully soon arrived at Arbutus Road, parking a few houses shy of number 9, even though there were spaces closer. His car tax was out of date. No need to give the lads in blue any more cause for upset. He knew they found him a pain in the ass.

Any attempts to discern anything meaningful about the murder at Myrtle Crescent two months ago or last month's murder at

38

Friary Lane had been met with both derision and resistance. 'Scully, why don't you piss off back to covering garden fêtes and weddings, like a good fella?' Superintendent Sean Begley had said. 'This investigation lark doesn't suit you at all.'

Didn't suit gardaí at Coleman Street, more like. Contrary to Begley's pronouncement, Scully found his spell of crime reporting was suiting him just fine. It was a welcome distraction.

Reaching into the back of the Land Rover, he grabbed his rain-coat. The rain was holding behind the Black Pins for now, but the coat would serve to cover goose-fat splatters. Pulling a wipe from the glove compartment and tilting the rear-view mirror, he tidied himself as best he could. He regretted not heeding his daughters' requests to shave. Slipping a notepad into his pocket, he hopped out of the car, flung his door shut and set off up the road, purpose in his step.

Swagger was the key. Presenting himself with confidence would suggest he had the right to be there. It could be a while yet before Paudie pitched up. The guy had sounded very hungover on the phone. Scully took long strides to shake off the chill. He counted four marked garda cars parked on the roadside. There were proba-bly unmarked cars as well.

Nearing number 9, he saw a cordon had been set up around the house. Two uniformed gardaí were at the gate. He approached them as if fully anticipating they would step aside. It was all in the attitude.

'They're expecting me,' he said, the way his contact had advised. He lifted his chin in the direction of the garda standing at the front door.

'OK . . .'

The two gardaí stood aside as he pushed the gate. Exactly the response he'd been hoping for. It had worked. And what he'd said wasn't a bald-faced lie – gardaí were bound to expect some report-ers, weren't they?

He noticed the garden was nicely landscaped. Phrases for his report were forming in his head. Well-kept neighbourhood. Manicured lawns. Affluent area. He proceeded down the path curving through shrubbery to the front door, which stood open. The young garda eyed him nervously.

'Don't worry, Garda. The lads at the gate said it was OK.' Scully pulled out his notepad.

The garda twisted his head over his shoulder, looking into the dark blue hallway, uncertain. Scully spotted a sitting room off to the right. Voices were echoing down the stairwell. 'It's all right,' Scully reassured him. 'I won't be going in.' He wouldn't stretch his luck. 'Just a few basic questions, Garda. The victim was a bride, another woman in a wedding dress, right?'

'Ehmmm . . .'

The young man's hesitation confirmed Scully's suspicions. Tall Dark hadn't filled him in on much, only that a young woman had been discovered. Dead.

'Was the woman found in her bedroom, like the other two?' Scully looked up from his notebook.

A flicker in the eyelids. Another silent confirmation.

'Any signs of violence or a struggle?'

The policeman shifted from one foot to the other. 'We're wait-ing for Constance Kiely.'

'She'll be getting the Freedom of Kylebeggan next,' said Scully drily. It would be the pathologist's third visit down from Dublin.

The young garda gave a half smile.

'Who called it in?' Scully pressed ahead.

'The fiancé. Arrived back from his stag today.'

At last. Something. Tall Dark had been unsure who had contacted Coleman Street garda station.

'Name?'

'Dylan Coyle.'

'I see. And, Garda, can you tell me if there's an estimated time of death? Did death occur last night or today?'

The garda scratched above his ear. 'Last night, I think.'

Voices inside the house were growing louder. Scully could hear footsteps on the stairs. He flipped the notebook shut, bid the garda thanks and took off up the path, snapping a few photos on his phone as he went. There wasn't a lot to go on. But it was a start.

On the street outside, Paudie from the radio station had pitched up. He was slugging back a can of full-fat Coca-Cola. His eyes looked like two piss holes in the snow.

'A scoop or two too many last night, my man?'

Paudie grunted. He drained the can and busied himself setting up a live link to Skellig FM. Scully concentrated on putting together a carefully worded piece with the few details he'd gleaned, while Paudie set things up with Teresa in the studio.

When the interview concluded, Scully wanted to make himself scarce and to head off home for his Sunday lunch. He wanted to clear out of Arbutus Road before 'a nuisance of journalists' descended. It was an expression favoured by his source that ignored the fact Scully himself was part of the self-same 'nuisance'.

But before going home Scully would have to put in an appearance at Coleman Street garda station. He had to make it look like he was seeking information. He needed to protect his source. If Tall Dark's superiors got wind he was leaking, the policeman could face a jail term of up to seven years or a fine that would ruin him.

Scully's stomach rumbled. As he proceeded back to the car, he tried not to dwell on the garlic roast chicken and the goose-fat roast potatoes at home at the cottage. Unwrapping a stick of gum, he sensed he was being watched.

Across the street, he clocked a collection of faces casually staring from a parked car. Through foggy windows, he was able to make out three uniformed gardaí. On closer inspection, he thought there was another person in the car. Staring into the distance. A guy with a haunted look. Scully knew that face. It belonged to the fiancé of the woman in the house. The woman lying dead, most likely murdered. It was the groom-to-be, Dylan Coyle.

By the time Scully got back into the Land Rover, the rain had stolen back in over the mountains. He turned on the wipers. They made a mournful sound.

7

Outside Coleman Street garda station, Scully hesitated. Should he hold the heavy door open for the woman coming in behind him? She might appreciate it, or she might as easily chew the head off him. Would the action be seen as chivalrous or chauvinist? Navigating social niceties was becoming increasingly complex. Going on instinct, he held the door.

'Thank you,' said the woman, passing through, seeming preoccupied. She made straight for the counter. The reception area was bustling with gardaí, rushing through one set of swing doors to the next, bearing folders. There was an air of something afoot. The garda at the desk looked up at the woman in the grey fitted dress.

'Yes?' He wore a pained expression. He clearly wondered what fresh hell was headed his way.

'Oh, it's just that,' the woman began, 'well, the thing is . . . I happened to be listening to the radio in my car. I heard the tail end of some news report on Skellig FM – something about another body being discovered in Kylebeggan?'

'Oh yeah?' The garda stopped short of rolling his eyes.

According to Scully's source, every bewildered, bored citizen had seen fit to descend on the station with all kinds of ráiméis in recent weeks. Yet the slight blonde woman at the counter seemed neither bored nor bewildered. She spoke well and was smartly dressed.

'The thing is' – she cleared her throat – 'I drive a taxi.'

The policeman at the desk sat back.

'I was working last night,' the woman continued. 'And it's just that the report mentioned Arbutus Road.' She hesitated. 'Well, the thing is, I dropped a group of women there last night, you see. A hen party. Actually, I didn't drop all the women. Only one got out, well, it was two at first and—'

'Hold on there a moment.' The garda was interested. 'And your name is?'

'Ellie. Ellie Gillespie.'

Scully followed the exchange between the woman and the garda at the desk from where he'd parked his bum on a bench against the wall. No one in the garda station had paid him a blind bit of notice yet.

The petite blonde taxi driver ran a distracted hand through her hair. 'One of the passengers lives at number 9 Arbutus Road. I don't know if that's relevant, or even if it's the house in . . . in the news.'

The garda at the desk was suddenly all business. He spun his chair towards the back office, calling out, 'Superintendent Begley, can you come here a minute?'

Scully gave an involuntary shudder. He looked in the other direction to avoid being recognised by Begley but kept his ears wide open. He might just pick up something useful.

'What can I do you for, ma'am?' said Superintendent Begley with faux conviviality.

Scully listened in as the taxi driver recounted how she'd dropped a female passenger home and had taken two remaining female passengers onwards to Godiva's nightclub. Unfortunately, the taxi driver didn't mention any names.

'Maybe you'd like to come with me, Ellie?' said the superintendent. 'We might just take a statement, if that sounds all right to you?' Begley scanned the reception area, his eyes coming to rest on Scully with displeasure. He must have realised that much of this exchange had been overheard.

'Actually, Ellie, Garda Galvin here will take your statement and any other necessary details.' Begley lifted the counter, ushering Galvin out. 'I'll just have a word with this gentleman here.'

The taxi driver turned around to see the cause of the superintendent's consternation. A pair of enquiring eyes landed on Scully. Scully studied her in turn. Her face looked drawn and pale.

Garda Galvin indicated the taxi driver should head for the swing doors to the left of the counter. Ellie Gillespie did as directed, unaware that Superintendent Sean Begley was watching, his eyes drinking in her shapely legs and figure. Begley turned the full weight of a less appreciative stare on Scully.

'What's up, Scully?' He was terse.

'I'm here to see if there's any information on the murder in Arbutus Road.'

'And who says it's a murder?'

'I've just come from there. Given the level of garda activity it certainly looks like one.'

'Well now, Mr Scully, you'll have to wait for a statement from the garda press office like everyone else. Tell me, how did you end up in Arbutus Road anyhow?'

'I happened to be passing.'

'Is that right?' he sneered.

'Superintendent, I don't see why we can't collaborate, or why this always has to be so adversarial. Surely we can share information?'

'It doesn't work like that, Scully.'

Scully knew it didn't. The force kept tight control of information, disciplining those who released news without a sanction from senior positions. All the more reason for Scully to be careful to protect his source.

'Surely it's in the public interest to disclose that we now definitely have a serial killer on the loose?'

Begley exhaled long and slow. His expression changed. There was a twitch above his eye. The reception area had emptied and there came the sound of phones and keyboards from the back office, but no low hum of chatter. Scully sensed they had an audience.

'Now you listen to me, Mr Scully. You let us decide what's in the public interest. We've enough to be doing to solve this carry-on with the crowd from Dublin breathing down our necks. Trying to make us lot look like eejits below in Kerry. We don't need you stirring things up as well, getting everyone all excited with your talk.' He eyeballed Scully. 'Use of the term "serial killer" is incorrect and ill-advised.'

Scully held his gaze. He responded with a measured tone. 'With a murder in January, a murder in February and now this latest murder in March, you can be certain most news outlets are going to raise the spectre of a serial killer. Are you really saying you want to let everyone else report on this, and us local gombeens should stick our heads in the sand?'

Begley blinked.

'What I'm saying to you is to go handy, Mr Scully.'

'I've a job to do as well as you do, Superintendent,' said Scully, airily. 'If you give me nothing to go on, I can but speculate.'

The superintendent clamped his jaw. Scully was getting what was known in the force as the mushroom treatment. Being kept in the dark and fed manure.

'Have it your way.' Scully shrugged. 'I'll check back in for the press statement later.' He turned to leave but Begley was muttering something.

'What's that?'

Begley shook his head. 'The very notion of you as a crime reporter. The irony of it.'

Scully's glare was icy. 'I have three words for you, Superintendent,' he said. 'Pot. Kettle. Black.' Turning on his heel, he swung open the main door and loped angrily down the steps.

The path was slick with rain as he made for his car, two blocks away. His mood wasn't helped by his rumbling stomach. He needed to eat.

In the Land Rover, he started the engine, driving back to the empty space he'd noted, directly opposite Coleman Street garda station. It allowed him line of sight to the main doors. Turning off the throaty engine, Scully sat back and waited.

His stomach growled again. There was a bag of red apples in the passenger footwell. *Ideal for lunchboxes*, declared the packaging. *Fun-size*. He reached for one. With an eye on the doors across the road, he chomped down on the fruit. He suddenly stopped, mid-chew, and squinted.

Was that the mayor pulling up in that shiny black Mercedes? There, going up the steps? He'd swear it was.

Rain spittled a path down his side window. He returned to the apple, gnawing it down to the core. He waited some more. It was a full twenty minutes before the taxi driver eventually came out the main door. Scully had begun to fear the woman had exited the rear of the station.

He pulled himself together, trusting he looked agreeable, got out, buttoned the raincoat and made it across the street in a few strides. His footsteps smacked off the wet pavement as he closed in on the departing woman.

8

'Excuse me . . .'

'What the—'

The unshaven man with a jagged scar on his chin had appeared out of nowhere. He took a step back, aware that he had startled her.

'Sorry . . . let me introduce myself.' He held out his hand. 'Cormac Scully. Everyone calls me Scully.'

Ellie recognised the name. It was the guy who'd been on the radio with news of the grim discovery at Arbutus Road. The same guy she'd also seen on TV. She'd thought he looked familiar as he held the door open at the garda station.

'I know who you are,' she said, ignoring the outstretched hand. She pulled up the collar of her wool coat against the wind.

'I couldn't help but overhear you in there.' He tilted his head towards the station. 'I wonder if we could have a quick chat? I'd say the tearooms are shut by now but they do a reasonable coffee around the corner in the Three Hags.'

This guy had reported on the body found at Myrtle Crescent in January and the body found at Friary Lane a month later. A conversation might not hurt.

'Or a drink, if you'd prefer.' He sensed her hesitation. 'Can't remember the last time I was in a pub.'

'I only have a few minutes.'

'That's all it'll take.'

Ellie wanted to get home. It had been a long day, driving to and from the prison, followed by her giving a statement in the stuffy, impersonal interview room. She'd hated garda stations since she was a kid. Reluctantly, but curiously, she accompanied the reporter around the corner to the Three Hags. The painted sign creaked in a gust of wind.

Inside, a huddle of old boys sat on barstools, some of them reading the Sunday papers. There was a smell of burning peat, and a small TV hung precariously over the bar on an angled bracket. A Gaelic football game was playing. As Ellie and the reporter entered the bar, one lad turned and eyed them up with a despondent eye, before returning, somnolent, to his paper.

At the counter, Scully asked the barman for two coffees. He studied the lone wholemeal scone in a basket and offered to take it off the barman's hands. 'Nothing but a fun-size apple since breakfast.' He patted his stomach. 'Fun-size. Who thinks up such crap? Should we expect fun-size turnips and parsnips next?' He turned to Ellie. 'Fancied myself as a copywriter once . . . not much call for that around here.'

Ellie moved her mouth into what she trusted was a polite smile. As the barman clattered about with cups and saucers, Scully indicated that they should move away towards the fire. She followed to a table in an alcove and perched on a low stool opposite the reporter.

Scully gave a rueful smile. 'Instead of a stellar copywriting career, I took myself to Asia, backpacking and teaching English.' The smile accentuated the scar across his chin. 'Then home to Ireland to do a diploma in journalism . . .'

He looked away, withdrew some gum and put it into a curled-up piece of foil.

'Apologies if I smell of garlic.' He smiled again. 'So, that's a bit about me. It's what brought me to *The Kylebeggan Echo*. Sales and Advertising first, followed by general-purpose reporting. Oh, and I also have a gig going with Skellig FM. You have to earn a crust if you have kids, right?'

Ellie looked at him stone-faced. If this guy thought furnishing her with a potted biography was going to lead to any disclosures from her, he was mistaken. She remained silent.

The reporter studied the smouldering peat in the grate with a wistful look. 'Now, it appears I've become a crime correspondent. Not a moniker I ever thought I'd have . . . certainly not in this town.'

'Strange times for sure.' Ellie hadn't meant to sound sarcastic, but she wondered where his spiel was going.

The reporter cleared his throat, picking up on her impatience.

'The thing is, I couldn't help overhearing you back there in Coleman Street. You said you'd dropped a passenger home to Arbutus Road last night.' A knot appeared on his forehead. 'It must be distressing to learn that someone was murdered in the place.'

Ellie gave him a considered look.

'What makes *you* think it was murder? The gardaí didn't say anything about that.'

'You're right.' He was quick. 'I'm not a hundred per cent. But I think it's a reasonable hunch. I'll be checking in with a source later. Tell me, did you notice anything out of the ordinary last night?'

Ellie paused.

'And why would I share that with you?'

The reporter took a moment to consider her question.

'Because, Ellie,' he said, his tone dropping, 'things around here have a peculiar habit of being hushed up.' His eyes drifted to the bar counter, checking for eavesdroppers.

Ellie followed his gaze, taking in the men on the high stools. They were engrossed, blinking quietly at the TV.

'People here keep stuff quiet,' Scully said under his breath. 'Unless you were living on another planet, you'll have heard all the stories about what went on in Lisquinna Industrial School For Boys. And that's not so long ago. The outside world didn't get to hear much about that now, did it? The starvation, the forced labour, the beatings, the rapes—'

Ellie shifted on her seat.

Scully hesitated.

'Go on,' she directed.

Undoing the buttons of his coat, he continued. 'Lisquinna Lodge is billed as a luxury hostel nowadays. A charming Victorian house, with woodland fairy paths, a nine-hole pitch-and-putt course and a lake stocked with trout.' His lip curled. 'What they don't tell guests is that self-same lake was the watery grave of the broken-up, skeletal remains of five teenage boys.'

'More of Ireland's dark history,' Ellie murmured.

'*History?*' Scully blinked. 'If that were so.'

She raised an eyebrow.

'Look around you,' Scully instructed.

Couples were huddled in low conversation at tables around the bar. Ellie realised then that Scully was pointing to framed photos of Kerry football teams around the walls.

'Gaelic football is everything in this county. Every single lad in those photos is a legend . . . can do no wrong.' He checked over his shoulder at the men sitting at the bar before swinging back to Ellie. 'Remember what happened last year when Jack Cusack was found with evidence of stolen, blank vehicle registration books on his computer?'

Ellie cast her mind back. 'I may have heard talk about it in the taxi a while back. Or I may have read about it.'

'You certainly didn't read anything about it in my paper.' The reporter's expression darkened. 'I was all set to do a piece when someone leaned on Bradshaw, my editor. Cusack's computer had been seized but had somehow disappeared. Then it transpired that the records that had been entered into the garda records system, PULSE, had been tampered with.' Scully shook his head. 'Cusack's old man, Ned Cusack, owns that fancy Mercedes dealership out by the racecourse. Know the one?'

Ellie nodded.

'So, to answer the question I just put to you, Ellie, I'll tell you precisely what happened to Jack Cusack, cross-border importer of stolen second-hand cars and football legend. Nothing. Nada. Fuck all.'

Ellie thought a moment. 'In the same way there was nothing much done about that judge who crashed into those cyclists down by Coosheen Cross? Circuit court judge, Donegan? I collected one of those cyclists from the train station recently. I had to help him with a wheelchair.'

Scully nodded. 'You get my drift.' He cast an eye to the bar. 'Our friend is taking his time with the coffee.'

'I think he's watching the game,' said Ellie.

'While we're sitting in here, I can guarantee you that Mayor Halligan is rounding up the troops.' Scully was sombre. 'I'll bet he, the gardaí, along with the council and the board of trade, are all in conclave, wondering how to deal with all the additional media that's coming into town. Getting all their stories ready. A media storm is on its way, Ellie. More broadcasters. More cameramen. More reporters. More sound engineers. The whole shooting match. I'm telling you, Ellie, they're all on their way.' He pulled at the sleeves of his raincoat. 'And I, for one, am going to do my best to see the truth gets out this time. Not some damage-limitation hogwash. I'd like to know *who* murdered those three women. Wouldn't you?'

'I'm sure everybody would.' Ellie nodded.

'I'm not so sure.' Scully shook his head. 'I was in O'Shea's café a while back, working on something for the Friary Lane murder, when Mayor Halligan sidles in beside me, spluttering away, his coat all snowy with dandruff. "You're a talented journalist," he goes. Praise from Halligan is no praise at all, the guy's practically illiterate. "I liked your coverage of the Christmas races and the golf Pro-Am," he goes. "Your coverage of the teachers' conference above in Shanaglish Mountain Lodge was top-notch. Not many could make something dry sound interesting. Fair dues, you did, Scully."' Scully grimaced.

'And I'm there, wondering where all his shite talk is going. "Now, Scully," he goes, "why get everyone excited over the deaths of those poor women? What good will it do local trade and business? Kylebeggan all over *Sky News* again. On the map for something sick like this." Like the guy expected me to fill the pages of *The Kylebeggan Echo* with parish notes? Like people aren't going to find out anyway, somewhere else? "You leave all this to the gardaí, son. They know what they're doing," he goes.'

'You obviously *don't* think the gardaí know what they're doing,' Ellie countered.

Scully gave her a blistering look.

'Technically, this inquiry falls under Southwestern Division. There's something like eighteen gardaí of varying ranks in Coleman Street. Senior management has been careful not to disgruntle the force on the ground, reckoning the division and Coleman Street are competent on day-to-day operations but not in dealing with crimes like this. The town has never had a murder case before, at least not one they've openly *acknowledged*. That's why they've sent down experienced investigators from the Serious Crime Squad.'

Ellie was puzzled. 'If you have no faith in what the gardaí are up to, what were you doing in Coleman Street?'

Scully suddenly seemed stumped for an answer. He traced a finger along his scar.

'I'm going to go out on a limb here.' His eyes met hers.

Ellie crossed her legs.

'I have a friend . . .' he began. 'A source,' Scully half mouthed, half whispered. 'In order to protect him, it has to appear that I'm going to the gardaí at Coleman Street for my information.'

He gave her a moment to digest this.

'This is a person with a genuine interest in the truth,' he added. 'In making sure someone is caught for these murders. But not just *any* convenient someone. Not some scapegoat. The *right* someone. The perpetrator. My source has seen what goes on inside that station. There are . . . irregularities, shall we say.'

'This is someone who's leaking from inside Coleman Street garda station?' Ellie wanted to be sure.

'Someone needs to tell the truth.' Scully leaned closer. 'Remember Donegan, that circuit court judge you mentioned? He's been driving around half pissed out of his head for years. Not one penalty point. And the policeman who tried to blow the whistle on his carry-on? He's been ostracised. Out on stress leave for the last six months. Where's the justice in that?'

Ellie pursed her lips. Scully wasn't the only one interested in justice. She was interested too. Her brother Owen didn't get justice. Neither did her brother Johnny.

Scully fumbled in his raincoat pocket. He checked his phone and slipped it back in the pocket. 'The long and the short of all this is that I'd like your help, Ellie.' He placed two weather-beaten hands on the table. 'Can I ask you again, did you see or did you notice anything out of the ordinary at number 9 Arbutus Road last night?' He paused. 'Anything at all?'

Ellie jumped to her feet, scraping back her stool. Scully blinked, surprised.

'I'll be back in a second,' she said.

She needed a moment to think.

9

'You all right, love?'

Ellie jumped. She hadn't noticed that one of the cubicles in the ladies' washroom had been occupied. Her face dripped where she'd splashed herself with water.

'I'm fine, thank you.' She spoke in the mirror to the dark-haired woman who'd appeared beside her.

'If you're sure,' said the woman, proceeding to wash her hands.

Ellie didn't know how long she'd been there, staring at her reflection. Little wonder the woman had expressed concern. Ellie looked pallid, with dark, veiny hollows under her eyes. The dark-haired woman smiled as she eased past her, exiting the washroom.

Alone, Ellie leaned against the basin, rubbing her temples, trying to think. Her eyes were drawn above the speckled mirror to a picture depicting three cloaked and hooded figures with shadowy faces. An accompanying script told the story of the Three Hags.

Long ago, there were three hags who lived in Kerry. The first lived on the Paps of Danú, the second on Mullaghanattin, and the third hag lived on Carrauntoohil, the highest mountain in all of Ireland. They shared a hair comb between them. When the Hag of the Paps died, the two remaining hags began to fight over the comb. At the time, the Hag of Mullaghanattin was nursing a baby. To keep the baby safe, she jumped from Carrauntoohil towards Eisc Caillí but failed to stop and instead she landed on Carraig na Lathí (Rock of the Enclosure).

She landed so hard that her feet were imprinted in the rock and the baby slipped out of her grip. The baby's footprints were also imprinted on the rock. Mother and baby's footprints can be seen today on Carraig na Lathí. The Hag of Mullaghanattin then launched herself from the rock into a lake and disappeared, never to be seen again. From then on the lake was known as Loch Callaí (Lake of the Hag).

Feeling like a hag herself, Ellie splashed herself again with water. She knew she shouldn't trust the likes of a reporter and wondered what, if anything, she should say.

This reporter was local. He was on the ground. He was best placed to source the news, to gain the inside stories. The guy was plainly trying to further his career and was obviously looking to use her. Despite that, he could be a useful guy to know. Ellie pulled her shoulders back, took a deep breath and made a decision.

In her absence, the barman had deposited coffee, a scone, a pot of jam and a small pot of whipped cream on their table.

'Everything OK?' Scully looked up from his phone.

'Fine,' she said, sitting down.

Scully cut the scone, spread both sides with jam and cream and offered half to Ellie. She declined.

'Sunday dinner.' He raised the scone to his mouth.

'I suppose there were one or two things that struck me as a little odd last night,' Ellie began.

She told him about driving the women back to Arbutus Road. About how she'd waited outside the house while two of the women went indoors. About the van in the street with no lights, behaving oddly. Scully studied her as he ate.

She broached her unease about one of the women. She'd been mulling over the previous night's conversations in the car, on her journey home from seeing Johnny in the prison.

'The woman who was to have been a bridesmaid – Jen, I think her name was – she was saying how it was her third time being asked to be a bridesmaid. She sounded a bit regretful, to be honest. Or maybe even slightly jealous.'

Scully set the scone down. 'How so?'

'Well, you know what they say—'

'I don't.'

'*Three times a bridesmaid, never a bride.*' Ellie trotted out the old adage a little impatiently.

'Ah . . .'

'From what I gathered, not only was Jen going to be bridesmaid to this woman, Marina. She was *also* supposed to have been a bridesmaid to the woman murdered in Friary Lane last month.'

'Imelda Gannon?'

'That's right.'

Scully fiddled with the crumbs on his plate.

'I take it you didn't know?' Ellie prompted.

He shook his head. 'Interesting, though. A lot of these people were in school together. Like Dylan Coyle and Harry Kirby, for example.'

'Dylan Coyle came in for several mentions last night,' Ellie told him. 'He was the stag, right?'

'Marina Willoughby's husband-to-be.' Scully dabbed his chin with the paper napkin. 'And Harry Kirby was the husband-to-be of Imelda Gannon. Neither what I would have called marriage material. I guess that's why they remained single for so long.'

'Dylan Coyle and Harry Kirby were friends?'

Scully was a tidy eater and didn't speak with his mouth full, a habit Ellie couldn't abide. Good table manners were one of the first things the foster home had taught her. She waited for him to swallow.

'Yes,' he said, after a second or two.

'And you think it's significant in some way?'

'Maybe.' Scully folded the napkin neatly back on the plate. He continued to fold it in ever-decreasing triangles. 'I know one thing' – he lifted his cup – 'those two are not a good influence on one another.'

After a mouthful of coffee, he went on to tell her how Dylan Coyle and Harry Kirby had been involved in an incident, way back when they were in school. Doing odd jobs to fundraise for a school rugby trip, they'd been tidying the garden of a retired member of the board of trade. Along with other lads from the Comprehensive, they'd been cutting away brambles and overgrown fruit bushes when they came upon the shell of an old stone outhouse.

Kirby had suggested they all return after nightfall for a bit of craic, for a séance, he suggested. Kirby had a fixation with the occult at the time. Coyle managed to get hold of a ouija board, and that evening, by a flickering candle, they made the board spell out a message to timid Patrick Shaughnessy – known as 'Shocks' to his mates.

The message warned that Old Silas Keane was coming for Shocks. Keane had operated a pony-and-trap business around the town up until the day he'd died. Kids around the town said he'd never truly passed over, and the story was that he could be seen on foggy nights, riding about the town with his distinctive long grey hair, constantly blessing himself and looking out for company in his trap.

Learning this, Shocks ran like a scalded cat out of the ruin, tripping over an abandoned lawnmower and breaking his leg in three places. Shocks's parents threatened to sue. However, the plaintiffs, Dylan Coyle and Harry Kirby, were represented by Coyle & Coyle Solicitors, Dylan's father's practice. The case was settled out of court.

'Coyle and Kirby sound like a charming pair.' Ellie was sarcastic.

Scully pulled a face. 'The irony is some people think they are. You didn't grow up around here, did you, Ellie?'

'I grew up in a lot of places. Mainly in a small place about fifteen kilometres from here. But you're not from around here either, judging from the American twang.'

'You have a good ear.' Scully raised his cup, saluting her. 'Not many pick up on that. Yeah . . . my folks bailed in a recession and we headed to cousins in New Jersey. But Ma missed the farm and home.' He shrugged. 'For good or ill, we came home to Kerry when I was fourteen.'

'I'll bet you were the man.' She smiled.

Scully shook his head. 'When I came back, all the kids around the town were smoking. They said I was a tight arse, too mean to buy cigarettes. I'll show them, I thought to myself. Off I went and bought a pack of twenty and I handed them round. Would you look at this flash wanker, they said. Look at your man, Scully, flashing all his Yankee money about. So, Ellie, I was damned if I did and damned if I didn't. Damned, either way.'

Ellie rolled her eyes. She knew exactly what that was like. What it was like to be an outsider.

10

'Coyle and Kirby are definitely worth following up on.' Scully pulled his stool in closer. 'As is this bridesmaid woman, Jen.' He circled his thumbs, one around the other. 'I'm just not sure if they'll agree to talk to me.'

He looked into the middle distance.

'You could always say you're doing a tribute piece on Imelda and Marina,' Ellie suggested. 'A sensitive piece to remember the victims by, rather than . . . instead of . . .' She trailed off.

Scully brightened. 'I get you. Yeah, that might just work. In fact, I don't see why it wouldn't. I could certainly see Coyle and Kirby going for that.'

'And it would give you an excuse to record any interviews.'

'It would. And this bridesmaid—' Scully was momentarily distracted by his phone pinging. 'You said you dropped Jen and the other woman off at Godiva's nightclub?'

'I did. The two were dithering about going in.'

'I don't blame them. You been?' His eyes dropped to her hands. Ellie's ring finger was bare.

'Not my scene, I'm afraid.'

'Good call. It's a meat-market.' He pulled a face. 'From what I hear,' he added.

Ellie crossed her legs. 'I read your article about Imelda Gannon's murder.' She had no desire to talk about her personal life.

'That was a first.' He grinned. 'Murder coverage is a bit of a departure for *The Kylebeggan Echo*.'

'Was the woman . . . or were any of the women –' Ellie hesitated – 'were any of them assaulted? Sexually, I mean?'

'I have some information, stuff I can't put into print,' Scully responded guardedly. 'I can't jeopardise the investigation or my source.' She felt him appraising her, making a judgement on how much he could trust her.

She would have to offer up something more.

'Imelda Gannon was popular,' she ventured. 'Just like you said in the article. The thing is . . . I'm not altogether too sure how happy she was.'

'Yeah?'

'I do a school run for a couple of kids who live out beyond Dunseally Castle. A brother and sister. Up to St Columba's Primary and back each day. The parents are GPs, busy all the time. As you can imagine, the kids were devastated at what happened to Imelda. They loved their teacher.'

His navy eyes locked on hers. She had him now.

'You know how kids talk,' she added.

'Especially after a long day at school,' he agreed.

'More especially when they think no one is listening.'

Ellie had found that she became invisible when she was driving the taxi. People seemed to forget she was even there.

'I think there was something up with Imelda.' Ellie paused, mindful of what she was about to share. 'Ava sometimes remarked on how sad her teacher looked. She'd complain that Imelda had changed her mind about playing games with them out in the school playground. Latterly, I heard a lot about

Imelda arranging games, cancelling them, then setting them up again.'

'Maybe Ava just likes sounding off. Kids hate being cooped up. My girls do.'

'That's possible. But instinct tells me there was something to it. A visit to the school might be in order.'

'Maybe.' Scully gave her a considered look. 'Imelda was into sports, so it does seem a little odd. All right, I'll do some digging around.'

'Maybe I could unearth a little more,' Ellie offered. 'I'll be taking the kids to school in the morning.'

'Excellent.'

Ellie fixed him with what she hoped was a meaningful stare.

Scully cleared his throat. 'You asked if any of the victims had been sexually assaulted?'

He'd twigged that this was now an exchange of information.

'My source said that the pathologist's report indicated it wasn't the case. Not in the murder of Isolde Hanly at Myrtle Crescent in January or the second murder in Friary Lane with Imelda Gannon. It's going to be a while before I find out anything about last night's murder of Marina Willoughby.'

Ellie blinked. 'You know they're calling him "The Bride Collector"?'

'Is that so? Puts me in mind of the Fowles book *The Collector*.' Scully rubbed his chin. 'The mayor would have a stroke if I printed something like that.' He chuckled. 'Well, he's going to have zero control about what other media outlets say when they arrive in town.' His gaze was steady. 'Where did you come across that expression, Ellie?'

'In the taxi last night. It's what detectives in Coleman Street are calling him, apparently. There was mention of something else too.

Or someone else, to be exact.' Ellie was keen to reinforce her usefulness to him.

Scully cocked his head.

'Someone called . . . Joseph Liston?'

He shook his head.

'My other passenger, Rose I think her name was, she has some connection to Coleman Street and she mentioned that this guy was of interest. The guy used to drive a taxi or a minibus and may have attacked women in the past?'

'I don't know, as I say, but I can certainly look into it.'

They were interrupted by another pinging. This time Scully got to his feet, gathering up his raincoat. He reknotted his fringed scarf.

'Got to head home to my girls.'

'And I should get home to Henry.' Ellie picked up her bag.

Scully shook the crumbs from his jeans and smoothed his T-shirt over his stomach.

'Cake retention.' He gave a rueful grin.

Ellie smiled.

'If you don't mind me saying, you don't strike me as someone who drives a taxi,' he said.

'And you don't strike me as a crime reporter,' she said tartly.

'I didn't start out as one. I take opportunities as they come along.'

'Likewise.'

Scully pulled a card from the sleeve of his mobile. 'If you think of anything. Or come across something you think may help.' He handed it to Ellie. It had his name and number.

'The girls said I should shave more often.' He rubbed a hand over his stubble. 'That I'll have to smarten myself up before any more slick media types descend.'

Unsure how she was expected to respond, Ellie said nothing and followed him back through the main bar, heading for the door.

64

The old boys were still in residence, perched on their high stools. They were looking up at the TV, absorbed in the early evening news covering the previous night's deadly event in Kylebeggan. Scully paused to watch. Ellie waited beside him.

The newsreader had scant details. Footage moved from shots of tearooms and coffee shops with coloured awnings to the pubs, restaurants and craft shops all along Main Street. There were file images of Brannock Square with its ivy-clad Georgian buildings and fountain, followed by images of pathways by Lough Avulla with picnic tables, and shots of the bowling greens and cycle tracks. The coverage rolled back to the February murder of Imelda Gannon, showing footage taken at the time from Friary Lane. File pictures of Scully – the reporter at the scene – beamed out at them from the TV.

'It's yer man,' said one of the old boys, his back to them.

'Would you look at the cut of him,' remarked his companion.

'A face for radio,' added another.

Outside, the light had all but gone. Ellie and the reporter took a moment to adjust to the cold after the sultry heat of the fire. The sun, which had hardly made an appearance all day, vexingly came out as the day was ending. There were streaks of red across the sky.

'You think those old boys knew you were standing behind them?' asked Ellie.

'Of course they knew.' Scully buttoned his raincoat. It billowed in the breeze as if it were a cloak. 'That lot have eyes in the backs of their heads. You must know by now that you wouldn't get a compliment in Kylebeggan if your life depended on it.'

Ellie watched as Scully marched off with a wink and a grin. She slung her handbag over her shoulder, squeezing it tightly under her arm. When she looked at the sky again, the sun had slipped down behind the white-topped mountains. Like blood on snow.

11

Sitting in her car, in a side street facing Coleman Street garda station, Ellie turned up the heat in the Škoda, wishing she could have her old life back. It had been a dark, unsettling day that made the events in her podcast sound benign. Staring through the rain-grimed windscreen, she shifted in her seat and straightened up.

A number of cars had drawn up outside the station. Ellie turned the wipers on to clear the screen. Two of the cars were emblazoned with *Armed Response Unit*. Her eyes were drawn to shadows moving behind the panes of a third-floor window. She sensed she was being watched. Clipping her seat belt in place, she signalled and joined unusually heavy Sunday traffic. She'd noticed a lot more rental cars on the roads lately. Media, she guessed.

Instead of making for Botany Row and home, she drove down Main Street, passing cafés, tearooms, Kenneally's Food Emporium, Buckley's Bakery and craft shops, all closed for the day. The shop fronts were painted in tangerine, raspberry red, ochre and blue. They should have looked garish but they worked together harmoniously. She drove past the bow window of *The Kylebeggan Echo* with its traditional gold lettering carved into the burgundy frieze above the window.

At the end of Main Street and not far beyond the humpbacked bridge the road began to climb. Three-storey over-basement terraced houses soon gave way to small neat housing developments. Further on again, on either side of the climbing road, the houses grew once more in size and grandeur. Individually designed homes on landscaped plots, each with views over the valley. Approaching the sign for Pottershill, she felt a flutter. She followed the signpost and drove past a number of smaller roads branching right and left.

The moon was coming up behind the Black Pins as she pulled into the cul-de-sac, parking behind another car for cover. The taxi gave her an excuse to sit, to watch, to reminisce. The intervals between her visits were getting longer, yet she was careful not to stay too long. She didn't want attention.

All eight houses were detached residences, each house with six or seven bedrooms, elegant public rooms, spacious gardens and views out over the foothills of the mountains. Some homes had been turned into guesthouses. Ellie's former home sat in the right quadrant of the semicircle. And it was, in her opinion, the finest.

She recalled summer cocktails on the terrace outside the French windows of the drawing room. It was hard to tell from here if anyone was taking care of the gardens. The front looked more unkempt than usual.

Ellie studied the façade of her old home, the sting of tears burning her eyelids. The light closed in as clouds scraped across the sky, making it harder to see. Suddenly the front door opened.

It was him.

With her.

She hadn't expected that. She slunk low in her seat.

Even from this vantage point, she could make out her pinched, mean-eyed, money-grabbing face. Five years younger than Ellie, she swanned down the front steps in thigh-high boots and the vulgar confidence of a bleached blonde with laser-whitened teeth. He followed behind.

He looked well, as always. Trim and fit. He ambled down the steps, heading to the car in that loose, languid way he had. Neither of them gave Ellie a passing glance as they whizzed past in a sporty new BMW.

Ellie's eyes welled up. She thought back to her happy times here, to times that would be no more. She thought of her brother's words earlier, 'That house should be yours, you know.'

She couldn't face more pulling and dragging through the courts. She had one more battle in her, and she would save that energy for Johnny's appeal. She pulled herself together and turned the engine on.

By the time she got back home to Botany Row, there was rain and the beginnings of a westerly wind. As she crossed the cobbled street, she observed the now familiar twitch of Pauline's net curtains.

With her key in the front door, Ellie stopped. She stepped back, smelling paint. Mervyn had been busy. His nameplate was returned to its original condition, now reading *The Snug*. She turned the key and went inside. She'd had plans but she was too drained for anything else just now. Henry would have to wait.

She switched the fire to full, turned on the lamp and padded to the fridge. She deserved a drink after the day she'd had. On the settee, wine glass in hand, she mulled over the encounter with the reporter.

Though he was new to crime reporting, Ellie had a feeling Scully would be good. He'd seen she could be useful to him. Well, that could be a two-way arrangement. Scully could be very useful to her as well. He'd taken up her suggestions nicely. And he was going to make recordings of his interviews, so she could listen in.

Later that night, Ellie was roused from her sleep by the sound of her mobile ringing. She propped herself up on her pillow, rubbing her eyes and feeling for the phone in the dark. She had forgotten to put it on silent.

She stared at the number sliding across her screen. Not one she recognised. An unknown number ringing her at two in the morning? It kept ringing. She turned the phone to silent, concerned it might wake Mervyn.

The call rang off. She let her breath go and sat wide awake against the pillow, listening to the creaking noises inside the house. Outside, the wind was whirling. It rattled against the bedroom window. She waited, wondering what to do. She had a tightening across her chest when the phone lit up again, casting a spectral glow on the sloping ceiling. The same unknown number as before.

She swiped a trembling finger across the screen.

'Hello?' she whispered.

'Ellie . . .' The voice was breathless. Hushed. 'Ellie, is that you?'

'Who's this?' Her voice shook.

'It's me. Johnny. I got my hands on some lad's phone . . . he's sleeping.'

'Jesus, Johnny,' she whispered.

Would her brother never learn?

'You'll get your head caved in—'

'Never mind about that. Listen, Ellie, I've something for you. About this guy, Joseph Liston . . .'

Hugging her knees to her chest, listen she did, for the next two minutes with no interruptions.

12

The Land Rover dipped and bounced over the brown, rain-swilled potholes as Scully drove down the boreen towards the lights and back to the cottage. The forecast on Skellig FM had warned of swells by Valentia Island and of strong winds in the south of the county. A twig from a nearby branch got caught in the wipers. He'd have to get the scythe out and cut those briars. He flicked away some lingering crumbs on his T-shirt. That scone in the Three Hags had barely taken the edge off his hunger.

The tyres made a crunching sound on the gravel as he swung up by the outhouses. He flung his door open to the sound of a hooting owl. The sound was coming from the copse of trees down at the river behind the cottage.

Turning the key in the cottage door, he entered the small lobby, tossed his coat on a hook, pulled off his shoes and lifted the latch to the kitchen. The scene before him filled him with alarm. His wife was slumped in her chair and the girls were trying to deal with her.

Straightening her up and making her comfortable, Scully confirmed she didn't want to go upstairs just yet. The kitchen was tidy enough and the girls had left the remains of the chicken in a red enamel crock on the dresser. He'd liquidised a separate meal for Jill that morning. Maude informed him they'd both finished their weekend homework and had set out their uniforms for school. They were trying hard.

Scully fixed himself some food, leaving enough for lunchboxes for the following day. Carrying his plate to the sofa, he moved aside the mess of newspapers and turned on the TV, going to Netflix. Scarlett and Maude snuggled in next to him, one on either side. These days they were a lot less chatty, keeping their thoughts to themselves. And for the next while all four sat in their own private worlds, supposedly watching *Bleak House*.

Scarlett looked up at him. 'About our sandwiches, Dad . . .'

'Yes?'

'Can you buy gluten-free bread? I think I might be coeliac.'

'What?'

'Rebecca Collins is coeliac. Says she feels so much better now she's gluten-free.'

'Coeliac, my arse.' Scully snorted. 'You're no more coeliac than the man in the moon. That Rebecca Collins is a proper little notice-box. Don't pay any attention to her.'

'Mum . . .?'

Scarlett looked to her mother.

Jill blinked but didn't respond. Her eyelids drooped lethargically.

'Bedtime, girls.' Scully got to his feet. 'I'll get Mum organised. She must be tired.'

He lumbered up the stairs with Jill in his arms. The girls followed behind, to their shared bedroom across the open landing.

It was gone eleven by the time he'd made Jill comfortable for the night. Downstairs, he was arranging things for the week ahead and had just put the washing machine on when he heard something. He turned around.

Moonlight was streaming through the rooflight on to the mezzanine landing. Scarlett was standing in her nightdress looking down on him through the wooden slats, her eyes dark hollows.

'What's the matter, Scarlett?'

'You're going to stay in the house, Dad – you won't go out again tonight?' She pulled at the hem of her nightdress.

'No, Scarlett, not tonight. I've had a busy day and it's wild enough out there.'

She never used to check up on him. It was affecting them all in different ways.

The following morning at St Columba's Primary, Scully thanked the principal for seeing him at short notice. Having asked about signs of stress in his girls, he chanced a few, concerned queries about tragic teacher Imelda Gannon.

The principal offered him tea. She assured him his girls were doing fine. Unlike some other pupils in the junior cycle. 'We've had the school psychologist in,' she said.

'I passed the floral tributes outside.' Scully stirred his tea, ignoring the phone pinging in his pocket.

The principal turned her gaze to the window. 'It's difficult to know when to bin the flowers. To know what's a respectable amount of time. I think they're ready for the compost now.' She paused. 'Imelda started our school garden, you know. The garden was her idea. It's just so sad.'

'Tragic,' Scully agreed.

'Whatever we as adults make of what happened, the younger ones can't get their heads around it at all. They imagine it's like Imelda being off sick. That she'll be back after a while.'

'Did Imelda take much time off?'

'On and off. We used to joke in the staffroom that hockey

would be the death of her. She was always spraining or tearing some muscle or other. Had a path worn to Finbar Deasy's.'

Scully raised his brow.

'Sick notes,' she explained. 'We used to tease her that she was holding him back from retirement.'

Long past normal retirement age, everyone knew that Deasy was fond of the gargle. Same as everyone knew there'd be no problem getting a sick note from him. That's where Paudie, at Skellig FM, got his.

'What position did Imelda play?' Scully asked. 'I've covered hockey in my time.'

'You'd have to ask her team-mates at the hockey club.'

Scully had asked enough. He'd made that cardinal error before, seeming too interested. As he shook the principal's hand, he became aware of something going on outside. There was activity. He directed his gaze through the Venetian blinds.

'You've got company.' Two white vans had pulled up outside the school's electric gates. The outside-broadcasting vans were from a national news channel. A high-calibre outfit.

The principal's face set in grim lines. She lifted her chin. 'There's no way that lot are setting up camp out there. This is an educational establishment.'

'Well, they can't film while children are in the yard. That's off-limits,' Scully offered. 'Cite them the Data Protection Act.'

'Excuse me.' She picked up the phone. 'I need to call the board of management.'

Scully knew it had merely been a matter of time. The story was growing by the day. As he pushed the buzzer and exited the school gates, he was approached by a heavily made-up woman.

'This is the school where Imelda Gannon taught, right?'

'Ah no, love.'

73

He adjusted his scarf against the biting wind.

'This is St Columba's junior school,' he explained. 'Imelda Gannon taught in St Columba's middle school a few kilometres back, on the Ring of Kerry road. God rest her.'

Agitated, the woman raced past him without a word of thanks and shouted new instructions to her crew. Scully would have to move fast to stay ahead of the pack.

Back in the Land Rover, he blew on his hands to warm them up, then pulled out his phone. Now, what was troubling Ellie Gillespie? It was the third text from her this morning. Maybe best to call her.

She answered straightaway.

'I've come by some information,' she said. 'On Joseph Liston.'

'Fire ahead,' he said, feeling her adrenaline.

'Well, this guy has form. Used to run a minibus service, not a taxi, back in the day. About twelve years ago, he raped a couple of women, allegedly. Kylebeggan women.' She let out a long breath, followed by a sharp inhale.

'I was out of the country at that time,' Scully mused. 'I suppose it explains why it doesn't ring a bell with me. Then again, in a small town people don't always talk about stuff like this.'

'That's true.' Ellie appeared to consider his point. 'My information says that one of the women had been on her way home from a bowling outing. The second . . . incident . . . happened about three weeks later. This time, it was a woman who'd been on her way home from a wedding.'

She went on to tell him how both women had been the last ones to be dropped to their stops. The first woman had been a pensioner. The second had been a woman in her twenties. 'For some reason the cases never went to trial.'

'Curious.'

'It is, isn't it? As you might expect, Liston lost his minibus business and only got odd jobs after that. You might get a chance to look into it a little more?'

'Let me see what I can dig up. I'm going to follow up another lead first.'

'Yeah?'

'Something doesn't stack up with Imelda Gannon, as you thought. I've a feeling she was hiding something.'

'Let me know, won't you?'

'I will.' He hesitated. 'I'm sure I don't need to say this, but take care out there, Ellie. I reckon you're safe enough in the town where it's lit and busy, but the country roads around here are dark as soot at this time of year.'

13

Trish Walsh worked on the reception desk at Shanaglish Mountain Lodge. She also happened to be the ladies' captain at Kylebeggan Hockey Club. She was about to go on her lunch break when Scully rocked up to her desk. When he explained that he was doing a tribute piece on Imelda, she agreed to talk to him. The hotel was expecting a deluge of guests, she cautioned. It would have to be brief.

They sat on deep-seated, squashy sofas in the foyer, looking out on a waterfall, the far side of the valley. Melting snow at the top of the Black Pins was adding to the force of the flow. Scully could see white spray being highjacked by the wind. The spray glistened in a rainbow of colours in a sudden burst of sunshine.

'Imelda was a keen gardener,' Scully opened. 'I've just been up at the school.'

'She was always in her element, gardening with the kids.' Trish's eyes watered. 'The kids loved Imelda too.' Her tears threatened to brim over. 'She got such a kick out of training the younger ones in our club. She was a real team player, you know, an inspiration and—'

'Accident-prone, so I hear,' he interrupted gently.

She looked at him blankly.

'Prone to injuries?' he prompted. He bit into the costly triple-decker sandwich. He'd felt obliged to order something.

'No more than anyone else. The last time I remember Imelda being injured was Christmas a year ago.' Trish cut into a plump chicken breast. 'She had to ice an ankle. Nothing dramatic.' She chopped her salad with vigour. 'Imelda did have a few falls out at the construction site though, if that's what you mean.'

Scully stopped mid-chew.

'The house,' said Trish. 'The new house they were building at Ardeevin Cross?'

'Right.'

Scully had heard that Harry Kirby had become involved in construction. Building golfers' villas.

'I hear Harry's not doing so good himself,' he said softly. 'That he's in a bad way.'

Scully had heard no such thing. He was fishing.

'Would you blame the poor man?'

Trish turned the conversation back to Imelda's hockey career. It was more a monologue than a conversation. She rattled off match anecdote after anecdote as Scully resisted the urge to glaze over.

'Trish?' A nervous lad in uniform approached. 'Can you come back to the desk?' he asked, apologetically. 'There's a mis-understanding about an online booking. Three journalists in from the UK—'

'I'll sort it.'

She turned to Scully. 'That's it, I'm afraid. I hope I've given you something you can use.'

'You've been very helpful.' Trish Walsh had given him more than she knew.

The front desk was swarming. A coach-load of US visitors had arrived, vocal in their admiration of the views. And a rabble of reporters, equally vocal in their dispute about a booking. Trish looked like she could do with her hockey stick to sort them out.

Instead of exiting through the revolving door, Scully slipped through the one to the side, following the person in front. Her head was bowed, a laptop case slung over her shoulder.

Scully had spotted the woman as soon as she'd stepped out from the lift into the lobby. Constance Kiely, state pathologist. A black jeep swung up to the steps to meet her. She got in swiftly and the jeep pulled away.

He checked his phone. Nothing that needed urgent attention. Just a couple of texts in from Ellie.

Good luck with the Imelda Gannon queries. E

And another one she'd sent an hour later.

And the Joseph Liston queries too. E

He made it back to his desk just after 2:00 p.m. When Gerry Bradshaw, his editor, came back after lunch, Scully apprised him of his plans. As long as the pages of *The Kylebeggan Echo* were filled, Gerry was largely indifferent to the contents. Gerry didn't really give a shite.

The owner and editor had sold the ailing newspaper to Lir Media Group, and in so doing had pulled off a masterstroke. The middle-aged editor got a lump sum and a contract to keep him in employment until retirement. In fairness, Gerry did put in the odd appearance, but more often than not he was found enjoying a round of golf out at Finneran's Dip.

Scully had a number of calls to make. There should be something in by now. He avoided using the landline on the desk, scrolling instead to the number they'd agreed to use.

His call was answered gruffly.

'Hello, my friend, it's me,' said Scully.

'Right you are,' came a less abrasive tone, 'just a sec . . .'

There came the sound of footsteps and doors opening and closing, followed by the outside rumble of traffic. In light of recent revelations about garda stations around the country being bugged, Tall Dark was taking precautions. He was freaked out by what had happened to a colleague who'd tried using normal channels to expose a cover-up of Judge Donegan's drink-driving offences.

'OK, shoot,' said the sergeant.

Scully asked Tall Dark if results were in from Forensics on the weekend's murder at Arbutus Road. The sergeant confirmed they were indeed treating Marina Willoughby's death as murder. Her body had been posed in the same fashion as Isolde Hanly's in Myrtle Crescent and Imelda Gannon's in Friary Lane. As in the previous cases, there was no evidence of forced entry at the murder scene. A file was being prepared on the case for the Director of Public Prosecutions.

'A case of the Bride Collector strikes again?' Scully quipped.

'Doesn't take the brightest brains in the country to figure that one out,' responded Tall Dark.

Scully tapped his feet. He needed more. He needed details. Tall Dark hadn't come across the toxicology report. Yet.

'The first two victims, can you remember if there was anything about bruising on their bodies?' Scully asked. 'Did Constance Kiely make any remarks on that?'

'Dunno, pal. Not off the top of my head anyway. Give me a minute . . . I took some screenshots of the preliminaries—'

Scully drummed his fingers.

'Yeah, actually there's some stuff in the reports all right. Both women had bruising. Old bruising. One had bruising on the hips.

Consistent with a possible slip or fall, it says. The other victim, Imelda Gannon, she had unexplained bruising around the abdomen and torso.'

'Interesting.'

The fuzzy outline of a theory was beginning to take shape in Scully's head. A little visit to Harry Kirby might be in order.

'Before I go, do you have anything on a guy called Joseph Liston? I'm hearing he's a suspect and that he was accused of raping a couple of women years ago but never stood trial?'

'That's right. His name is being tossed about here in Coleman Street. Both women reported the assaults at the time. Statements were taken, but the women dropped the charges. I don't think either of them wanted the stress or publicity of a rape trial. Who could blame them? God forbid, if it happened to anyone belonging to me, I'm not sure I'd advise going to court. I've seen what goes on.'

'What's Liston up to nowadays?'

'Not much. On social security, probably. Living down in Lowertown, tinkering about with old wrecks of cars. Listen, I gotta go . . . I've been out the back of the station here for long enough. If it got out that I was talking to you, I'd be in Traffic for the rest of my days.'

'You'd still get early retirement and a civil servant's pension.'

The sergeant snorted. 'I didn't join the force to spend my time directing traffic.'

'I owe you, pal.'

Scully hung up.

They'd agreed no names. Not that the sergeant had any idea his nickname was Tall Dark. Scully knew he was no oil painting himself, but the unfortunate sergeant looked as if he'd been assembled from spare parts, thrown together from a height.

Scully checked the time and grabbed his coat from the back of his chair. There might just be enough time to pop over to the Fiddler's Arms before he headed home.

14

The March wind buffeted the Škoda as Ellie swung in behind the pillars of the Old Manse. She left the engine of the taxi running as she waited. It was coming up to 8:30 a.m.

A magpie eyeballed her from the portico above the front door, strutting from one end to the other before taking off. The door opened a fraction and Ellie observed a dark-skinned young woman adjust the beanie hat of one child, then another, before ushering them out in the cold. Gabriella did not wave to Ellie as she usually did, but quickly shut the door. Liam immediately ripped off his hat and kicked at loose stones as he made his way towards the taxi.

'Good morning,' Ellie said cheerily. Early morning did not bring out the best in Liam. 'How are things with you guys?'

'Mum's going mental.' Ava leaned over to buckle her brother's seat belt. 'Gabriella said she wants to go home to Spain, that she's too scared to stay around Kylebeggan.'

'That's a shame.' Ellie turned in a semicircle and headed back out on to the tree-lined road. 'You should tell Gabriella not to worry. That they'll catch that nasty person soon.'

'I don't want another au pair,' Liam moaned. 'I like Gabriella.'

Ellie pointed above the tree line. 'Is that a hawk?' She couldn't be listening to whingeing this early in the morning. A winged creature swooped and disappeared from view. There was no engagement from Liam. In peaceful silence, for the next kilometre or so, Ellie tried to overtake a laundry truck while listening in to the radio. It was down low.

> The atmosphere in the Kerry town of Kylebeggan is tense this Tuesday. Hoteliers and guesthouse owners report above average occupancy due to international news crews but are said to be worried. They normally see a surge in summer bookings this time of year, but say that cancellations are on the increase.
>
> Despite a division of the Special Crime Squad being dispatched to Kerry, it appears detectives are no closer to apprehending a suspect for these sinister killings. The latest woman to be murdered has been named as Marina Willoughby, a solicitor who worked locally with Coyle & Coyle solicitors in Kylebeggan. As the days go by, local residents are on high alert. In the parks, in the food markets and the many cafés and tearooms they all ask the same thing. Who is the Bride Collector? And when will he be caught?

As Ellie pulled up outside the school, a group of women with prams checked over their shoulders. Their eyes lingered on her taxi sign before turning back to their group. They snuggled their scarves in around their necks. Ellie had seen it. She felt it too. The fear. That gnawing unease. That sense of being watched.

The apprehension that had gripped her did not let go all week and she was glad to be busy. Midweek was her Blue Rinse Brigade. After the school drop-off on Wednesday, she drove to a neat housing development to collect Doreen.

Thanks to Doreen, Ellie had other senior citizens on her books. Ladies who liked to get their hair done once a week, but who could no longer drive because they'd proven a hazard to themselves or others on the road.

Doreen was Ellie's first-ever Blue Rinse lady. She'd put the word out about the taxi service. Before long, Ellie had found herself with requests from many families, keen to have a female driver for their ageing mothers. It was a reliable stream of business. She enjoyed the company of the ladies and they in turn felt safe with Ellie.

Doreen waited at her door, clutching her handbag and umbrella. Ellie greeted the pensioner, took the walking frame and umbrella and helped Doreen into the passenger seat. She set the walking frame in the boot and got into the front.

'Thank you, Ellie,' said Doreen. 'You're a little angel. You know that? Oh Lord, it's bitter this morning. That wind would rip the face off you.' Doreen strapped her seat belt on and settled her bag on her lap. 'I don't know how I'd get to the hair saloon without you, love.'

For some reason, Doreen insisted on calling Klassy Kuts a hair 'saloon'. To her, Klassy Kuts was more than just a hair salon, it was the Ministry of Information, and the veracity of any news gleaned inside was not a consideration.

'You're the daughter-in-law I wish I had, you know.'

'All I do is give you a lift to Klassy Kuts.' Ellie laughed. 'It's nothing.'

'It's not nothing. You make me feel like a lady, my dear.' The pensioner smoothed her skirt over her knees. 'Because you're a lady yourself.'

Ellie felt a burst of pleasure. Wouldn't Bessie from the foster home have loved such praise?

'As I keep telling you, Ellie – my son is a gentleman. You'd make such a lovely couple.'

'I'll bear that in mind. Thanks, Doreen. I'm doing OK on my own for now.'

The journey to the salon took fifteen minutes, usually. It took longer than that today because of traffic. Doreen tutted and checked her watch. 'I wouldn't like to miss my appointment, love.' She opened the clasp on her handbag. 'Just let me get my phone and I'll send a text.'

'I'll do that, Doreen.' Ellie phoned ahead to let the salon know of the delay.

'Isn't it shocking what's happened, Ellie? If you ask me, I think we have one of those, what do you call them . . . those sequel killers. You know where it all went wrong, don't you? There's no such thing as right and wrong any more. It's all gone out of fashion. There's no heaven. There's no such thing as hell. Sure, no wonder the world is gone to the dogs.'

Ellie kept her smile to herself. On these journeys, she was not generally required to talk, only listen.

'Word has it that Marina Willoughby was laid out the very same as Isolde.' Doreen fiddled with the buttons of her coat. 'Same as that teacher, Imelda Gannon, too. Laid out, just like in that wedding rhyme. You know the one.'

Ellie glanced at Doreen.

Doreen sighed.

'So much has changed with all you young people. I don't know what you know any more.' She shook her head. 'The rhyme goes, *Something old, something new, something borrowed, something blue, and a silver sixpence in her shoe.*' Doreen rubbed the handles of her bag, up and down, down and up. 'Poor Isolde. The poor craythur. She didn't deserve to go like that, you know.'

'None of the victims did.'

Ellie craned her neck to check the line of traffic ahead. She'd have to allow extra time for this trip in future. It was fifteen minutes more before she finally turned into Limekiln Road, pulling up at Klassy Kuts.

The salon was right next door to Minerva's. Ellie had been hoping to set her passenger down discreetly. Minerva's was Mervyn's tanning salon, and right by the half-open door stood the man himself, blowing cigarette smoke out into the street.

'Now there's a God-help-us, if ever I saw one,' Doreen muttered. 'God forgive me, only a mother could love a face like that.'

'You could be right,' said Ellie, springing out of the taxi, pretending she hadn't seen her neighbour.

Doreen swung her legs out on to the pavement. 'Did I tell you I'm thinking of getting my veins done?' She looked up at Ellie. 'There's this new lady doctor down at the Aurora Clinic that does them. A nice woman—'

'I'll be back to get you at half past, Doreen.'

Ellie helped the pensioner to her feet and busied herself with Doreen's things. She felt Mervyn's piggy eyes boring holes into her back. With Doreen handed over to Jacinta in the salon, Ellie slipped back inside her car and checked her phone. One missed call. One text. It was Scully. She sat back, took a breath and dialled.

The reporter answered straightaway.

'Do you have a few minutes?' It sounded urgent.

'I do, as it happens. I'm between fares.'

'I'm at Mountain View community centre,' he said. 'There's plenty of parking and it's quieter than the centre of town. Away from prying eyes. I'll meet you at the Coffee Station.'

'See you as soon as I can. The traffic's awful.'

'Get used to it. Things are only kicking off. It's going to be that way for a while.'

As Ellie pulled off, Mervyn beamed and waved. He'd been standing there, watching her, all the time.

15

Ellie pulled up her collar and knotted the belt of her wool coat before hurrying across the car park. It felt an age since she'd been at Mountain View.

Giant ferns in stone urns stood on either side of the sliding glass doors. The filigrees of green swayed in the wind. Under the long slate porch of the annexe to her right, picnic benches sat empty.

The community centre was a marriage of nineteenth-century and contemporary architecture, and one of the more ambitious projects embarked on by Kerry County Council. Adding a glass and steel structure to the side of the refurbished Victorian railway station had inspired debate. The result was pleasing to Ellie's eyes. She admired the fusion of old and new.

The modern building housed a swimming pool on the ground floor and sports halls on both levels, while the original structure housed the Coffee Station where she was now headed.

She was met by wafts of chlorine as the doors parted. A glance at the digital timetable told her the pool was reserved for a Mother and Toddler swim session. No other activities were scheduled for that morning. A good choice of venue on Scully's part, she thought.

Her winter boots echoed off the tiled floor as she passed by the turnstile, the reception desk and the central staircase, proceeding towards the low lighting and flagstone floor of the Coffee Station. Seating was arranged around a number of small round tables and more was provided in booths along one wall.

At the sound of footsteps, a man emerged from a booth and came towards her in a long, smart coat and fringed scarf. He looked very different to the unshaven reporter she'd met the previous Sunday.

There was a sparkle in his eye. 'It's my funeral coat. My only coat. I do scrub up occasionally.'

'I see you've got the coffees.' She pointed to the cups, embarrassed he had clocked her expression.

He directed her to the seat opposite. She noted he'd chosen a booth with a line of sight to the concourse and the main entrance.

'Thought I'd bring you up to speed.' He slid a cup towards her. 'And maybe you can confirm a few things.'

She tipped some milk into her coffee. 'If I can.'

'First up, I called on Harry Kirby, Imelda Gannon's fiancé, at his parents' place. It was hard to get the guy alone with his mother clucking over him.' Scully stirred thoughtfully. 'The guy was cagey. But when I put it to him that I was doing this tribute piece on Imelda, he changed his tune.' He raised his cup. 'Kudos to you, Ellie.'

She shrugged off the compliment.

'Kirby tells me how he and Imelda had been going out together on and off for a couple of years. I tell him I've just been up at Imelda's school, St Columba's. That they'd been telling me all about her work with the school garden, but that she'd had an accident a while back, ending up black and blue. She'd tripped over clay pots, I said. Harry, he's nodding away, going yeah, yeah, I remember that . . .'

Scully ripped the wrapping off a biscuit that accompanied their coffees.

89

'And?' Ellie prompted.

Scully took a bite. He chewed. He swallowed. 'I don't imagine Imelda Gannon was in a happy situation. You were right. According to my source, she had bruising. Old bruising. Imelda didn't have a fall at the school. I made that up . . .'

He leaned out, scanning the other booths, checking that he and Ellie were the sole customers.

'My feeling is that Harry might have been . . . coercive. Agreeing so readily that Imelda had had an accident at the school was very telling.'

'The kids were right,' said Ellie softly. 'Liam and Ava *had* picked up on something.'

'According to preliminary reports, there was old bruising on Isolde Hanly's body as well.'

Ellie gripped her cup .

'Of course, none of this suggests that Harry Kirby is guilty of anything more than domestic abuse, awful enough as that is.' Scully sat back, running a hand through a thatch of wiry hair. 'We know he has an alibi for the night Imelda was murdered. He was on his stag with Dylan Coyle and his old rugby mates.'

'And I imagine Dylan Coyle has an alibi in Harry Kirby for the night Marina Willoughby was killed?'

'To be confirmed. But there's something else. I asked Harry about this bridesmaid who keeps popping up everywhere – this girl, Jen.'

Ellie set her cup down.

'It took an amount of wheedling to get the woman's address out of him. Jen hasn't moved out of the parental nest either.'

'That generation stay with Mum and Dad for ever. Helps them save for a deposit, I guess.'

'I was turfed out of home soon as I hit eighteen.' Scully grinned.

'I was turfed out of lots of homes long before I was eighteen.' Ellie was homeless more times than she cared to remember, before Bessie's place.

Scully widened his eyes.

'I grew up in foster homes,' Ellie said, and quickly pursed her lips. She hadn't meant to be so revealing.

Scully carried on. 'When I pitched up at the home of said bridesmaid, Jen Healy, it turned out Ms Healy had taken time off work. She was in pyjamas and a dressing gown when I called. The mother tells me her daughter is in shock. Depressed, she says. That in between the garda interviews, all her daughter's doing is watching *Downton Abbey*. I felt like telling her that would depress the hell out of anyone.'

Ellie felt her mouth pull into a smile.

'Jen struck me as assured and capable,' she remarked. 'How did she come across to you?'

'There was a nervousness. Could be shock or she's possibly hiding something, I don't know. I moved quickly to the night of Marina Willoughby's murder, last Saturday.' Scully paused, pulling his eyebrows close together. 'You did say you dropped Marina's two companions outside Godiva's nightclub?'

'Yes.' Ellie nodded, following closely.

'I thought as much.'

Scully explained that neither woman had actually gone into the nightclub. Jen told him that they'd stood in the queue for a bit and changed their minds. They'd split the money Marina had given them and taken separate taxis home, or so she said. She also said she was too drunk to remember the name of the cab company she had used.

Ellie pulled a face. 'She was fairly tipsy when I dropped them off, but I wouldn't say she was roaring drunk.'

Scully explained that he had checked in with his source to see if Jen's story was corroborated. His source had confirmed a taxi driver did indeed remember collecting Rose Moriarty, but no one could recall collecting Jen Healy. Nothing was captured on CCTV in the area. Scully sat back and placed both hands on the table.

'The fact is that Jen Healy does not have an alibi for the night of Marina Willoughby's murder,' he said softly.

Ellie stretched her leg out. She had pins and needles.

'I wonder, Ellie, if you could do a bit of digging around with the other taxi drivers?' Scully prompted.

'Maybe.' She loosened the belt of her coat and undid the buttons. She was hot. 'To recap, you're saying there was bruising, old bruising, on the first two victims, Isolde Hanly and Imelda Gannon. You're also saying that Jen Healy doesn't have an alibi. And if I understand, you're suggesting that Harry Kirby may have been . . . abusive . . . to Imelda?'

'You have it in a nutshell.'

'Anything on Joseph Liston?'

'Keeping a low profile, I hear, tinkering away with cars down in Lowertown.' Scully checked the time. 'Unfortunately, I now have to head over to Skellig FM for my slot. Folk still want their birthday and anniversary requests, regardless of whether we have a Golden State Killer or a Jack the Ripper in our midst.' He gathered the cups and saucers and returned them to the guy who was refreshing the menu on the chalkboard behind the counter.

Ellie walked slowly towards the concourse. Scully caught her up. 'I meant to also say that I'm hoping to hear something on toxicology tests.'

'You'll let me know?'

'I'll probably have had an update from my source by the time you hear back from any other taxi drivers,' he said, pointedly.

It was clear Ellie wasn't going to be updated free of charge. 'Well, good luck with your investigations. I'll leave you here.' They were standing outside the ladies' washroom. 'Thanks for the coffee.'

'You're welcome.' He smiled. The navy-hued circles underneath his eyes matched the navy of his long coat.

When Ellie emerged from the washroom, Scully had departed. And yet she had a sense of someone watching. She looked about but there was no one. Through the sliding doors, the wind caught her hair. She tidied it behind her ears, swiping a quick look at the nearby picnic benches outside. No one. An abandoned polystyrene cup tumbled across the tarmac in the breeze and an empty crisp packet tumbled across the surface of one table, floating on to the ground, only to be whisked into winter-shrivelled hedges that separated the parking bays.

She spotted something and quickened her step. She couldn't be certain but it had looked like a van with a satellite dish antenna. She kept her head down the whole way to the car. Pulling out of the car park, Ellie knew exactly what she needed. She had time before going back to the salon to collect Doreen.

She went to Boots the Chemist. To the middle aisle. The aisle that sold expensive body creams. In her hand she held a foot cream. A spa brand, on special offer. She had often paid twice the price.

Her heart was racing like a fucked clock. She gave an inward grin. It was one of Johnny's lines from his favourite film. She'd promised they'd watch it again as soon as he got out of prison.

Some things were second nature to her. This was one. Ellie sometimes wondered about their father, if he too had been good at thieving. Their mother had never spoken of him.

A security guy was standing by the razors. Built like a brick shithouse, as Johnny would say. The guy hadn't as much as looked in Ellie's direction. Why would he? She was well dressed, well spoken. She'd already embarrassed him into looking well away from her by asking him to point out where the tampons were. What reason would he have to look as she slipped two tubes of sea-algae foot cream into her expensive bag? She'd always been much better at this than Johnny.

Outside on the street, the pounding in her ears abated and her heart returned to normal. She felt a deepening calm, as relaxing as any spa treatment on any cruise ship. Back in the Škoda, she felt good. She'd needed that.

She checked her phone. Doreen normally texted to say if she was finished early. There was nothing. All good. As she rounded the corner into Limekiln Road, she saw blue flashing lights outside Klassy Kuts.

She felt her chest tighten. No. She was mistaken. The garda car was not outside the hair salon. It was parked outside Minerva's. Along with even more cars. Ellie pulled in on the opposite side of the street.

As she watched, the door to Minerva's opened. Two uniformed gardaí exited the shop and got into the flashing car. They exchanged some words before driving off at speed. Two other cars followed in convoy. Ellie reached for her phone.

Her call was answered on the first ring.

'That was quick. Didn't expect to hear back from you so soon.'

'There was bruising on two of the victims' bodies,' Ellie said. 'That's what your source told you, right?'

'Yeah, that's right,' Scully replied, sounding curious.

'Was there anything else about the bodies?' Ellie's heart was thumping.

'You'll need to be more specific. Why do you ask?'

'I'll tell you why. I'm here in Limekiln Road collecting a fare from the hair salon, and a bunch of gardaí have just left Minerva's.'

'Minerva's?'

'Minerva's is a tanning salon. And now I'm wondering if any of the victims had been using sunbeds?'

'It's possible, I guess.'

'The reason I ask is because the guy that runs the place is very odd. I know him. He lives beside me in Botany Row – he's my next-door neighbour.'

16

He usually met his contact in the woods, about a kilometre or so in from the entrance. It was a good place to meet without it looking suspicious. Part ancient woodland, part sitka spruce, Doone Wood's numerous trails were crisscrossed by runners and cyclists.

Tall Dark had informed Scully that the path was known locally as Brokeback Mountain. Scully didn't give a crap what it was called, as long as the sergeant kept his shovel-like hands to himself and kept up the steady supply of information.

Scully's nostrils filled with the fresh scent of pine and his ears rang with the chatter of the high-up birds. Above him, swirls of cloud clipped the treetops. As he ran along, the woodland air felt cool and damp on his legs.

Following the latest phone call from Ellie, Scully had put in a call to his contact. The taxi driver had been unnerved about her neighbour and had asked Scully to find out what he could. He was happy to follow up. Their little arrangement was working out quite nicely.

He clocked Tall Dark in a clearing by the water. What was the guy wearing? Scully had never seen kit like it. Emerald green nylon running shorts, knee-high black socks and red running shoes. The guy could be arrested for crimes against fashion. Tall Dark looked about him before saluting.

Scully clapped his back. 'Thanks for coming, pal.'

'No bother, I needed the air. It's been mad down at the station.'

'I can only imagine.' Scully cut to the chase. 'Manage to find out anything about that tanning place, Minerva's?'

'As I told you on the phone, the Serious Crime boys are checking out *all* the tanning salons.'

Tall Dark squinted into the trees as if there might be someone lurking. He'd already informed Scully that detectives were trying to identify what the murdered women might have had in common. When two victims were found to have tan lines on their bodies, checking out tanning salons for further attention had seemed a reasonable approach to Scully.

Tall Dark sniffed. 'I have to say it didn't strike me as a particularly significant line of enquiry.'

Having his old friend as a contact inside the force was helpful, but the sergeant had his limitations.

'Are there many tanning salons in town?' Scully asked.

'Three, believe it or not. Young fellas use the beds as well, I hear.'

'I'd be tempted myself.'

'I'd prefer to go out foreign.'

Scully couldn't imagine himself anywhere foreign any time soon.

Tall Dark stretched his arms behind his head. 'Begley's wound very tight, with the Serious Crime Squad in town.' He limbered up with a sideways bend. 'Those boys are awfully fond of their Venn diagrams. The whiteboard in the Incident Room is covered in them.'

Scully could see how they'd be useful. 'What happened when the detectives went to visit the tanning salons?' he prompted.

'Turned out that both Imelda Gannon and Marina Willoughby had been using the beds in Minerva's, preparing for their weddings.'

Scully whistled. Ellie wouldn't be pleased with this news.

'Superintendent Begley caught up with the detectives when they came back to the station. The lads reported that the owner is a single bloke, not keen for his old dear to find out about his visit from the gardaí. Begley thinks the guy is harmless. I think the superintendent is cooking up some ideas of his own.' Tall Dark took off in the lead. 'I don't rate Begley's judgement,' he said.

Tall Dark continued talking as he lumbered along. The trail was wide enough for two of them. 'In fact, I wouldn't believe daylight out of that fucker . . . but he has his eye on someone. He and Mayor Halligan want an end to the publicity. They want their town back.'

Scully's chest was burning, out of practice with the uphill jog. 'Would you look at that view,' he huffed. Tall Dark obliged by panting to a stop. Above the tree line, jagged snow-topped arêtes pushed into the sky. Beyond the peaks and deep into the mountain range Scully knew there were more corries, U-shaped valleys and even more arêtes and ridges. Where the snow was melting, water cascaded down.

'Ever consider coming back to us?' Tall Dark asked softly, as if he'd mysteriously read Scully's thoughts.

'I'd love to.' Scully sighed. 'In the next life, maybe. I've the girls to think of now.'

'You do know that what happened that day up on the ridge was pure bad luck?'

'Every accident is bad luck, my friend. And when the Rescue gets into trouble it's a fucking disaster.' Scully ran a finger along his chin, where he'd smashed it against a rock.

'The Mountain Rescue guys often ask for you. They miss you on the team.'

Scully gave a rueful smile.

'How are the girls?' Tall Dark asked. 'And Jill?'

'Not great. And not great,' he answered. 'Jill's sister Lou comes every afternoon and I have a Polish lady coming to the cottage in the mornings. It's not ideal but we'll keep going for as long as we can at the cottage. Jill had said she wanted to be at home.'

Tall Dark patted Scully on the back. 'Motor neurone disease is a bitch,' he said gruffly.

'A bitch is what it is,' Scully agreed.

Tall Dark moved on tactfully, filling Scully in on other developments. The toxicology results were back, he said. He had some screenshots on his phone. The lab results made little sense to Scully.

Tall Dark followed with another screenshot. This time, a more helpful narrative of the results. It described the pharmaceutical findings in relation to all three victims: Isolde Hanly, Imelda Gannon and Marina Willoughby.

Scully wiped a film of sweat from his brow. 'You got the nuclear codes on here as well?'

'Begley would blow worse than Chernobyl if he knew just what I have.'

'Can I take notes?'

'Fire away.'

Scully pulled paper and a pencil from the pocket in his shorts. They couldn't risk an electronic trail between them. While his friend held the phone, Scully jotted down what he needed. Tall Dark also filled him in on what he'd seen in the evidence room. Scully took more notes.

As their feet crunched on cones and pine needles, the last kilometre passed by without either man saying very much. A theory was forming in Scully's head. A worrying theory. It had been flitting in and out of his head these past few days.

His mind felt clearer as he hit the bottom path. Fresh blood was rushing through his veins. Back on the main trail, he turned to Tall Dark.

'I've been thinking –' he sucked in a lungful of air – 'about all of this.' Another breath. 'About what you've shown me . . . about the reports. I don't want to be alarmist, but something strikes me.'

'Spit it out,' huffed Tall Dark.

Between breaths, Scully voiced his fears.

Tall Dark blinked, wiping sweat from his eyes.

'Funny. That's pretty much along the lines of what I've been thinking. I didn't say anything about it at the station because I didn't think anyone would believe it.'

'If I didn't know what I know now, I wouldn't want to believe it either,' said Scully.

17

Ellie paced up and down the kitchen, wondering if she was simply being paranoid. She bit her nails, a habit she despised and hadn't done since her days in care.

The previous evening, unusual sounds from the back yard had prompted her to slip out of bed and peek through the landing rooflight. The sight of Mervyn in a boiler suit, lifting slabs in the moonlight, had sent a chill right through her.

She'd padded back to bed, still hearing dull thuds and then the sound of Mervyn eventually moving back indoors. She managed to doze in fits and starts. When she awoke, she reached for her phone and sent a text to Scully, describing what she'd seen. She received a prompt reply:

> I can be there @ 30 minutes. Text me your
> address. Few things to sort here first

She messaged back:

> Leave an hour to be sure M has left for work.
> Park on Cornmarket Street. Botany Row
> permit-holders only. Look for nameplate
> The Snug at M's. I'm house before. E

She turned the radio down low to listen out for the sounds of any vehicle departing. When the doorbell rang, she jumped. She checked through the fanlight before opening the door.

'I guessed this must be it.' Scully grinned, his eyes pointing to something on the wall outside. 'I wasn't sure.'

Poking her head round the door, Ellie saw that, once again, Mervyn's nameplate read *The Slug*. She glanced up and down the street before directing Scully indoors.

As soon as he stepped into the living area, Ellie noted his eyes travel from her open laptop on the coffee table to the settee with its cushions and herringbone throw. He cast a casual eye over the compact kitchen area.

'You'd better come straight upstairs,' Ellie said.

'Isn't that a bit quick?' There was a twinkle in his eye. 'We hardly know one another.'

Giving him a cool look, she grabbed the banister. Scully followed, mumbling something.

Upstairs, light was spilling through the slanted roof window on to the landing. There was a hatch cover into the attic, and on either side of the narrow landing was a door. One with dimpled glass to the bathroom, the other to her bedroom.

Ellie placed a foot on a stool and stood up to yank the lever of the roof window, pushing it open. Scully didn't need a stool. He poked his head through the opening. Outside, the slate roof fell away and there was a view to the back yards all along the row.

'What do you make of that?' Ellie pointed to the back yard to their right.

Leaning against a breeze-block wall was a pickaxe and three bulky, knotted, heavy-duty sacking bags. A cloud of flies swarmed above. Paving slabs had been stacked in a pile in the corner, with a square of earth visible where the slabs had been dug up. In the middle of the yard was a cardboard box, roughly a metre square. The box was secured with packing tape and printed with the letters *B&Q*.

She followed Scully's eyes as they moved to a clothes line strung across the yard. Pegged out was a backpack, a towel and a skimpy pair of men's swimming trunks. His gaze shifted to the camping chair at the back door.

A rolled-up magazine poked out of the cup holder in the arm. The magazine displayed skin-like tones. On the ground sat an ashtray with a cigarette butt floating in rainwater. Next to that was an upturned crate. Scully swatted an insect that had landed on his nose.

'So, what do think?' she asked again.

He looked back out to the yard. 'He's not going to be on *Gardeners' World* any time soon.'

She smiled. 'Not what I meant.'

'What are you suggesting, Ellie? That he's burying bodies in the middle of the night?'

'Not necessarily bodies. I don't know. Gloves or something.' She caught his eye. 'I feel a bit stupid now.'

'To be honest, it looks innocent enough to me.'

'Maybe . . . in daylight.' She shrugged. 'It's unnerving to hear him hammering away in the dark. He goes ballistic if anyone else makes noise.'

'Listen, I don't really think you have anything much to worry about here, Ellie. The feeling in Coleman Street is that this guy is harmless.'

She stepped down off the stool, suddenly aware of the narrow space between them.

'Can I get you a cup of tea – for coming all the way out here?'

He pulled the window shut. 'I'd murder a cup.'

As they turned to go downstairs, she saw him hesitate. Her bedroom door was ajar. The force of shutting the rooflight had blown it open and something had caught his eye.

She spotted what had caught his attention. Sticking out underneath the bed was a see-through plastic stowaway box, packed with silver. The tea service and the candelabra were clearly visible.

'Downsizing comes with storage problems,' she said.

He started down the stairs.

'We'd been thinking of a change of home ourselves, last year,' he said. 'To that new development in Abbey Court.'

'I know the one,' she said, following. 'Looks nice. Open-plan, American-style homes?'

'That's right. Turned out it didn't suit my wife.'

Smiling politely, Ellie signalled she didn't want to hear about his wife. She wasn't interested in anyone else's marriage difficulties. As she busied herself in the kitchen, Scully headed for the small settee.

'I was talking to my contact down at the station,' he said, checking his phone.

'Anything new?' Ellie filled the kettle under the tap.

'He had a look in the evidence room, where the victims' clothing and jewellery is bagged and tagged.'

She looked up.

'They have three wedding rings in evidence. Each of the victims was wearing a ring when they were found. One is tagged at 18 carat.'

'And the other two?'

'Both brand new yellow gold, 9 carat each. Identical.'

'OK . . .'

'The 18-carat ring belonged to Isolde Hanly,' Scully added.

Switching on the kettle, Ellie set out a tray on the coffee table. Scully watched as she placed cups, saucers, a sugar bowl and milk.

'There's something else in evidence too,' he said. 'Something curious.'

'Yeah?'

'Two of the victims had a coin placed underneath a foot. Between the sole of the foot and their shoe.'

Ellie tilted her head.

'Weird, I know. Have you ever come across an old sixpence reul coin?'

'Dunno.' She scrunched her nose. 'I don't think so.'

'One side has an Irish wolfhound. On the other is a harp. The coins in question were dated 1964. That suggest anything to you?'

'Nothing comes to mind.' She perched on the end of the settee. 'What do the detectives make of it?'

'The Serious Crime Squad say they're looking at all areas of commonality between the three murders.'

'Any other news?'

'A few results from toxicology.'

The kettle whistled and Ellie went to the kitchen. She returned with a teapot.

'Results showed all three victims had significant doses of sleeping pills in their systems.'

Ellie poured.

'Imelda Gannon and Marina Willoughby had other substances in their systems too. I don't think sleeping pills alone killed those women.' He reached for a teacup. 'From one report I learned about, one of the victims, Isolde Hanly, suffered injuries consistent with suffocation.'

'And the other two victims?'

'I don't think either of them was suffocated.'

'Do they know if the women suffered?'

He sipped the tea. 'There wasn't anything in what I saw. There

105

was evidence of old bruising on Imelda Gannon, as you know. And there was also evidence pointing to old bruising on Isolde Hanly.' Scully studied her for a moment. 'To be honest with you, Ellie, I've been working through a theory of my own.'

Her phone rang loudly on the coffee table. It flashed *Unknown number*. She looked at it, expressionless, and darted Scully a look of apology. He indicated she should take the call.

'Hello.' She took the phone into the kitchen. 'Yes, of course I remember. What time?' she said. 'I know, it's such a pain when they let you down.' As she spoke, she separated the slats on the kitchen blind, checking on something outside. 'That's no problem. See you in the morning. Yes, I have that. Yes, yes. St Malachy's at nine.'

When she turned around, Scully was already at her front door.

'Some Holy Joe wanting a lift to Mass?'

'Something like that,' she said.

'Well, thank you for the tea.'

'It's always nice in a china cup. And thank you for coming over.'

'No problem.' He smiled. 'Henry at work today?'

Ellie was confused.

'That day in the Three Hags? You said you had to get home to Henry—'

She let out a peal of laughter. 'Want to see Henry?'

He followed as she made towards a door under the stairs.

'*Et voilà!*'

Scully stared into the musty cupboard. He was looking straight at a vacuum cleaner with a smiling decal face inscribed in large letters, spelling 'Henry'.

'Henry helps me clean the taxi.' Ellie grinned.

Laughing, they both walked to the door. About to set a foot outside, Scully pointed. There was something on the step. Ellie stared. It was a plant. Accompanied by an envelope. She looked at Scully. Picking up the envelope, she opened it tentatively and pulled out a card.

'I thought that was him,' she whispered. 'Passing by the window earlier when I was on the phone. He's usually at work by now.'

'Who?' asked Scully.

'Mervyn.'

Scully blinked. 'What does the card say?'

'Apologies for any disruption,' Ellie read. 'Project nearing completion. Mervyn.'

She looked up.

'Well then, there you go,' said Scully. 'Like I said. The guy is harmless. Either that or it's all part of a game plan.'

'Game plan?'

She caught a sparkle in his eyes.

'You know . . . create a disturbance, send flowers to apologise. The next step is dinner and an engagement ring.'

'Jesus.' Ellie winced. 'The very thought of it.'

Scully left her on the doorstep, chewing over the card.

18

Ellie held the potted plant at length as if it were a suspect device. She tried telling herself it was an act of kindness, that she should take the offering at face value. She placed the begonia on the window-sill, next to the washing-up liquid. It was not a plant she admired, finding its pink, tuberous stalks disturbingly flesh-like. If past experience was anything to go by, it would be short-lived. Plants never thrived in her care. In Pottershill, a gardener had done the needful.

As she cleared away the tea tray, she sniffed at something in the air. Aftershave. She'd had Scully down as a scruffy sort on first impressions, but as he'd pointed out – to her embarrassment – he scrubbed up not too badly. He came across surprisingly well on the TV.

Should she put away the other cup and saucer? Her stay here would come to an end just as soon as she'd saved enough. Repacking the crockery in old newspaper in a box in her bedroom, she stopped on the landing for another peek outside.

Pauline was out there, hanging up clothes. Hermano was draped along a back wall, idly watching on as she pegged out belly-warming pairs of knickers. Pauline's hair was set in rollers. It must be her night for cards. How her neighbour could stop her chatter for long enough to play was nothing short of a miracle.

Ellie had her own jobs to get on with. Wash the taxi for a start. There was a half-price deal in the garage at Scarteen Meadows. After that, there was her regular fare to the medical centre, and by then it would be time to collect Liam and Ava from school.

Ellie's afternoon went smoothly and she was at St Columba's in time to get a good parking space, having stopped at Buckley's on Main Street to buy freshly iced doughnuts. Observing the goings-on in the schoolyard was a good indicator of what was going on in the classroom.

As the school bell sounded, swing doors opened to release a swarm of buzzing kids and Ellie spotted Liam straightaway, making his way heavy-footed towards the gate. Ava was hopping spritely behind, chirping away with a friend.

Ellie turned to Liam as he climbed into the car. 'What's up?' she asked.

'School is boring.'

Ava climbed in beside him. Ellie held aloft the paper bag from Buckley's Bakery on the seat beside her. 'Who would like a doughnut?' she asked. Things could always be improved with a sugary doughnut.

The road out to the Old Manse was strewn with twigs and fallen debris. Ellie ploughed through troughs of brown slush on the mountain road outside the town, regretting wasting money on washing the car. As the kids tucked in to their treat, she tuned in to the radio.

Met Eireann has issued a red weather alert for the south-west of the country. The alert is in operation from 8 p.m. this evening until 8 a.m. tomorrow morning. There is the possibility of force 8 gales inland, reaching violent storm force 10 at sea. There is also a likelihood of structural damage to property, and homeowners are advised to secure their homes and make sure that items such as trampolines are tied down.

'Hear that, kids?' Ellie looked in the mirror. 'Check your trampoline.'

'That's already gone.' Liam licked the sprinkles on his doughnut. 'It blew away in the last storm.'

'You're very exposed to the wind outside the town, I guess.'

With the kids dropped off, Ellie headed for home and pulled back into her space on Botany Row. She thought back to earlier in the week. To the strange noises she'd heard. She thought they could be coming from above her in the attic or on the roof. She wondered if some slates were loose. Either that or there was a creature nesting in the crawl space.

The forecast she'd heard on the radio proved accurate. From eight o'clock that evening, rain pummelled and lashed against the window panes. Later, as she burrowed underneath the bedclothes with her book, she tried her best to ignore scraping noises overhead.

Jen Healy insisted she couldn't remember the name of the taxi company that had taken her home from Godiva's the night of Marina Willoughby's murder – according to Scully's information. Curiously, the woman who'd lamented being 'three times a bridesmaid' *had* been able to remember the number for Ellie's taxi service. When she'd phoned Ellie the day before, Ellie had been in her little sitting room in Botany Row, deep in conversation with Scully.

Ellie was now on her way to collect the woman at her flower shop, having cleared the worst of the overnight debris from her windscreen. Jen had told her she had to make a delivery of fresh wreaths for a wedding, and her car had gone into the garage for a

110

service. She'd been assured the turnaround would be swift. To her annoyance the service was turning out to be protracted, with the mechanic waiting for parts to be delivered. When Ellie pulled up, Jen was standing outside Blooming Vales with a number of cardboard boxes at her feet. Ellie popped the lever for the boot.

'Morning.' Ellie hopped out of the car. 'Let me get one of those for you.'

'Thanks.' Jen handed her a box. Ellie's eyes lingered on Jen's gloves.

'Occupational hazard.' Jen rolled her eyes. 'It's a pollen allergy. Some get hay fever. I get this awful skin reaction.'

'That's a shame.' Ellie shut the boot. 'Do antihistamines work?'

Jen shook her head. 'I'm on a mission to find something that will.' She slipped into the back of the taxi.

Easing into the driver's seat, Ellie buckled up and set off in the direction of St Malachy's church.

'Thanks for helping out.' Jen leaned forward. 'I've been trying to keep myself so busy ever since it happened . . .' She trailed off and stared darkly through the window to the side.

Ellie said nothing.

'It's been the week from hell,' Jen muttered as if to herself. 'Everything going wrong. Horribly wrong. And on top of it all, the bloody car letting me down.'

Ellie focused on the road but felt herself being watched.

Jen cleared her throat. 'Lucky that I remembered I'd taken one of your cards.' She held up a business card. Ellie kept a supply in a sleeve at the back of the driver's seat. They came in handy for repeat business.

'I'm really sorry about your friend,' Ellie ventured.

'Friends,' corrected Jen. '*Both* of them were friends of mine. Imelda *and* Marina.'

'Of course. I'm sorry.'

'I can't get my head around what's happened. It's all so horrible. We should have stayed with Marina that night. I know that now. I feel so guilty.'

Ellie allowed a few moments to pass.

'You're not to blame. You took precautions. You went into the house with her. You checked it out.'

'I did, didn't I? You saw that. You were there. You waited outside. Both of us checked that house. I was convinced there was no one there. No one but the two of us.'

Stopping at traffic lights, Ellie checked her passenger. Her dark eyes wore a strange expression.

'You shut the front door when you left?' Ellie asked in the mirror. 'I mean there wasn't any possibility you could have left it open, was there?'

'I'd had a bit to drink but I distinctly remember pulling it, yanking it shut. It's a heavy door.' She frowned. 'The gardaí asked me that too.'

'Do you think it's possible anyone could have been in the bushes? There's a lot of shrubbery in that garden.'

'Gardaí asked me that as well.' She sighed. 'So many questions. I guess it's possible. But if there was someone there, I didn't see.' Jen paused. 'Did you? Did you see anything, Ellie? I'm assuming the gardaí questioned you as well. Did *you* notice anything out of the ordinary that night?'

'Like what?' asked Ellie.

'Oh, I dunno. I mean you were sober, not like us. You may have noticed something outside the house that we didn't . . . ?'

Ellie thought a moment.

'No, I can't say that I did. I didn't notice anything out of the ordinary.'

'Did any other taxi drivers mention seeing anything to you? There had to be other drop-offs around Arbutus Road that Saturday night. You guys must talk. Someone had to have seen something—'

'Sorry. I keep myself to myself.'

'Oh.'

There was a pause.

Ellie checked the mirror. 'But if I do hear or remember anything, I'll be sure to let the gardaí know.'

Jen Healy blinked slowly. 'Of course.'

When they arrived at St Malachy's, Ellie helped Jen to carry the boxes of flowers into the church.

'Back to the shop?' Ellie asked her.

'I have to tie the arrangements on to the pews.'

'I can always wait.'

'Not at all.' Jen chewed her lip. 'I'll settle up with you now.' She reached for her bag. 'Anyway, a walk back in the fresh air will do me good.'

'If you're sure. I hope you get your car back soon.'

'What?' Jen fumbled for her purse. 'Oh, yes. Thank you.'

'And as I said before, I'm very sorry about your friends.'

Jen nodded. 'I hope they get the bastard.'

19

Ellie sat outside the train station with the engine idling. It was a low-slung building in red brick with tall Georgian windows, named to honour a fallen 1916 patriot. Dainty snowdrops shook their heads in tubs along the taxi rank. A painted sign welcomed travellers in Irish and in English to the town.

FÁILTE GO KYLEBEGGAN
WELCOME TO KYLEBEGGAN
JEWEL IN THE RING OF KERRY

The Dublin train would be in shortly. Ellie knew exactly what she was looking for. Indoor pallor, scruffy laptop case, bad shoes. Journalists could be enlightening. She spotted someone fitting that description heading in her direction right now. A woman with hair that hadn't seen a blow-dry in months. Scuffed high heels. An overnight bag.

'For hire?' The woman looked in through the open window.

'Where to, madam?'

'Just a sec.' The woman slid her glasses down her nose. 'It's a guesthouse. I had the address on the tip of my tongue.' She peered at her phone. 'Ah, here we go, first line, Myrtle Crescent, second line—'

'I know the place.' Ellie was short.

The journalist bundled into the back, setting her bags on the seat beside her. Wrestling with her seat belt, she edged towards Ellie. 'You know it's the place—'

'Where Isolde Hanly lived. Yes, I do.'

'Where she was murdered.'

Ellie nodded.

'Well, I'm headed to the guesthouse next door to that.'

'Right you are.' As Ellie indicated to pull out, her passenger's phone rang.

'Well, I don't know, do I?' the woman exclaimed. 'Ask your father. He's not a bloody ornament. He's supposed to be looking after you – he's what? Jesus Christ. Listen, Becky, I don't know what else I can do. There's probably a customer care number some-where. I've just arrived down here in the arsehole of nowhere. Oops—' She held up a hand in apology to Ellie.

'Husbands,' said the woman when she finished her call. 'Can't live with them. Can't shoot them.'

Ellie gave a pained smile.

'The wind down here is something else, isn't it?' The woman's head all but disappeared into one of her bags. 'Straight off the Atlantic.' She pulled a comb from the bag. 'My editor sent me all the way down here to see if I can get a fresh angle on the murders.' She dragged the comb through her bed-head hair. 'Is there anything you can tell me about Isolde Hanly, anything at all? Anything that'll let me get home before my kids burn the house down?'

'All I know is what's already common knowledge, I'm afraid.' Ellie was apologetic. 'She was living with her nephew, Freddy Hanly. And Regina, Freddy's wife, who was on holiday with her girlfriends when . . . when it happened. Lanzarote, so I believe.'

'Lanzarote, you say?'

'Apparently so. Freddy Hanly had stayed behind to keep Isolde – the woman who was killed – to keep her company.'

'And this guy, the nephew, his story is that he'd popped out for some shopping, and when he returned he found her . . . like that. Is that it?'

'So they say.' Ellie shrugged.

'Forgive me for saying so, but you sound a little . . . cynical?'

'Oh, I don't know.' Ellie waved a hand. 'The nephew and his wife are supposed to be a little . . . strange.'

'Mmm. I heard they didn't like people visiting the house.'

'I wouldn't like to be quoted on anything.' Ellie glanced over her shoulder at the journalist. 'It's a tight community here.' She tried her best to sound pleasant.

'Of course. Just one thing. Freddy Hanly was the last one to see Isolde Hanly alive?'

'Again, so they say.'

The journalist took a moment to consider this.

'You know what they say about the last one to see the victim alive?'

Ellie could feel the woman's breath on her neck.

'I do,' she said.

She checked in the mirror. The journalist sat back, produced a compact and attempted to apply some lipstick.

Of course Ellie knew. The last person to see a murder victim was the one most likely to be the killer. She had been thinking about little else for days.

Every time Ellie walked through the portcullis doors, an invisible weight tugged on her. It was hard not to think of Bessie. How the woman's heart would break to see Johnny in prison here. It was a good job Bessie had passed away. Just as well she was dead and gone. Along with their mother. Along with baby Owen.

'Jaysus, Ellie, what's the story in Kylebeggan? I don't scare easy and even I'm creeped out.' Johnny scraped out a chair from underneath a table. 'The place should be twinned with Twin Peaks, not to mind Lake Annecy across in France.'

It was busy in the visitors' room.

'You don't need to tell *me* that.'

Ellie scanned about, making sure no one was listening in. The chair felt hard beneath her. She spoke under her breath. 'When you borrowed that phone . . . and rang me the other night' – she looked around again – 'I didn't want to delay by going into everything that had happened.'

'Well, I'm all ears now.'

'OK.' She held his gaze. 'Get this. The woman who was just murdered, the night before my last visit to you – she was in my taxi that night before she was killed.'

Johnny sat back.

Ellie lowered her voice even further. 'I found out about the murder, listening to the radio on my way back home from here.'

'Fuck . . .'

Johnny whistled, drawing attention from other visitors. He waited for them to turn away. 'Jeez, Ellie. That's freaky. How awful for you. On top of everything else as well. And especially after—'

'I told you I don't want to talk about that.' Ellie was firm.

'OK.' Johnny swallowed. 'I take it you've been to see our pals, the gardaí?'

Ellie nodded. 'As I said, I heard about Marina Willoughby on my way home from here. I went straight into the gardaí. Into the station. I spoke to a Superintendent Sean Begley.'

Johnny's eyes narrowed. 'Begley in Coleman Street?'

'You know him?'

Her brother had acquainted himself with a number of gardaí over the years.

'Not personally, no. But I know the name. He's not too popular in here. A bloke I work with in the kitchens, Wayne, is from a farm somewhere around Kylebeggan. Says Begley cooked up evidence in a drug charge on him because he wouldn't rat on someone.' Johnny grinned. 'The same lad is no saint but I'd say there's some truth to the story.'

'Superintendent Begley is heading up the investigation. According to Cormac Scully, a guy I've been speaking to. He's a reporter.'

'That's not like you – blabbing to reporters.'

'I'm not exactly blabbing. And maybe I can help.'

She filled Johnny in on her conversations with Scully and the latest developments around the town. 'What do you think Bessie would have made of it all?' Ellie asked. Their visits often took this tack. It was a way of keeping Bessie alive.

Johnny raised his arms, putting his hands behind his head. 'She'd have been devastated about Isolde Hanly, for sure.'

'The locals are traumatised,' Ellie said. 'That woman, Imelda Gannon, used to teach a couple of kids I take to school. And the kids are just like the rest of us, trying to make sense of it all. But it doesn't make sense.'

As she spoke, she could see Johnny was listening, but he also looked distracted. He was staring at her strangely. 'This must be so stressful for you,' he said.

She gave a bitter smile.

'You're not keeping anything from me, are you?' he asked. 'Because I'm stuck in here?'

'Of course not.'

118

'Take care of yourself out there, Ellie. You may think that hurt has made you hard, that you're tougher than you are. Whatever's going on is not someone involved in a bit of robbing or dealing. This stuff is weird. If I was you, I'd stay a million miles away from any of it, and I certainly wouldn't hang around with reporters. You never know who's watching you.'

'You should take care too, Johnny. Pinching someone's secret phone doesn't strike me as particularly clever.' Ellie shifted the focus to him.

Johnny shook his head in mock exasperation.

'OK, have the last word as usual. But some advice on Liston, give that guy a wide berth if you happen to come across him. He's a nasty piece of shit.'

Ellie assured him she would. Although, she had been thinking of a little trip to Lowertown later that week, an idea she declined to share with her brother.

On the journey home, Ellie found her concentration slipping, her eyes going in and out of focus. Sleep did not come easily these nights. Mostly she lay awake, her thoughts churning over what had brought her to a small rental house in Botany Row. She wondered if she'd make the same decisions again, given another chance. Throughout the hours of darkness, scrabbling sounds coming from the attic would echo the thoughts scrabbling about in her head.

Back home in Botany Row, Ellie unpacked her shopping. She opened the back door to place discarded packaging in the bin. She was startled by someone clearing their throat. *Bloody hell.* How did he catch her every time?

'More bad weather coming in tonight.' Mervyn's bald head glistened over the wall in the flickering yellow of his outside light. 'It might keep those with bad intentions indoors . . .'

119

'I hope so.' Ellie could see his eye whites were flecked with tiny blobs of yellow. She squashed the cardboard packaging into the bin.

'Coleman Street don't appear to be making much headway.'

'I wouldn't know.'

'I wonder if the next murder will be on the twenty-eighth of the month?'

Ellie froze. 'What do you mean?'

'There's usually a pattern to these things, isn't there? Maybe this is a numbers thing. Think about it, Ellie. There was a murder on the twenty-first, the fourteenth and the seventh. All multiples of seven. Maybe the next murder will be on the twenty-eighth.'

Ellie backed up to her door. 'Let's hope the gardaí catch whoever it is long before then.'

'Maybe they will. Maybe they won't. Maybe they should have a word with that bridesmaid, Jen Healy.'

Ellie didn't react. She could see a glinting in his eye.

'I know a thing or two.' He smirked. 'A few things Miss Healy doesn't want anyone else to know.'

Ellie pulled up the collar of her cotton shirt against the chill.

'Why don't you put the kettle on, Ellie? I can pop over and tell you all about it?'

Ellie stood, saying nothing.

'Miss Healy left her mobile phone on the counter at my tanning salon.'

Mervyn smiled, raising what he appeared to think was a tantalising eyebrow.

20

Scully explained that he was running late. The woman sounded polite but irritated. Regina Hanly had a nasal, superior way of speaking. He apologised once again, agreeing it had been tough to find a time to suit all three of them, Scully, Regina and her husband, Freddy.

The woman had taken a fair amount of persuading to give an interview at all, but Ellie's proposal that he could do a tribute piece had done the trick again. On the way, he chugged past Victorian villas with shiny new cars in gravel driveways and neatly trimmed lawns. The garden around his cottage resembled a wild meadow, not through conscious design, but mainly through neglect. As Scully neared his destination, he reached for his phone.

He'd meant to call Tall Dark earlier, but had been distracted by events at home. Before he met with Freddy Hanly he wanted to know if the guy had indeed been in Tesco, where he'd professed to be the night of his aunt's murder. When the sergeant answered, Scully found his own sombre mood closely mirrored by the garda. The guy always sounded a few fries short of a Happy Meal.

Tall Dark was able to tell Scully that on the night of that murder, there were no recorded sightings of Freddy on any CCTV in the late-night Tesco Express in the area. Armed with this piece of information, Scully arrived at his destination, parking on a hill that led to the house in Myrtle Crescent.

He checked himself in the mirror. Before he'd left the cottage, he'd nipped to the bathroom to splash on some of the after-shave the girls had bought him for Christmas. He didn't want to give anyone an opportunity to dismiss him. Least of all snotty Regina Hanly.

Striding up the hill, he passed a number of guesthouses. Ahead of him stood a grand home with a large conservatory on a gable end. On the patio outside, a crew of tanned, white-shirted men sat at a garden table. Jehovah's witnesses, he thought. Although a foreign news crew seemed more likely. As he pushed the bell of the house next door, he felt a cannon of eyes bore into his back.

A woman answered. She was wearing a pair of animal-print trousers and a loose, white silky shirt-type thing. Scully reckoned she could be anywhere in age from twenty-five to forty. He supposed the woman was good-looking, if you liked the made-up look.

'Cormac Scully?'

'Yes,' he confirmed, putting out his hand.

'Regina Hanly.' She shook it briefly. 'This way,' she indicated. 'My husband's in the drawing room.' She directed Scully through an airy hallway with parquet flooring, dotted with boxes and tied black refuse sacks. He followed the length of the hall and into a bright room with large windows overlooking a lawn. It struck him that his cottage would likely fit into this one room.

Scattered about were more cardboard boxes. And slouching up against a marble fireplace, his back to Scully, relaxed a man in check trousers. He was on his phone. At the sound of approaching footsteps he turned and slipped the phone into his pocket.

Scully extended a hand. 'Cormac Scully from *The Kylebeggan Echo.*' He made a show of admiring the elegant room. 'What a beautiful house.'

'Freddy Hanly,' said the guy, taking his hand. 'I hope you're going to put together something fitting for Isolde. She wouldn't like to be remembered as a victim, if you know what I mean.'

'Of course.' Scully hastened to reassure. 'I believe your aunt was an interesting woman.'

'A wonderful person.' Freddy Hanly looked at his wife. 'We were fond of her, weren't we?'

Regina Hanly nodded. She directed Scully to a winged chair by the fireside and proceeded to the low-back sofa opposite, beckoning her husband to join her.

'What exactly would you like to know?' Freddy Hanly draped an arm along the back of the sofa and spread his legs.

'Maybe a little about Isolde's life before she came to Kylebeggan?' Closed questions were unlikely to yield anything of value.

Freddy lifted his chin. 'Aunt Isolde liked languages,' he said after a moment of consideration. 'French, Spanish, Italian, she was fluent in those. One of her first appointments was to the diplomatic service in Brussels.'

Scully retrieved his notepad and the Montblanc pen Jill had bought him for his thirtieth birthday. He'd have liked to record this conversation for Ellie as she seemed keen to keep abreast of things, and he'd agreed with her that another pair of ears was always useful. However, something told him these two would be less guarded without a recording device in view.

'According to Isolde, she was in line for a senior position but was passed over. It went to a man less qualified, or so she said. My old man always told us Isolde was the brains of the family. Got a scholarship to Trinity.' He angled his head towards the chess

123

set on a table by the bay window. 'Loved chess. Very celibate, so she was.'

'Cerebral,' came his wife's quick correction.

'Yeah, that.'

Scully's eyes were pulled to the well-stocked bookshelves on the back wall behind the sofa.

'They're going.' Regina darted a look over her shoulder. 'I'm making room for a sideboard.' She rubbed her husband's hand. 'This is going to be a breakfast room. We're turning the place into a guesthouse.'

'Nice spot for one.' Although Scully did wonder how prospective guests would feel about the fact that a woman had been ritually murdered in the house. 'Isolde didn't stay in Brussels?' he asked, turning his attention back to Freddy.

'No. She went to Dublin to the Department of Foreign Affairs. That was where she met my uncle, Clement Hanly. He was ten years younger than her. I believe my father used to tease her, calling her a cradle-snatcher.'

'Any romances before that?' Scully looked up from his notebook.

Regina crossed her arms. 'You said this was a tribute piece.' She fixed Scully with a stare. 'I think it would be in poor taste to speak of old boyfriends.'

'I'm just trying to build up a picture of the lady.'

Freddy cleared his throat. 'Yes, well, she loved ballroom dancing, good food and, of course, her gin and tonic and—'

'A bon viveur, then?' Scully poised his pen.

'God no,' said Regina. 'Please don't write that.'

Scully scored it out. He'd always thought it a polite way of describing someone as a drunk, glutton or both. Perhaps not an accurate reflection of the person Isolde Hanly had been.

'I'll make tea.' Regina stood. 'Isolde loved her *tea*.' Her shoes clacked on the floorboards as she left the room.

Freddy looked at Scully apologetically. 'She's tetchy. All this business . . . it's been very upsetting.'

'That's understandable.'

With Regina gone, Freddy filled Scully in on queries he'd jotted down. He learned something of Isolde's wide circle of friends, that she had a love of fashion and that she belonged to many clubs.

'There won't be anyone like her again,' said Freddy as his wife returned with tea and biscuits. 'Am I right, babes?'

'Isolde was one of a kind.' She set down the tray, poured tea and handed a cup and saucer each to Freddy and Scully. She offered them biscuits.

'She gave us the deposit for a house when we got married.' Regina exchanged a look with her husband. 'The least we could do was to move in to be with her when she got sick.'

Scully was about to dunk his oatmeal cookie but thought the better of it. 'Freddy's been telling me all about Isolde's social engagements. You must have been kept busy.'

'I did my best.' Regina looked thoughtfully into her tea. 'We tried other arrangements, but they didn't really work out. And to tell the truth, Isolde wasn't able for company towards the end. I gave in my notice because she really needed round-the-clock care. Isn't that so?' She glanced at Freddy, irked by his sudden lack of engagement. He'd moved and was standing by the fireplace, checking his phone.

'Sorry, babes. I'm going to have to scoot.' He turned to Scully. 'I've a lesson in less than ten.'

'Freddy's the club pro over at Finneran's Dip.' Regina looked at Scully.

That explained the clothes and the weird tan line on his forehead. Scully stood to shake his hand.

'Don't let me keep you. And once again, I'm very sorry for your loss. I'd like to have known your aunt. She sounds like she was quite a character.' He kept a grip of Freddy's hand. 'I'm sure you must feel guilty.'

Freddy pulled away. 'What?'

Scully stayed where he was. 'Wondering what might have happened, or not, I guess, if you hadn't had to pop out that night to Lidl . . .'

'Tesco.' Freddy's gaze was steady. 'I went to Tesco. We don't have a Lidl around here.'

'Of course. I meant Tesco.'

Freddy opened his mouth but closed it just as quickly. Stepping away from the fireplace, he pulled at the neck of his polo. He planted his feet hip distance apart, clasped his hands together and took an air swing with an imaginary golf club. He turned to his wife. 'Later, babes.'

At the door, he checked Scully one more time with a sideways flick of his eyes. Seconds later, the front door slammed.

'Was that necessary?' Regina Hanly turned to Scully.

'That came out wrong.' He did his best to look sheepish.

She folded her arms across her chest. 'You know that we haven't given interviews to any other reporters, or to any of that lot staying in the guesthouse out there?' She pointed through the window. 'You know *The Kylebeggan Echo* is the only paper we've given an interview to? Isolde always said charity begins at home.'

'Good to know. I'll include that in the article.'

He made towards the hall. Regina followed. As he skirted around a cardboard box, he spotted books and frames inside. 'I imagine there's a ton of sorting out to do,' he said sympathetically.

'What happened here was unspeakable.' She was terse. 'I want to give this place a new lease of life. Until probate's sorted I can't do much, but I can make a start.'

Something at the top of the box caught Scully's eye. 'Mind if I take a look?' He picked up the photo frame without waiting for an answer. 'This is Isolde?' He pointed to the figure on the right.

'That's her.'

She had undoubtedly been an attractive woman. Not conventionally beautiful but handsome with an intelligent face.

'And next to her – that's Clement Hanly, her husband?'

'Yes. Isolde spoke about him all the time.'

'That's the dress they found her in?'

Regina stiffened.

'Detectives haven't said. But she kept her wedding dress in a case under the bed, and now the dress is gone.'

Scully nodded.

The dress in the wedding photograph was high-necked, fitted and looked to be fashioned from white lace. The groom wore a look of pained endurance. Scully understood, remembering the protracted shenanigans of the photographer on his wedding day.

'What year did Isolde and Clement Hanly marry?'

Regina frowned. '1969. I think.'

'So' – Scully glanced about – 'this is going to be a guesthouse?' He imagined Regina would be the type to manage by delegation. With perfect nails, not for her the hard graft. 'You mind me asking what you did before you looked after Isolde?'

'I worked in the hospitality industry.' She took the picture from him and laid it back on the top of the box.

'Ah, so the guesthouse business won't be entirely new to you.'

There was something at the back of his mind, something else that he'd wanted to ask. Try as he might, he couldn't remember. No matter, he had plenty to be getting on with. At the front door, he thanked the woman for her time and headed off downhill to the Land Rover, a briskness in his step.

He put in a call to Tall Dark. The sergeant answered, the sound of traffic in the background. 'Hey, pal, I'm just leaving the Hanly place up at Myrtle Crescent. Listen, is there anything you can tell me about Regina Hanly? You have anything on her? Where she and the husband, Freddy, lived before? Any information at all?'

He could hear Tall Dark breathing heavily.

'Well, let's see.' A pause. 'There's not too much on them. All I can tell you is that Regina used to work in the gift shop at Shanaglish Mountain Lodge. Oh . . . and before moving into Myrtle Crescent the couple were renting one of those villas at the golf course at Finneran's Dip. You know the ones. And that's about it.'

So much for the hospitality industry. Regina Hanly had made her job sound much more grandiose.

'They were renting?' Scully was puzzled. 'She's just told me they were given a deposit for a home of their own from Isolde when they got married.'

Tall Dark let go a rare chuckle. 'Her other half wouldn't have been too long in going through that. Fond of the gee-gees is Freddy. That's not official though. I like a flutter myself. All I can say is any time I'm in Paddy Power's, your man is there as well.'

'Thanks, my friend. I'll be in touch.'

Scully rattled down the hill, fishing rods and waders crashing about in the back. His brain was chugging away. The nephew and his wife had said all the right things. But there was something almost too slick about the neatly groomed, well-spoken Regina Hanly.

Nearing the bottom of the hill, it came to him what it was he'd wanted to ask. He cast an eye on his fuel gauge. It was nearly empty. The march up the hill would do him good and he'd walk off the oatmeal cookies. A few minutes later, he arrived for a second time at the door of 7 Myrtle Crescent. He wiped his brow and rang the bell.

'Yes?' Regina answered, phone in hand.

'Sorry to bother you. Just one more thing I meant to ask you . . .'

'Go ahead.'

When she answered, he was stunned. Before Regina could register the shock on his face, he turned his back and waved his thanks over his shoulder.

21

The summer Ellie turned eighteen, Bessie took her to the house in Pottershill. The woman had done as much as she could, and it was coming time for Ellie to move on. She had done her Leaving Cert exam and had applied for a college course to start that autumn. According to Bessie the placement in Pottershill would be a nice little summer job for her. Ellie felt a bittersweet sadness that part of her life was over. She was sad to leave Johnny behind.

Joe and Bessie Moloney's had been the best home they'd ever had. The Moloney home had its downsides too. In a village a fair bit outside Kylebeggan, it was a little remote for Ellie's liking. *Deliverance* country, Johnny said. They'd been wary about the Moloneys at first. They knew that foster parents got money from the state to mind them. Happily, Joe and Bessie proved themselves different to the others.

Joe grew sunflowers in his cottage garden. A retired HGV driver with a little finger missing, he'd regale Johnny and Ellie with stories of places he'd been in Europe, of driving past plains swathed in sunflowers, fields with acres of vines. Sights they'd never seen. Johnny used to help Joe in the greenhouse behind the gooseberry bushes where Bessie hung the washing.

Ellie had a photo of him standing next to his first ever tomato plant. Joe had helped her brother with his reading, not in the

130

conventional way like teachers with their schoolbooks, but from the backs of seed packets, boxes of fertiliser and gardening DIY books.

For a time, they both enjoyed the novelty of being the only foster kids in their small village primary. Johnny vied for position of class joker, but fell in with the messers and alickadoos, the want-to-be-hard-men who were always up for a laugh. Bessie was often called to the school and was driven half demented. And Joe, well, Joe was stoic. He's being a lad, Bessie, he'd say. Leave him be. Give him space. He'll grow out of it.

But Johnny didn't grow out of it. And worse again, Johnny would always get caught. Ellie knew the thrill of stealing a fistful of jellies or a packet of smokes, but Ellie never got caught. Later, Johnny's behaviour had more serious consequences.

There was Ellie's entrance exam to secondary. When she didn't pass the exam for school in Kylebeggan, she couldn't fathom it. She was one of the top two or three pupils in her village primary. She overheard Bessie and Joe talking in low tones in the cottage kitchen. Bessie was of a mind to challenge the comprehensive school board. She felt sure Ellie's exclusion was on account of small-mindedness, on account of her being a foster kid. At which point Joe reminded his wife that even though it had been a tiny news article with no names mentioned, Johnny's exploits had featured in the local paper.

'But the girl is smart,' Bessie protested. 'As God is my witness, she'll not be held back on account of this.'

Ellie had eased herself quietly from her listening post on the bottom step and tiptoed upstairs to her room in the eaves, confident Bessie would sort things out as usual. But Bessie couldn't convince the school board to overturn their decision. For the five years that followed, Ellie had to take a ninety-minute bus journey to another school in a city sixty kilometres away.

Bessie's response to such injustice was to launch into a full-on extracurricular programme of her own making. On Saturday mornings, she'd drive Ellie to Kylebeggan for drama lessons. Afterwards, they'd go for lunch to tearooms by the bowling green. Saturday afternoons were set aside for bridge lessons. As Ellie's bridge improved, she was asked to make up a four in the village hall on a Saturday night, if they were short of partners. Sunday mornings were set aside for tennis lessons. Ellie was doubtful there was anything left in Bessie's foster allowance with all the money she spent on her.

She could easily have driven herself to all her activities in Kylebeggan. Unbeknown to Bessie, Ellie had taught herself to drive. She didn't have the heart to tell her that on the Sunday evenings Bessie and Joe walked off to the village pub, Ellie and Johnny would take the keys to the old blue Nissan and hit the back roads beyond the village. Johnny would approach the Gortbrack Road, head down and burn up the tyres, making figures of eight.

School in the city was not without its advantages. Ellie could make up whatever kind of stories she liked about her background and no one could challenge them. She lived in a village the city kids had never heard of and were even less likely to visit.

On the days she was bored, she'd head into the shops on a forged lunch pass to indulge in a spot of stealing. She could at least defray the cost of all the toiletries she wanted. Bessie was spending way too much on her already.

Ellie looked forward to English classes, in particular Shakespeare's plays. She enjoyed poetry too. Not that Wordsworth stuff about clouds and daffodils or Manley Hopkins' gloomy verses. But poetry like Seamus Heaney's, steeped in reality. When Miss Kelleher read 'Mid-Term Break' aloud, the whole class was silent as she finished, but Ellie was the only one to experience the truth of those poignant lines.

Baby Owen would for ever haunt her. She'd made a promise and she'd broken it. Johnny always maintained Mam was too far gone to understand what she was asking. Ellie had been a kid, and way too young to make that promise. It was kind of him to say so, but Johnny was not the one who broke the promise.

She remembered her mother's rheumy eyes. Promising her they'd stay together. She'd never allow the three of them to be split up. Blood is thicker than water, remember, Ellie. Remember that after I'm gone, said Mam.

For two days and two nights they'd stayed in that cold bedroom with Mam's body before the gardaí arrived. The blood was thick all right, on the legs of the old witch who came to drag baby Owen away from them. Ellie bit and kicked her, but it served no purpose in the end. It did ensure that she and Johnny were placed in a home used to dealing with kids with violent behaviour. Baby Owen went to the Quigleys.

Two years he spent there. During that time, Ellie and Johnny were allowed to visit, but only by appointment. Looking back, Ellie understood how it gave the Quigleys time to tidy up, time to make things nice. What had happened in their home was no accident, no matter what they said. That kind of thing doesn't happen by accident. One day, when Johnny was out of prison and things were sorted, they would go again to visit the Quigleys.

They didn't put Owen in next to Mam. The grave was full, or so they said. He went into a new section of the graveyard. He was the first one to go into a brand-new row. They lowered him down in his little white box. Watching on were Ellie, Johnny and a social worker. And like the poet said, it was a four-foot box. A foot for every year.

Ellie approached that summer job as a favour to Bessie. She wanted to repay some of Bessie's kindness. She promised she'd stick the job for a month at least. Although it didn't sound like much of a job to her. Since her broken promise to her mam, any new promises she intended to keep.

Bessie had a friend in Pottershill, who had an active social life. The problem was, she didn't drive. Years earlier, the woman had an accident someplace foreign where they drove on the other side of the road, and hadn't driven since. The woman needed a driver, among other things.

Ellie'd passed her driving test after a few formal lessons. Well, aren't you the finest girl, Bessie said, a twinkle in her eye. Imagine, passing your driving test with a bare handful of lessons? Aren't you the clever one? Ellie then realised that her foster mother had known all along about the Sunday-night antics on the Gortbrack Road.

The initial meeting with Bessie's friend was at the bowling-green tearooms. Over smoked-salmon sandwiches, Bessie and her friend swapped stories of visits to gardens around the country. They exchanged gossip about some retired nurse in the bridge club who inspired their dislike. Bessie's friend declared the woman had likely killed more than she had cured. The women's teacups rattled as they shook with laughter.

When Bessie's friend reached for a finger sandwich, her serviette floated off her lap. 'Your serviette,' said Ellie, retrieving it from the floor. 'It's a paper napkin, my dear,' the woman said. 'Our American friends call them serviettes.'

Had it been anyone else, Ellie would have told them where to stick their paper napkin. But she liked this person. She admired her sharply cut trouser suit, her square emerald ring and her steel grey, wavy hair.

'She's a ticket, isn't she?' Bessie said afterwards. How a woman who'd lived all over the world had ended up in Kylebeggan was a source of wonderment to Ellie. She was widowed, and though Ellie thought she was pushing sixty, she was taken aback to learn that the woman was in fact seventy.

Ellie's job was to be her personal assistant. To drive her to her activities. To her reading circle, to talks of note in the library. To Kylebeggan Bridge Club and the Horticultural Society outings. There was grocery shopping and basic cooking. There would be visitors to the house too – former colleagues and acquaintances of the woman's dead husband. Refreshments would be needed.

When Bessie dropped Ellie off outside the big house in Pottershill, she promised her foster mother she would give a good account of herself. The month duly passed. Ellie found she liked the job. It was varied. She could eavesdrop on visitor conversations. Politicians en route to a conference in the town or retired diplomats. Artists and writers travelling to summer festivals.

Ellie would be sent down to Kenneally's Food Emporium for crabmeat, or to Buckley's Bakery for fresh soda bread. She would assemble salads herself. She'd dress the table in the conservatory with a linen cloth and set it with rose gold cutlery that had come from Kuala Lumpur.

Visitors burst with stories and anecdotes of recent travels. They'd talk in hushed tones of scandals involving government ministers. Some stories took longer in the telling, and sometimes Ellie would be asked to make up a guest bedroom.

She grew to anticipate these requests. They generally followed requirements for sliced lemon and sprigs of fresh mint from the garden. This was Ellie's cue to fetch the gin and the Waterford glass from the cabinet in the drawing room. Ellie would head to bed to the sound of laughter drifting up the stairs.

At the end of that first month, when Ellie was asked to stay on, she did so without hesitation. The prospect of a trip to Venice had been mooted. Her employer was meeting an old friend and fancied company on the journey. Was Ellie interested? Perhaps she'd been there before? The notion was laughable. Of course she wanted to go.

One month became two. The deadline for Ellie to accept her college course came and went. Though she missed her life at the Moloney home, and though she missed her brother, Ellie liked her new life in the beautiful old house at Pottershill. And as time slipped by, she grew just as fond of its owner, Isolde Hanly.

22

There was a polite knocking at her door. Ellie groaned. Not Pauline again. She grabbed her raincoat from the coat stand and threw it on, making ready with an excuse about heading out. But when she opened the door it wasn't Pauline standing there. It was Scully. He took a step back, looking awkward.

'Scully, everything OK?'

'Yeah . . . think so. Just a bit confused, that's all.'

'Well, that's not good for an investigative reporter.' She smiled. 'Can I help?'

He noticed her raincoat. 'You look as if you're on the way out?'

'It can wait. Come in.'

She shut the door as he stepped inside. She had half an inkling what this might be about and directed him towards the settee. He seemed happier to stand.

'I'm here about Isolde Hanly.' He faced her. 'I've been to see her nephew, Freddy, and Freddy's wife, Regina.'

Ellie perched herself on the arm of the settee.

'You never told me you had worked for Isolde.'

'You never asked.'

'Don't you think it might have been relevant?'

'Relevant to what?'

He blinked. 'To all our discussions about the murder victims. To the company Isolde Hanly was keeping. To who might have wanted her dead.' His eyes locked on to hers. 'I don't understand why you didn't tell me.'

'You're the one who approached me, remember? I agreed to tell you if I came across anything that might be helpful in finding out who killed these poor women. Telling you I'd worked for Isolde would only have distracted you from that. How did I know what you would write? How could I trust that you would respect Isolde's memory? I worked for Isolde for over two decades. She was like family to me. You are a journalist, after all.'

'Christ.' He shook his head. 'I'm not some scumbag hack who'd sell his granny for a story.'

'Maybe not. But look at some of the personal stuff the other hacks are printing. It's disgusting. At the end of the day your job is to find column inches and sell a story.'

He looked pained.

'Listen.' Ellie looked up at him. 'If I'd told you that I'd worked for Isolde, that would have found its way to all the other newspapers. In my job I deal with the public all day long, but when I come home, I want privacy. You think I want the media outside my house?' She gave him a pained look. 'The only person who'd relish that around here would be my friend next door.' She jabbed a finger towards Pauline's wall.

'Do the gardaí know?'

'That I worked for Isolde? They haven't asked. As I said, I left Myrtle Crescent eighteen months ago. I don't see why they'd be remotely interested.'

He was silent a moment.

'Why did you leave, especially after all that time?'

'OK.' She sighed. 'I was asked to go. I suppose you could say that I was fired.'

'By Isolde Hanly?'

'God, no.' Ellie let out a mirthless laugh. 'By Regina.' She paused. 'You've met her.'

'I have.' Scully's expression didn't change. 'She's the one who told me you had worked for Isolde.'

Ellie shook her head slowly. 'Isolde loathed Regina. She was fond of Freddy because he was her husband's nephew, even though she felt he was led by his wife. Isolde and I would go abroad at Christmas so she didn't have to endure Regina's company. The woman only made a show of caring for Isolde. Arriving with big bouquets of flowers any time Isolde was unwell. Always one for the grand gestures. But behind the scenes, Regina had no real affection for Isolde.'

Scully looked dubious. 'She spoke very warmly of her when I was up at the house.'

'I'll bet she did,' Ellie retorted. 'I can tell you now you wouldn't leave a geranium in Regina Hanly's care. You saw the cut of her. She's not really the loving type.'

Scully smiled as Ellie continued talking.

'You can't exactly imagine the lovely Regina giving someone a bed bath, changing soiled clothes or clipping toenails, now can you?'

'They lived in that house with Isolde Hanly for over a year. Don't you think they must have done so?'

Ellie's expression darkened. 'I don't like to think what Isolde must have gone through,' she said, lowering her voice.

'After you left, did you ever visit Myrtle Crescent again?'

'I tried once. I called to the door and I could hear Isolde calling out in the background. I knew she had heard me and that the sound of my voice had distressed her. That was the last thing I wanted to do.'

Scully ran a hand over his chin. Ellie noted the dark shadows under his eyes. 'You didn't say *why* you were fired. Why after twenty years were you told to leave?'

'Because of what Regina found.' Ellie blinked. 'What she found in the study.'

23

The small sitting room felt suddenly cold. Ellie got up to switch on the fire. Apart from her brother, she hadn't told anyone about what happened the day she left Myrtle Crescent.

'You want to know why I left. Ellie sat at the kitchen table. Scully took the chair opposite, his eyes following her. 'All right, I'll tell you.' She swallowed. 'One morning when I was grocery shopping, Regina Hanly paid an unannounced visit to Myrtle Crescent. I spotted her car outside the house when I got back. I thought it was a little strange as I wasn't expecting her—'

Ellie checked to see if Scully was taking notes. His pen was idle, but he was listening.

'When I entered the hallway with the shopping, I could hear a ruckus and lots of rooting about. I wondered what on earth was going on. When I went to investigate, there was Regina in the study. While Isolde was upstairs resting, Regina was going through all her stuff. She didn't try to hide it. There were documents everywhere. Drawers open from the writing desk. Clement Hanly's correspondence from the Department of Foreign Affairs strewn about the floor. There was Regina sitting in the middle of it all, holding a sheet of paper. As I stood in the doorway, she stared at me with poison in her eyes.'

Ellie shuddered.

'Go on . . .' said Scully.

'The sheet of paper in her hand was a handwritten will, not yet notarised. A new will, one where Isolde bequeathed everything to me. The house in Myrtle Crescent, the contents, the lot. This was the first I knew about it. I didn't take any part in that side of Isolde's affairs. Freddy was responsible for all that kind of thing.'

Scully set the pen down.

Ellie carried on. 'Isolde had given Freddy power of attorney about ten years before she died. As I said, she had a bit of a blind spot for him despite her reservations about his wife. Freddy's father had been her husband's younger brother and he'd died of cancer as a relatively young man. That left Freddy as Clement's only living relative and I think Isolde felt obliged to overlook his shortcomings. Towards the end of my time in Myrtle Crescent, Isolde had been keen for me to drive her into town. Into Ormsby and Goodwin, her solicitors. I never asked her why. It was none of my business. The way things happened, I never got to take her.'

'You hadn't known anything of this new will?'

'Nothing at all,' Ellie confirmed. 'Not until Regina confronted me with it that day. She started waving this sheet of paper at me like a lunatic. I'm standing there, with bags full of shopping, and she comes screaming at me . . . that I'm a . . . what did she call me . . . ? A scheming cow, I think. She ordered me to drop everything there and then and to go straight upstairs to pack my things. I didn't even get to unpack the shopping.'

'You were fired on the spot?'

'That was pretty much what happened, yes.'

'You didn't get a severance package?'

'A severance package?' Ellie scoffed. 'Regina gave me what I was due, nothing more. I always knew I wouldn't work for

Isolde for ever, but I'd never really planned for it.' She shrugged. 'My own fault. I was too busy enjoying life. Isolde was great company.'

'Did you never fancy a family of your own?'

'I beg your pardon?'

Scully held up a hand. 'Sorry. That was rude. None of my business.' He cleared his throat. 'The long and short of it is that you were left high and dry?'

'I had some savings,' Ellie nodded. 'Not much.'

'And a suitcase full of silverware.'

This guy was sharp. He didn't miss a trick.

'Isolde wanted me to have them,' she said defensively. 'She told me many times. I made sure I took them when I left.

Scully's lips twitched in amusement.

Ellie found herself protesting. 'I wasn't going to let Regina undo everything that Isolde had wanted for me. That wedding service and that silverware were mine.'

'These too?'

Scully pointed to a china cup and saucer on the table.

'Those too.'

'Isolde thought a lot of you.'

'You don't get to spend two decades of your life with someone and not develop an affection for them.'

'That's true.' A shadow crossed his face.

'I never had designs on Myrtle Crescent. I know Isolde meant well but I wish she'd never attempted to change the will. I could have stayed with her and given her the company she enjoyed.' Ellie's voice cracked. 'Instead of the unnatural end she had.'

'If what you say is true, and Regina really didn't care a jot for Isolde, why didn't she land her in some nursing home? There are plenty in Kylebeggan.'

'I can only surmise she wanted the carer's allowance and to hang on to Isolde's pension.'

Scully frowned.

Ellie explained. 'Between Isolde's pension and her husband Clement's, I'm sure the amount was sizeable. Both gold-plated civil service pensions. Freddy had power of attorney, remember. He would have been collecting that money, or perhaps it was Regina. Nursing homes aren't cheap. If they'd put Isolde into one, it would have cost a lot of money. And when Isolde eventually passed on, they'd have had to sell Myrtle Crescent to pay back the debt. You know, under the rules of the Fair Deal scheme.'

Scully chewed this over. 'When I was up at the house, Regina mentioned turning the place into a guesthouse.'

'That adds up. She was always full of plans.'

Scully ran a hand through his thatch of hair. 'I've been doing a little digging around on Freddy,' he volunteered. 'It seems he may not have been in Tesco like he said, the night Isolde died.'

Ellie widened her eyes. 'Where was he?'

Scully shrugged. 'I believe gardaí have invited him in for further questioning. If I hear anything, I'll let you know.' Smoothing his trousers, he stood up.

'You get my personal interest, don't you?' Ellie asked. 'I was terribly fond of Isolde. I really need to know who killed her . . . and the other women.'

'I get it.' Scully headed to the door.

'There's something else you should know,' said Ellie softly. 'It's about Jen Healy, the bridesmaid.'

Scully turned. 'I'm listening.'

'I don't know whether this is a fabrication, but Mervyn' – Ellie angled her head towards the adjoining wall – 'told me that Jen had left her phone on the counter in the tanning salon when she was paying for her sessions. Some time back in January. She had gone into one of the tanning booths when her phone rang. Mervyn said a name flashed up on her phone. That name was Harvey Specter.'

Scully clearly didn't watch as much TV as Ellie.

'Harvey Specter? From the legal drama *Suits*?' Ellie prompted.

'Ah, OK . . .'

'Mervyn said he knocked on the booth door and slipped the phone in to her. He heard giggling. "Of course she doesn't suspect. We've been careful," he heard her say. And, "What she doesn't know can't hurt her."'

Scully rubbed his chin. 'Jen Healy is not a woman I would warm to, personally.'

'Maybe you can do a bit of digging?'

'Will do.'

'And can you assure me what I've told you about working for Isolde is going to remain between the two of us, right?'

'Ellie, I'm not a scumbag who'd abuse the trust of a source or, indeed, a friend. It really wouldn't get me far. I'm not going to write about anything you've told me.' He paused as if deliberating whether to share something more. 'I'm moving on from the tribute pieces to another angle on the killings.'

'Oh yeah?'

'I've been working something up the past few days. A theory I think there's substance to. Or should I say, I *fear* there's substance to.'

'What's the theory?'

'In my opinion, whoever is killing these women . . . this Bride Collector . . . is not one person. I've been thinking about it, and I'm not convinced the same person killed all three women. I think we could be looking at a killer and maybe a copycat killer, or possibly even two people working together. The MO is similar in all cases, but with enough differences to make me wonder. I certainly think there's more to this than meets the eye. And I'm worried that there's more to come.'

Ellie felt a spike of fear. Scully was not alone. For some time now she'd feared the same.

24

Scully agonised over the final copy. If he had an editor worth his salt, he'd insist on oversight before the copy went to print. Gerry Bradshaw's office was empty. A phone call found him bursting with bonhomie at the nineteenth hole.

Scully explained he wanted a second opinion on a piece he was going to run, but Gerry directed him to work away. 'I've a pint of Guinness going bad on me here so whatever you think yourself,' said Gerry. 'I've every confidence in you, ol' stock,' he said. He sounded like he'd had a feed of pints already.

Scully's eyes were gritty. He blinked at the screen. He pored over the article for the fifth time:

IS THERE A COPYCAT KILLER IN KYLEBEGGAN?

Crime correspondent Cormac Scully examines
the case for more than one killer

One question in particular has been hanging on the lips of this reporter. Although bound to cause anxiety, it's a question worth considering. Did the Kylebeggan brides meet their deaths at the hands of the same killer? To answer that question, we must look at the evidence at hand.

Tragic pensioner Isolde Hanly (90) was discovered dead by her nephew,

147

upstairs in the bedroom of her home at 7 Myrtle Crescent, Pottershill. Mrs Hanly was laid out on her own bed, dressed in the same white lace dress she had worn decades earlier in her marriage to Clement Hanly, a former Irish Ambassador to Malaysia and Turkey. On her ring finger was the 18-carat wedding ring he had given to her on their wedding day. It should be noted that, for many years before her death, Mrs Hanly had been unable to wear the ring, due to medication.

A post-mortem revealed that there was a high level of a substance consistent with sleeping tablets in her system. It also appeared that Mrs Hanly had been smothered. As was already reported in this paper, Mrs Hanly's hands were arranged around a posy of dried blue flowers. And placed across her chest was a book borrowed from Kylebeggan Library in Chapel Street, using Mrs Hanly's library card.

It has been suggested that Isolde Hanly's killer was observing some kind of ritual as suggested by the well-known wedding rhyme, 'Something old, something new, something borrowed, something blue.' Something old, possibly being her 18-carat gold wedding ring, and something new, possibly being a pair of white stockings the victim was wearing.

As there was no evidence of forced entry, it can be surmised that the killer gained entry through a door that was left open or, less likely, Mrs Hanly let the killer in herself.

Let's now turn to the case of Imelda Gannon. Imelda's body was found at 13 Friary Lane in Kylebeggan town centre in largely similar circumstances. Imelda's fiancé was attending his stag celebrations. Post-mortem results in Imelda's case showed that along with a common sleeping tablet, the drug amitriptyline (used for chronic pain and depression) and the drug tramadol (a powerful opiate used for pain) were also found in the victim's system. Due to the quantity and combination, Imelda Gannon was exposed to a toxic level of drugs and died as a consequence.

In Imelda's case there was no evidence of suffocation, although there was evidence of recent bruising on the body. Imelda was dressed in the white wedding dress she'd intended to wear for her big day. She was laid out with a posy of fresh blue flowers.

On her ring finger was a new 9-carat gold wedding band. Inside her shoe was an old silver coin, an old Irish reul 6d coin depicting an Irish wolfhound. There was no evidence of forced entry, once again suggesting that Imelda possibly knew her killer and let them in, or even that the killer had a key.

In the case of Marina Willoughby, found in the home she shared with her fiancé, Dylan Coyle, in Arbutus Road, there was no evidence of forced entry either. Like Imelda Gannon, Marina was murdered while her fiancé was celebrating his stag weekend. It appears possible that Marina also knew her killer and let that person in to her home, or again that the killer had a key to the house.

Marina's body was discovered laid out in the dress she intended to wear on her wedding day. She too had sleeping tablets and toxic levels of amitriptyline and tramadol in her system. Also given as the cause of death. There was no evidence of any bruising or of suffocation. Marina's ring finger bore a 9-carat wedding band – identical to the ring found on Imelda Gannon. Inside Marina's shoe was a silver coin, also an Irish reul 6d coin.

All three murder cases strongly suggest the killer was known to their victims. The killer knew the movements of the women and the movements of their relatives. On the face of it, all three killings look similar, but there are some striking differences.

The first and most obvious is the age profile. Isolde Hanly was an elderly lady. By comparison the other two victims were young women taken in the prime of their lives. Isolde Hanly was killed by suffocation. The other two victims died through toxic overdoses. Imelda Gannon and Marina Willoughby were planning to marry, whereas Isolde Hanly was already married, and in fact a widow.

Research shows that if a killer has a certain signature, he or she tends to work by that signature. Why then were the deaths of Marina Willoughby and Imelda Gannon observed by a different ritual, by the lesser-known wedding rhyme: 'Something old, something new, something borrowed, something blue, and a silver sixpence in her shoe'?

While detectives at Coleman Street, assisted by the Serious Crime Squad, are working round the clock to solve these murders, it is to be hoped that the enquiry is open to the possibility that there may be more than one killer operating in Kylebeggan.

It was time for Scully to head home. He hit Send.

He was hoping to get some time alone with his wife. His sister-in-law Lou had texted earlier to say the girls were at a birthday party.

In the months following the diagnosis, Jill had ignored what was happening to her. She didn't acknowledge it or even speak about it, as if it might somehow go away. But the doctors had been clear. The disease was degenerative. Very little, if anything,

149

could be done. Scully suggested they move from the cottage to somewhere more suitable. Reluctant at first, Jill agreed to move to Abbey Court, the new, wheelchair-friendly development in town.

They learned that, despite the bungalows being sold as wheelchair-friendly, the kitchens had been fitted for able-bodied residents. Not to worry, said the developer. There'd be another more suitable development coming on-stream soon. It was a moot point. Jill's decline had been more rapid than they'd feared, and there was no point in moving now.

Lou had done some asking around and had found Agnieska, a Polish physiotherapist, who came out from town to the cottage each morning. She did piecemeal work for a few private clients. Agnieska spoke English with a strong Cork accent. Lou worked part-time in a call centre in the mornings so she was able to look after Jill in the afternoons.

The scent of burning ash drifted through his open window as Scully chugged down the uneven boreen towards the cottage. In the clearing ahead, puffs of white smoke sailed into a break in the clouds over the trees. As Scully approached the cottage, he spotted the clay chimney puffing away. Lou had lit the stove.

He parked the Land Rover next to Lou's car at the outhouses, noticing that the door to the woodshed was swinging open. Lou must have left it unlocked. Securing the bolt through the hole, he marched across the yard and entered the cottage.

Lou was ironing. 'Nice to see you home in daylight, Cormac.' Lou glanced at her sister. 'Not a bad afternoon so far. We're just getting through the ironing and watching a spot of *Judge Judy*.'

Jill detested daytime TV. Never mind. Scully had a treat in store. Thanking Lou for her help, he confirmed arrangements for the following day and waved her off.

A short time later, he and Jill were sitting in the car on Bailey Strand, a stretch of shingle on the shores of Lough Avulla. No one but locals knew about the old dirt track that led on to the secluded strand. It was where he and Jill had come, back in the beginning. There was no one else here today. If they were lucky they might spot a corncrake. Jill had been excited to see one here the year before. He'd take one last look at his phone before switching it off. Some bad jokes in from Doyler at the paper, and a text from Ellie.

Hi S. Anything in yet on Ms Healy? E

A visit to Jen Healy was next on his list. He switched the phone off and reached in the back for the basket. He'd assembled a picnic of shop-bought sandwiches and a bottle of wine. He and Jill sat listening to the birds through the open window. Scully pulled a fishing rug from the back and laid it across Jill's knees. He offered her bite-size pieces, waiting in between for each slow swallow. After, he poured wine into her plastic beaker, securing the mouth-piece before holding it to her lips. He wiped whatever spilled.

'It's not Barbados, Jill, I'll give you that,' he said. 'But it beats the socks off *Judge Judy*.'

Her facial muscles didn't move. But he felt sure he saw a flicker in her eyes. He knew his wife. He knew that inside she was smiling.

25

'What the actual fuck, Scully?' Begley hissed.

They were standing in Bradshaw's office.

'Other rags are content to rant about a serial killer running amok, but you have to go one better. Scully has to put jam on it with talk of a copycat killer.'

The windowless office smelled stale and airless. Someone had made it worse by spraying sickly-smelling freshener from an aerosol. Gerry Bradshaw was under pressure. *The Kylebeggan Echo* was a small provincial newspaper that rarely upset anyone and his boss wasn't used to confrontation. The room hummed from the heated exchange.

Gerry was sweating like a racehorse, the result of Begley's fury, the early morning phone call from Mayor Halligan and his hangover. He blinked sweat away as he watched Begley and Halligan tear into Scully.

'You've lost the run of yourself writing this.' With his eyes trained on Scully, Halligan pointed a short, squat finger at the paper on the desk. He was a short, squat man. 'Are you trying to kill our tourist trade altogether? This sort of drivel brings weirdos crawling out from underneath their rocks. How does shite like this make things better?'

Scully was calm. '*The Kylebeggan Echo* is not a PR agency. It's a newspaper.'

A snatched glance to Scully's left confirmed that any support from his boss would be unlikely. Bradshaw had his head in his hands as he stared miserably at the back of the aerosol can.

'My job is to report the facts as I see them,' Scully explained. 'The way I see it, I've made a good case for the possibility of a copycat killer at work here.'

Begley's eyes bulged. 'That so? The way I see it, you're just putting bells and whistles on this to distinguish yourself from the big media outfits crawling through the town. Trying to make a name for yourself.' His expression mellowed. 'I can't say I blame you. I can't begrudge you your big opportunity' – he swept a disdainful eye about the office and out through the glass door to the floor beyond – 'it's hardly the *Boston Globe* here. No offence.'

With a nod of apology in Bradshaw's direction he turned his attention back to Scully.

'You're jeopardising my investigation with your fairy stories.' His eyes narrowed. He took a step back and studied Scully. 'You've always had a problem with authority. Setting fires in churches. Throwing rocks through stained-glass windows.'

Bradshaw darted a nervous look in Scully's direction.

Scully squared his shoulders. '*Your* investigation?' he said, icily. 'I thought this investigation was being headed up by the Serious Crime Squad.'

'The Serious Crime Squad is *assisting* us with the investigation.' Begley raised a hand to smooth an eyebrow. 'There's something else bothering me here, apart from your crackpot theory.' He eyeballed Scully. '*Where* exactly are you getting all your information from? *Where* did you hear about toxicology results? About the tramadol and the amitriptyline? *Where* did you hear about old silver coins?'

Scully looked up at the strip lighting. It flickered and he could

153

see the carcass of a dead fly on the inside of the tube. He turned to face his accusers.

'I'm not in a position to divulge my sources. You know that.'

Begley threw an eye over at Gerry, as if he might somehow intercede. As Gerry shrugged, Begley's features tightened into a scowl. A hush descended on the airless room.

Halligan was shaking his head like a disappointed school-teacher, waiting for Begley to take another tack. Leaning against the office wall, Scully picked imaginary hairs off his jeans, affecting an air of insouciance. Gerry yanked at his desk drawer, muttering something about paracetamol.

Begley blinked. 'You leave the investigation work to us, Mr Scully,' he said, his tone calm and measured. 'We have things under control here.'

'But do you?' Scully's tone was equally even. 'How can you tell there won't be another murder? And another one after that?'

Begley flushed. 'We're advanced in our lines of enquiry. We'll have an arrest soon.'

Scully straightened up. 'Someone local?'

'Someone that females around here are familiar with. Ask around, lad. Now there's something that should keep you busy.'

'It's not Joseph Liston by any chance?'

'You might think that.' Begley smirked. 'I couldn't possibly comment.'

Mayor Halligan cleared his throat. 'Be mindful what you print in here, lads. An arrest may be imminent, but it could take years to build the town's reputation back. We've worked hard on the council to make Kylebeggan the place it is today. You know that too, Gerry.' He nodded in Gerry's direction. 'You know Finneran's Dip is in the running for the Irish Open in two years' time. That's hanging in the balance now.'

'I hear you.' Gerry sighed.

Gerry played golf with the mayor. Right now, the thing caus-ing Scully's boss the greatest grief was his hangover. He mopped his shiny forehead and tossed another screwed-up tissue into the waste basket.

'Good to know you're on board, Gerry.' Begley held the door. 'Right then, we'll be off.' He waited for Halligan to leave and had just turned his back when he appeared to think of something. 'I nearly forgot.' He turned to Scully with a strange expression. 'Jill Scully – that's your good lady wife, right?'

'What . . . ?' Scully was caught off-guard.

'I thought as much.' Begley gave a sly smile. 'The name rang a bell. I spotted a form for counter-signature down at the station. Jill is looking for a disabled person's parking card, yes?'

Scully stared. He'd put in the application months ago.

'Well, no need to worry about it.' Begley smiled. 'We take care of routine work. Even in the middle of a murder investigation.' He took a breath. 'It's just a little slower, that's all.' He let the door swing shut.

'Prick,' said Scully.

'Jesus!' Gerry exclaimed. 'What have you been up to? I thought I left the paper in a safe pair of hands. Can a guy not take an odd afternoon off for a few holes around the golf course without all hell breaking loose?'

Scully refrained from pointing out that Gerry rarely spent a whole day in the office. There was nothing to be gained from claiming that he had indeed sought Gerry's prior approval. The guy was unlikely even to remember the phone call.

'I'm off home,' said Gerry. 'I'll be back later. We'll talk then.'

As his boss departed, Scully skipped down the fire exit at the back of the building. It was time for him to put in a call to Tall

Dark. Begley seemed to be pointing him in the direction of Joseph Liston while at the same time putting distance between himself and that suggestion.

Tall Dark answered after a few rings. When Scully recounted the tetchy exchange with Superintendent Begley and Mayor Halligan, the sergeant was scathing. 'He *really* said, "You might think that. I couldn't possibly comment"?'

'He did.' Scully examined the soles of his walking boots. There wasn't much wearing left in them. 'But all that stuff happened at least ten years ago. The investigation team doesn't seriously think Liston's involved?'

'It was twelve years ago actually.'

'OK, ten years, twelve years, whatever. The point is the guy has been quiet for years. All right, so he has an unproven history of rape. But none of our victims was raped. I dunno, pal. To my mind, none of this stacks up.'

'You don't think so?' Tall Dark sounded unusually cryptic.

'Am I missing something here?'

'Come on, Scully. Do your homework. I thought you'd have found out by now.'

Scully bristled. 'Found out what?'

'The name of the woman who alleged she was raped.'

'Tell me.'

The sergeant was breathing heavily. 'It was Connie Begley . . .'

'Not anything to Superintendent Begley?'

More breathing. 'Connie is Superintendent Sean Begley's sister.' The sergeant lowered his voice. 'The girl was no great shakes in the head department to begin with, but she's in a very bad way now, God love her. In and out of St Jude's all the time.'

St Jude's was a psychiatric hospital.

'Yeah, OK, I get you . . . I can't imagine Begley would leave that go.' Things were starting to fall into place.

'He hasn't. Joseph Liston gets pulled over regularly. The guy has been done for every traffic violation in the book. There were rumours, years back, that Begley and some of the boys got him in the back of a garda van on a quiet spot in the woods down there beyond Lowertown. They kicked the shit out of him. Left him half dead, by all accounts.'

Scully whistled.

'Begley wants an easy solution. A scapegoat. That's why there's no way he'll buy into your copycat theory.' Tall Dark chuckled drily. 'The Serious Crime Squad were taken with it though. I heard them kicking it about in the Incident Room but Begley poured cold water on it straightaway, making out that you were some small-town, frustrated wannabe Dan Brown. Begley wants results. And quickly. He's not too pushed on truth.'

Scully sighed. 'I think he and Mayor Halligan are living in their own parallel universe. All Halligan wants is warm and fuzzy headlines. I have a few they might like.'

'Be careful, Scully. Begley's not a fan of yours.'

'I'm well aware of that. It sounds like he has his hands full trying to stitch someone up.'

Back at his desk, Scully sat brooding at his keyboard. He scanned some local photos that had come in. His phone pinged on the desk. Another text from Ellie.

> Hi there. FYI Jen Healy's flower shop is called Blooming Vales. Between Main Street and Brannock Square. Ellie

He'd be in that direction later. He went back to the photos. In line with Begley's directive, he composed the most inoffensive offensive headline he could muster:

MINE'S THE BIGGEST IN KYLEBEGGAN

Underneath, he placed a link to the photo of a Kylebeggan gardener holding a parsnip at last weekend's horticultural show. He inserted a photo caption:

Kylebeggan man Bernard Ryan wins parsnip competition

He padded out the article with details of other contestants, and tips for the growth of parsnips. One contestant, he wrote, was in the third generation of a family of parsnip growers. The contestant put his success down to regular dowsing of holy water from the Marian shrine at Knock.

For the second front-page lead, he typed the line:

NEW LEAD IN KYLEBEGGAN BRIDES CASE

He followed with:

Detectives in Coleman Street are very happy with progress being made in the case. A person known to the gardaí from a number of years ago is helping them with their enquiries. Superintendent Sean Begley, assisted by the Serious Crime Squad, says interesting parallels are being followed up on at present.

Inserting a link to a photo of Superintendent Begley, he slammed the laptop shut. That should keep the fucker happy.

On his way out the door, he had a word with Shona in Layout. He'd be gone for the rest of the day, he said. He had an interview to conduct, followed by his radio slot at Skellig FM. If Shona could arrange the front-page layout so the two articles ran side by side, slapping the photo of the superintendent bang up against the headline **MINE'S THE BIGGEST IN KYLEBEGGAN**, then all the better.

'You're sure?' she asked.

'I'm sure.'

Shona shook her head and laughed.

A brisk walk in a stiff wind took Scully to the ivy-clad offices of Coyle & Coyle in Brannock Square. He was directed to a shelf-lined room smelling of polish and old books. Paned sash windows overlooked the fountain in the square outside.

The receptionist set off to locate the senior partner of Coyle & Coyle. She was confident Dylan was in the building somewhere. Scully sat and waited.

26

'Thanks for coming, Ellie. Another pair of ears is always helpful.'

Scully and Ellie sat in a booth at the Coffee Station in Mountain View community centre.

'A pair of female ears in particular.' Scully smiled.

'No problem,' said Ellie. 'I was in the area.'

Ellie had been dropping a fare to sheltered housing nearby when Scully had phoned to say he had a recording of the previous day's conversation with Dylan Coyle, conducted at the offices of Coyle & Coyle Solicitors. Marina Willoughby's fiancé had consented to a recording on his phone.

'I've got most of the conversation here.' Scully set his phone on the table, pressing Play.

Ellie settled in as she looked through the small paned windows of the converted railway station out to the foothills of the Black Pins. A guy in overalls glanced over at their table as he left the Coffee Station carrying a takeout cup. Scully adjusted the volume:

'It's been a while since school. I'm sorry for your loss.'

'Thank you. It's hard to believe.'

The sound of furniture being moved.

'Here . . . have a seat.'

'I wondered if I could do an obituary piece on Marina?' Scully clears his throat. 'We ran tributes to Isolde Hanly and to Imelda Gannon. You may have seen them?'

Silence.

'Or perhaps you'd like to write a few words yourself?'

'Maybe . . . maybe. We're heartbroken, it's hard to think straight. I couldn't sit at home and look at the walls though. I had to come to the office.'

A door opens.

'I'm trying to keep busy. Isn't that right, Aisling? Perfect – we can pour ourselves.'

The sound of a door closing and the sound of something being poured.

'That was a disturbing piece you did about copycat killers.' Something slides across a table. 'You always had imagination, Scully.'

'It's only a theory. I don't think the gardaí are pleased with it. They have their own ideas.'

'I'm happy enough to let them do their job. As long as they find the bastard that messed up my life.' Dylan Coyle sighs. 'It's ruined everything.' A heavier sigh. 'Her friends used to call her Little Miss Perfect, you know. Because she was. She really was. If Marina had any failing, it was that she was too kind. People took advantage.'

'I'm sorry.'

'We used to give Marina all the hard-luck or, should I say, distressing cases. Clients who'd been abused by the Church and such. My forte is not for tears and tissues, I'm afraid. I left all that to Marina. And now she's gone.' The chink of a cup against saucer. 'I guess you saw our place in Arbutus Road on the news?'

'I was the one who did the initial report from there.'

'Right, right. The place was a wreck when we bought it. Marina did wonders. She has . . . had . . . good taste. An artist's eye. You can see from the paintings hanging behind you.'

'Oh . . . I see that. Impressive.'

'She was a perfectionist in every way. In her personal and her professional life. A stickler for protocol.'

'I imagine you have to be, in your profession.'

'The wedding was going to be perfect. From the bridesmaids' posies to the first dance.' Dylan Coyle suddenly chuckles. 'You know she wanted me to take ballroom-dancing lessons so that we wouldn't fluff the first dance?' He chuckles again. 'Actually, that was one thing we did argue over. Me, ballroom dancing? Not on your nelly, mate.' More amused sounds.

'It's not for everyone.'

'I never stopped Marina going. Marina kept herself in shape. I always felt good around her. You'll know what that's like, Scully. Jill's a looker too. You got there in the end, my friend. Perseverance. That's the name of the game.'

'Marina was head girl at school, if I remember rightly.'

'That's right. She was. Everyone went to her with their problems. I'm sure you find this yourself but there are just some people that would suck the life out of you. Marina would listen to them all.'

A pause.

'It must have been difficult . . . having to cancel stuff – the venue, the photographs, the flowers.'

More pouring sounds.

'My mother stepped in and took care of a lot of stuff. The florist was Marina's bridesmaid, Jen – Jen Healy. A live wire and a bit of a minx, but really good fun and a good friend to Marina too. Jen's devastated, the same as us all.' A slurping sound. 'Totally devastated.'

'I'm sure.'

The sound of a chair moving.

'That it?'

'I wouldn't like to intrude on your grief.'

'Well, thanks for dropping in.' The sound of footsteps. 'And, Scully, sorry about your brother, by the way.' Dylan Coyle hesitates. 'I only got to hear about it after. It occurs to me as I speak that I may have been insensitive earlier. Sorry. No offence meant.'

'None taken.'

A pause.

'And how are your folks doing?'

'They passed away a number of years ago.'

'You still have the farm?'

'I lease it out. We live in my folk's place, in the cottage.'

'Give my best to Jill. Won't you?'

'Sure. Sorry again for your loss. I'll put together something for Marina.'

'I'm sure you'll do a nice job.'

Scully reached for his phone, clicked off the recording and turned to Ellie.

'You've got the gist of it there. Anything else as I was leaving was chat from our school days. Rugby matches, guys we knew, that sort of thing.' He looked pained. 'Oh, and how these days Dylan keeps himself in shape by going swimming and heading to the gym. So, Ellie, what do you think?'

She was momentarily distracted by someone peering in at them from the concourse. She looked away.

'Ellie?' prompted Scully.

'Yeah, well, Dylan Coyle is obviously in shock,' Ellie responded thoughtfully. 'You can hear that in his voice. Sounds like a bit of a charmer too.'

'You think?'

Ellie was feeling brave. 'None of my business, Scully, but he didn't happen to date your wife at any point?'

'Briefly,' said Scully tightly. 'I think she found the guy controlling. Used to tell her what to say, what to wear.'

Ellie raised an eyebrow.

'Dylan Coyle is a guy who's used to attracting attention. Male and female.' Scully shook his head. 'Always managed to get out of any scrapes. He studied law in Cork. Rumour had it that his final exam results had been in doubt there for a while before his old man intervened, blaming an injury in a college rugby game for his son's impaired exam performance.'

'Must be nice to be connected. Interesting, too, his comment about Jen Healy. A minx? Have you had a chance to speak to her or find anything out yet?'

Ellie had certainly sent him enough texts.

'It's next on my list.'

'There's definitely something about that girl. You won't know more until you talk to her. There could be a story in it for you.' Ellie made a move to put her coat on.

Scully was staring out at the slushy rain that had started to fall. Grey swirls of cloud rolled down wraith-like from the mountains. Only the lowest reaches could now be seen. Ellie's next customer wouldn't be enamoured at having to wait out in the wet. She grabbed her bag and swung her legs out of the booth.

'I'm sorry about your brother, Scully. I didn't realise you had lost someone too.'

'Old news. It was a while ago.' His expression was inscrutable.

'Was it sudden?'

Scully picked up his raincoat.

'He was an altar boy,' he said.

27

'My friend Sheila in number 6 was saying to me she has her doubts about them finding this killer – the way the gardaí are stopping the world and his father, going off in one direction then another.' Doreen fumbled with the seat belt. 'But my son says to take no notice. That Sheila thinks she's back in the days of the Raj with her own personal manservant, just because her bungalow has extras like a ramp and a handrail, and Brendan the warden checks in on her twice a day. She says he drops in every evening to make her hot chocolate.'

'The investigation doesn't appear to be making much progress,' Ellie agreed, manoeuvring out into the road.

'A right cluster-fuck.' Doreen snapped her buckle in place.

Ellie nearly rammed into a car in front.

'I believe that's a term you young people use?'

Ellie laughed. 'It's one way of putting it.'

Doreen looked into the distance, innocently.

Ellie still couldn't figure out any connections between Isolde and the other two victims. She couldn't make any sense of the murders, and when she darkly imagined Isolde in her dying moments, she blocked the images out.

There were just so many theories as to the identity of the killer.

Most tabloids ran with someone with a history of sex crimes fitting the killer's profile. Scully had been the first journalist to air his copycat theory in *The Kylebeggan Echo*.

All reports had one thing in common, suggesting the killer was a man. Ellie wasn't so sure. Imelda Gannon and Marina Willoughby had both been able-bodied and young. It was possible that they had willingly let their killers into their homes. Someone known to them, someone they were comfortable with, someone they liked, or even loved. That person could have been a woman.

She was plagued by thoughts of Jen Healy. Had the self-declared 'three-times-a-bridesmaid, never-a-bride' committed murder, while an unsuspecting Ellie had waited outside at 9 Arbutus Road? Had Ellie been an unsuspecting party to a woman's murder? It was entirely possible that she had unwittingly driven Marina Willoughby to her death.

While Ellie had been concerned only with her ticking taxi meter, perhaps Jen Healy had enough time to poison Marina and to stage her body in a manner disturbingly similar to that of Isolde's. Jen had certainly taken her time checking the house. She'd behaved as if she'd been drinking. But what if it was all a ruse, designed to deflect? Perhaps it had all been exaggerated, a grand pretence.

When Ellie had given her statement to the gardaí in Coleman Street, the gardaí had registered little to no disquiet at the length of her wait outside 9 Arbutus Road the previous evening. She wondered just how competent the Coleman Street gardaí were.

Ellie had another nagging thought. Jen Healy had parted company with her friend, Rose, outside Godiva's nightclub. So far, no other taxi drivers had come forward to say they'd driven Jen home, as she'd alleged. Perhaps Jen hadn't gone back to Arbutus Road. Marina would have been delighted to see her, thinking her bridesmaid had a change of heart and returned to keep her company, knowing how uneasy she was feeling.

But why would she kill two supposed friends? Perhaps she was jealous they had found partners to share their lives with. Ellie couldn't imagine such a thing, yet she believed there were women like that. Maybe Jen had been envious of her friends' popularity and career success. Both women had been well loved. Perhaps Jen had been motivated by simple jealousy.

Both Marina and Imelda had been laid out with arrangements of fresh blue flowers, something Jen Healy had access to, running a florist shop. Though, in reality, anyone could have bought fresh flowers.

And why had Jen specifically sought out Ellie for her taxi ride to the church? She'd told Ellie her car had been delayed while in the garage for a service. Ellie had since found out that this was untrue. Scully had learned from his source that a number of cars had been impounded by the gardaí as part of the investigation. Jen Healy's car had been one of those.

Maybe Jen had wanted to check up on Ellie. Maybe Jen's real purpose in arranging a ride had been to find out if Ellie had seen anything unusual the night of Marina's killing? Anything that could incriminate her.

More pressingly, was Ellie in any danger? The whole business was terrifying. She couldn't help feeling, as she had on many occasions these past few weeks, that someone was watching her. Watching her very closely.

Ellie jumped, though Doreen's touch was light.

'How are you doing, my dear? I know how close you were to Isolde.'

Ellie trembled with a sudden swell of emotion. 'It's hard,' she admitted. 'Very hard.'

'It is.' Doreen nodded. 'She was a lovely lady, may God rest her.' She patted Ellie's hand. 'I was only talking about her to my friend Ursula last night. I rang Ursula to tell her all about this fantastic new cushioned tray my son had bought to ease the pressure on my leg, and she started telling me about all the reporters staying with her up at Pottershill.'

'Is that right?'

'She says her lumbago's acting up from doing all those beds. But I said to her, "Ursula, there's no such thing as lumbago any more. It's gone out of fashion." Well, she didn't like that much. Ursula likes to keep up to date with everything, you see, likes to think she's so with-it.'

When Ellie pulled up outside Klassy Kuts, there was no sign of Mervyn outside his tanning salon, much to her relief. One less creepy conversation to be had. She imagined it was too cold for a smoke in the biting wind.

Arriving home for an early lunch, she could see Pauline vigorously bleaching her front step. Her neighbour wore furry ear muffs and a flowery apron over a quilted jacket. Head down, she was focused on her brushing action, her back to the street.

With luck, Ellie might just slip by her unnoticed. She closed the car door softly and headed on her toes across the cobbled street. Despite ear muffs, Pauline's head whipped to the side.

'There you are.' She leaned back on her haunches. 'My, you look tired, my dear. I know what's going on is a worry, Ellie, but you need more sleep.'

'Not so easy these past few nights with the wind, is it though? And all those noises in the attic – don't they bother you, Pauline?'

'Not a bit. But I'm asleep as soon as my head hits the pillow, love. Funny you should say that, though; the Australian used to say that too.'

'Australian?'

'Melissa – the girl before. A pretty girl but not as pretty as you.'

'Oh . . .'

The letting agency had told Ellie the previous tenant had left the house before the lease was up.

'What did Melissa do?'

'She worked in a bar in town, she said. Somewhere off Limekiln Road.'

'And where did Melissa go?'

'I have no idea.' Pauline rubbed her hands on her apron. 'But it might have been the neighbourly thing to say goodbye to me. The girl just upped and left. Here one day. Gone the next.'

Ellie looked up in the direction of the roof.

'I wonder if the noises I'm hearing could be loose slates.'

'Or birds, maybe.' Pauline brightened. 'We could have a residents' meeting to organise someone to take a look. I've always thought a street party would be a lovely idea. We could talk about the roof at the same time.'

Ellie gave an inward groan. The idea of a residents' meeting filled her with dread. The less she had to with her neighbours, the better. She'd prefer to finish decorating, and that was saying something. She wondered if paint went off. That paint may indeed smell of an elephant's breath by now, living up to its name on the tin.

'Mervyn has been saying for ages that he plans to have a get-together in his yard to show the neighbours his water feature.' Pauline's eyes sparkled. 'We could have our residents' meeting then.'

This was getting worse.

'A back-yard party in March?' Ellie blew on her hands. 'A little cold at the moment, don't you think?'

'Oh, he's getting a fire pit. As well as showing off the water feature, he wants to figure out who it is that's defacing his nameplate.

169

He has his eye on the lad at the top of the row. The young man with the noisy motorbike.'

'He'd be well advised to keep the noise down himself.' Ellie put her key in the door. 'I'd be more likely to get a proper night's sleep if he didn't clatter about so much outside.'

'Sure, Mervyn always has his projects, always tinkering away with something or other in the evenings.' Pauline got to her feet, pushing back her ear muffs. 'It was a lot quieter before he ran the tanning salon.'

'How's that, Pauline?' Ellie turned the key.

'Well, he used to work nights before he had his own business.'

'Oh, yeah. What did he do?'

'He was a night porter.'

'Seriously?'

'Perfectly serious.' Pauline set her scrubbing brush and bucket inside. 'Up at the hospital mortuary.'

28

Scully had left his mobile on his desk at *The Kylebeggan Echo*. By the time he got back from Buckley's Bakery, he had two missed calls. One from his sister-in-law and one from Ellie. Sinking his teeth into a bacon, egg and lettuce roll, he checked to see if there were any messages. He'd had every intention of buying a fruit salad and some yogurt, but it was pissing down and bleak outside and he deserved some comfort.

'How's the diet going?' cried Doyler, from across the floor. Doyler was in Advertising.

'Better than yours,' Scully shouted back. Doyler's wife always had him joining some slimming scheme or other. Despite that, the guy was getting larger by the day.

Scully ate just enough to assuage his hunger, wiped his mouth and hit Lou's number.

'Thanks for getting back to me, Cormac. It's a quick one,' whispered Lou when she answered. 'I know you're busy with all these murder cases but don't forget about the girls today.'

'Of course I won't . . .'

Scully tried to remember why today was different.

'The girls are on their school tour,' said Lou. 'They're not getting

171

the bus home as usual today. You're collecting them from the train this afternoon, remember?'

'Sure, I remember.' Scully hoped he sounded convincing.

'Good. See you all back at the cottage later?'

'Yep. You'd better go. I don't want you getting in trouble with your supervisor.'

The call centre was disapproving of any personal calls.

'Grumpy old cow is off today. Tummy bug. I hope she pukes her guts up.'

Scully hung up and looked at the remains of his breakfast roll. He suddenly felt a bit queasy himself. Bundling the roll in the wrapper, he raised his hand to lob it into the bin.

'You're not going to throw that away, are you?' Doyler looked alarmed. He held out his hand. 'Give it here.'

Scully chucked the roll over to him. 'Your wife would kill you.'

'What the wife doesn't know won't kill her.'

Scully went back to his calls, and this time he dialled Ellie. She sounded as if she was whispering too. A worried whisper, not like Lou's. She asked if they could meet.

'I've a few things to get off my desk first and I also have to swing by home. Let me think . . .'

He had a vox pop for Skellig FM in the afternoon, and there were the girls to collect. He had a brainwave.

'I could meet you around 12.30. Sound OK?'

'That would be great.'

'How about Lorrigan's Mill?'

Lorrigan's pub was in a converted grain mill, not too far from Skellig FM. It had a snug at the back overlooking the river. They could sit there.

'See you then.'

Scully scanned the office. Doyler was gawping at his screen, having made short work of the roll. A tail of shredded lettuce was hanging from the corner of his mouth. Shona was staring at her screen, a frown on her face. Scully felt guilty having to leave almost as soon as he'd arrived, especially as Gerry had cut him a lot of slack since Jill got sick.

He looked across at Doyler. 'Listen,' he said and tilted his head towards Gerry's office, 'if your man comes out and asks where I am, just say I'm off on a lead.'

'All right,' mumbled Doyler. 'I'm keeping my head down here. Gerry's had a bad dose of IBS ever since Mayor Halligan and Superintendent Begley called in.'

This was news to Scully. 'I didn't know that Gerry had IBS.'

'He sure does.' Doyler picked the lettuce from his chin. 'Irritable Bastard Syndrome.'

As Scully headed home to the cottage, he used the journey to make a call about Freddy Hanly. He was a guy worthy of further investigation. Did anyone know yet where Freddy had been the night of Isolde Hanly's murder?

Tall Dark was not in the best of form. In fact, the guy was seething. 'Do you know what these fuckers have me doing?'

'I don't.' Scully held his breath.

'Setting out traffic cones to block off Friary Lane and a section of Arbutus Road. Residents have been complaining about the media. They can't come and go about their daily business. Pity about them. I'm the eejit working away here in the pissing rain. Makes me wonder if Begley hasn't somehow got wind that I've been talking to you?'

'I doubt that.' Now would not be a good time for Tall Dark to dry up on him. 'How about we swap places.' Scully tried to humour him. 'How do you fancy a vox pop this afternoon with a bunch of octogenarians, followed by music from the eighties and the nineties back in the studio?'

Tall Dark grunted.

'Yeah, riveting stuff,' said Scully. 'I'm off up to the bowling green very shortly to ask the pensioners how they feel about the green being moved out to Lissfeakle Park to make way for retirement homes. How's that for exciting?'

'I'll stand by with water cannon,' Tall Dark muttered.

'Listen, have there been any further developments on Freddy Hanly? The last I heard the guy didn't have a solid alibi. There was no CCTV footage of him in any local supermarkets. Is that still the case?'

'There's been a bit of news all right—'

'Really?' Scully wished he didn't have to drag every last ounce of information out of the sergeant.

'Freddy does actually have an alibi. But it needs to be checked out. It looks like he was enjoying a little extramarital with some young female from the golf club. A junior he coaches.'

Scully whistled. 'Underage?'

'Just turned eighteen. Not quite jailbait. He came to the station and volunteered the information, begging us not to tell his missus. He says he was with the young one the night his aunt was murdered.'

'I don't think his wife would be too forgiving, from what I saw.'

'Freddy Hanly may have question marks hanging over him, but I can tell you here and now that Begley is still gunning for his man Joseph Liston.'

Talk of Begley made Scully edgy. 'Listen, thanks for all the updates, pal. I'm just on my way to check in on Jill at the cottage. We'll catch up for a run soon? I'd been thinking about going for one later, but the mist looks like it's on its way down for the day.'

'Soon then.' Tall Dark grunted as he hung up.

The further Scully drove away from town, the denser was the

mist crawling down the mountains. He switched his fog lights on as he took the turning off the main road for the boreen down to the cottage.

Agnieska came towards the door as soon as Scully put the key in the lock. He could see her frame through the frosted-glass panes of the inside door. Lou had advised him early on that it would be a good idea to call by unannounced from time to time. His sister-in-law prided herself on being a good judge of character. Though Lou considered Agnieska capable, there was no harm in being vigilant, she said.

'Nice,' said Scully, directing an ear towards the music coming from the radio.

'Dvořák,' she answered. 'Jill likes the Classics station.'

His wife sat secured safely in her wheelchair at the table. Scully had interrupted Agnieska feeding her. She looked serene. Perhaps the music did indeed agree with her. Scully kissed her on the cheek as Agnieska returned to the task in hand, still wearing her out-door coat. It was a habit Scully found annoying. It made her look like she was only passing through.

'Cold, Agnieska? I'll go out and get some more wood for the stove if you like.'

'I am not cold.' She kept her eyes trained on the spoon.

'Because you're wearing a coat—'

'Yes?' This time she looked up.

There was no point. Scully moved to the fridge and pulled a face behind her back. Jill's eyes followed him. He saw the merest suggestion of movement at the corner of her eyes.

'I haven't forgotten about Maude and Scarlett.' He directed his gaze to Jill. 'I'm going to get someone to collect them at the train station this afternoon.' He did his best to keep Jill up to date with all the girls' movements, so she wouldn't worry.

'They could walk,' said Agnieska. 'Many kids today are fat.'

'Thanks, Agnieska, but I think the walk out from town on country roads is a bit much. In winter too. And neither of my kids is fat, thank you.'

Spoon in hand, she raised an eyebrow.

'I'll be on Skellig FM later, if you want to tune in,' he said, heading to the door, a chicken leg in hand.

'I think we stick to Dvořák.'

'Fair enough.' He couldn't blame her. If he were Agnieska, he'd stick with Dvořák too.

29

Ellie sat at a window in the snug overlooking the mill wheel, waiting for Scully. She looked out at the steady flow of water below and let her thoughts turn to Isolde, as they often did. In particular, to her old friend's misfortune at having been lumbered with her nephew's wife, Regina.

When Ellie had called to Myrtle Crescent in search of a tax form to claim social security benefits, she'd listened to Regina's exasperated tones as she waited outside on the step.

'For goodness' sake, give it a rest,' shouted Regina. 'If it isn't your arse, it's your elbow.' When Freddy had eventually responded to the doorbell, Ellie preferred to think it was him Regina had been shouting at.

Ellie and Isolde's last ever excursion had been on the Orient Express. They'd chosen the route of Paris to Istanbul. It had been a bittersweet trip, Ellie sensing that any further travel would be confined much closer to home.

Isolde had spent her time casting her eyes about the dining carriage, visibly quaking at sights of check, pleats or cotton jersey favoured by the women of her age. Isolde's clothes were stylish and well cut. Later, in the confines of their shared compartment, Isolde would share her observations with Ellie, and they would laugh. Shoot me, she'd declare. Shoot me, Ellie, if you ever find me wearing fuddy-duddy clothes like that.

In her quieter moments, Isolde was given to introspection. God forgive me, she would say. What are you doing with an old bag of bones like me, Ellie? You should be off with a whole string of men. Ellie informed her she had all she wanted. Travel and good company. In any event, she said, she had yet to meet a man she'd like to live with.

'What about children?' Isolde asked.

'I don't want kids,' Ellie assured her.

'It makes me sad to hear that, Ellie,' Isolde said.

Whatever Isolde's sadness, it couldn't compare to that of Ellie's dying mother, knowing she was leaving three young children behind. Ellie had long since decided not to have kids of her own.

At the sound of footsteps she turned. It was Scully. She loosened her favourite purple and orange printed scarf and pulled her low-knotted ponytail from underneath her collar, letting it fall over her fitted jacket.

'I'd order tea if I were you,' she said. 'The coffee's dire.'

He cast an eye on her half-drunk cup.

'Sorry. I was trying to think of somewhere quiet. I'd half an idea this place didn't do food. I thought it'd suit – not likely to fill with lunch-time trade. I hope you're not too hungry?'

'I'm fine.'

'I'll order tea for two?'

'Thank you.'

Placing an order, Scully sat on a low stool on the other side of the small round table.

'I'm all ears,' he said, business-like. 'I've a vox pop shortly, so I don't have long.'

Ellie looked at him, widening her eyes.

178

'I got the impression you had something to tell me?' Scully angled his head in enquiry.

'Oh . . . not really. I rather thought *you* might have had some updates?'

Surely he'd spoken to Jen Healy by now? She'd sent him enough reminders.

'We must have got our wires crossed.' Scully shrugged. 'OK, let's see . . . I did do a bit of digging around on Freddy Hanly.'

Ellie pulled her shoulders back. Better than nothing, she supposed.

'Seems like he had something going on the side with some young girl at the golf club.'

Ellie rolled her eyes. 'I can't say I'm all that shocked. He seems the type, I guess. I can tell you one thing, though. Regina would kill him. And the girl too.'

'She doesn't know. What I've told you is confidential.'

'Well, well, well, Freddy Hanly.' Ellie shook her head. 'What a chancer.'

She jumped. The swing door opened and a surly-looking barman entered with a tray. He left without saying a word and Scully poured the tea. 'If you don't mind me saying, Ellie, you look a little strained.'

'Life isn't exactly a garden party just now.' She held up her hand. 'Sorry, I don't mean to be short.'

'No problem. We're all feeling it.'

'There's no let-up.' She cast a miserable eye on the river. 'Camera crews all over. Reporters stopping people in the street, outside all the coffee shops. I'm finding it hard to sleep. There's something in my attic, I think. And the guy next door is creeping me out.'

'Ah, don't go worrying about him, Ellie. I'm almost certain the investigation has ruled him out of any involvement in any of this.'

Ellie looked at Scully. 'My neighbour on the other side of me has just informed me that he used to be a night porter before he ran the tanning salon. Up at the hospital morgue.'

Scully pulled a face. 'Someone's got to do it.' Picking up the milk jug, he stopped and stared at the 'x' on his hand.

'The girls. I nearly forgot . . . Ellie, I wonder if I could call upon your services?'

It occurred to Ellie that she wasn't the only one who looked strained.

'Maude and Scarlett are on a school trip, coming back into the train station later. They usually get the bus as far as the top of the road and walk the rest of the way, but they'll have missed that bus today. I've my slot on Skellig FM. If I text the girls to say you'll be waiting for them, could you drop them back to the cottage? It's about four kilometres from town, out the Glanduff road, down towards the river.'

'Sure,' she said. 'Happy to help. Give me the postcode and I'll find it on Google.'

Scully insisted it was a business transaction and settled up with her in advance.

'How will I know your girls?' Ellie asked.

'Oh, you'll know my gorgeous girls.' His eyes crinkled as he smiled. 'I'm happy and relieved to tell you that the twins take after their mother.'

Back in the taxi, Ellie cleared away a crumpled paper bag and a copy of the *Daily Gazette* tabloid left behind by an earlier fare. She didn't imagine the front-page headlines were one a child should see:

Kylebeggan Murders

Who is next to say 'I Do' . . . and Die?

30

Having dealt with the concerns of Kylebeggan's bowling community, Scully made his way to Skellig FM. He sucked in deep lungs of air in advance of a two-hour slot in the airless, soundproofed studio at the radio station.

Mist rolled down the Black Pins in tombstone-grey. It billowed along the streets of the town. There was a stillness. Tonight would be an ideal night to pull on his waders and stand with his fishing rod in the slow-moving water behind the cottage. An evening alone with his thoughts.

He missed taking the short walk through the knot of trees while Jill and the girls slept. That pleasure had drawn to a close for now. The time had come, as they said it would. He had to keep a closer eye on his wife.

Arriving at the radio station, he first had a chat with Tara at the desk, then checked in with his producer, Shane. They ran through the order for the show, confirming the afternoon's vibe would be eighties nostalgia interspersed with some nineties hits. There were a number of requests he had to read at the top of the programme. Live phone-ins would be in the second half of the day's show.

Scully in the Afternoon was an easy-listening slot, tuned into by a middle-aged to elderly audience. Scully's first well-wishes were for a patient listening in from hospital who'd had a knee replacement, and another for a man who'd had a farming accident.

He kept one eye out on his phone for any texts from Lou or anything new from Ellie. He read out the updated vacancies from the Skellig FM jobs page. Pastry chefs, baristas and tour guides were sought in anticipation of the summer season. He played some tracks from Simple Minds and David Bowie.

'Linger' by The Cranberries had just finished when the lines opened for live requests. Scully asked his first caller to repeat their name. He still didn't make out the soft-spoken caller's name the second time around.

'Great to hear from you today,' he said, moving on. 'And who would you like to play a request for on *Scully in the Afternoon*?'

'Mmm . . . now let me see.'

There was breathing.

Scully looked at his producer through the glass. Why did callers phone in to make a request and seem caught on the hop?

'I'd like you to play something for a special person.'

More breathing.

'Something cheery and upbeat. Something special.'

'Well, that's what we're about here at Skellig FM.'

Scully didn't chance 'sir', still unable to confirm whether he was talking to a man or a woman.

'And who is this special person?'

'Someone I've been keeping an eye on.' The tone was pleasant. 'Someone I visit now and again. Someone who isn't terribly well.'

'That's very kind of you,' said Scully, his brows coming together. 'I'm sorry to hear that. Everyone here at Skellig FM wishes your friend a speedy recovery.'

Silence.

'Caller, are you there?'

Through the glass, he saw Shane put up his hands, puzzled.

'I'm afraid that is not going to happen.'

Scully felt a sudden chill in the soundproofed studio.

Through the glass, Shane angled his head to the side.

'My friend is not going to get any better.'

Scully stiffened, aware that the person in question was probably listening.

'I'm very sorry to hear that,' he said.

'I sit with my friend to keep her company when her husband goes out at night.'

Scully's skin started to prickle. He needed to wrap this up.

'We have an eighties feel to this afternoon's show. How about something from The Waterboys?'

'I'm sitting with my friend just now, actually. Oh . . . it looks like she may have nodded off. Just wait a moment until I check . . .'

Scully became aware of the hairs at the back of his neck.

'Are you there?' whispered the caller.

'I am. We're all listening.' Scully could barely get the words out. 'You're still live on *Scully in the Afternoon*—'

'I'm afraid my friend is unable to speak, but I do have one suggestion. You mentioned The Waterboys. How about "When Will We Be Married"? Yes, that's a nice one. I think my friend should be happy with that. I would like it too.'

31

It was gone four in the afternoon when Ellie parked up in the taxi rank outside the railway station. She locked the Škoda and headed across to O'Halloran's, on the corner with Griffith Square. Scully's girls were not due in for fifteen minutes.

O'Halloran's supermarket hummed with intending travellers, buying ready-to-go sandwiches and take-out coffees. At this time of day Ellie normally had a banana or some other piece of fruit, but she craved a blast of something nasty. Heavy-duty confectionery, full of E numbers and laced with all sorts of badness, the sort she would immediately regret eating.

Carrying a bag of pink and white iced sweets, and the double-shot Americano she had paid for, she weaved her way through the traffic and back to the car. Setting the coffee on the dashboard, she ripped apart the pack of sweets. The iced caramel was sickly pink and full of the sugar she craved.

Her nerves jangled. All day her head had swirled with memories, fragments of images and snippets of old conversations. As icing melted on her tongue, she cast her mind back. To Wednesday afternoons and tea dances at Mountain View community centre. To happier times.

She pictured Loretta Spillane arriving with freshly laundered tablecloths under her arm. Loretta's job was to look after the Burco boiler and make the tea. Isolde and Ellie were in charge of table decorations, and Bessie would bring home baking. Before anyone arrived, Isolde and Doreen would shuffle about, dressing and decorating the tables.

There would be excitement among the women in anticipation of men turning up. Any men who did arrive would appear sheepishly at the door before edging their way inside. Some were bereaved and strong-armed into attending by well-meaning friends or neighbours. They wore their Sunday suits. When the dancing started, the air would swirl with powdery notes of L'Air du Temps and L'Aimant and the brisker scent of 4711 cologne.

Most men came just once, their dance-floor antics proving too embarrassing for a second outing. A few were seasoned dancers. Two of note were the McElligot brothers, Stanley and George – bachelors from a farm on the Gorse Road. Their stamina was legendary. They worked a system whereby a woman who may have missed a dance one week was sure of getting one the following week.

Isolde told Ellie she was lowering the average age by forty years at least. She wasn't far off. Ellie and the teacher were the only non-pension-age citizens in the basketball hall at Mountain View on those Wednesday afternoons.

Ellie enjoyed two hours of dance routines – waltzes, foxtrots, quicksteps and the jitterbug. She partnered Isolde's friends. Bessie whispered how lovely she thought the teacher was. A gentleman, she said. In touch with his feminine side, Isolde said.

Loretta would call time for refreshments, and the smell of shortbread and homemade apple tarts would replace the tang of sweat and rubber soles. Ellie would listen to the pensioners' stories over cups of stewed tea. Some had spent their working lives abroad, in domestic service in residences in Boston, Chicago or the southern United States. Others had returned to Kerry from London.

Ellie heard all about London clubs in the sixties and seventies. About seeing bands like the Kinks and the Small Faces before they were famous. Not all the stories were happy. There were tales of isolation and prejudice. Of shop windows seeking staff but excluding people of colour and Irish. There were accounts of how difficult it had been to be Irish in London during the dark days of IRA bombing campaigns.

As Ellie waited for Scully's girls outside the train station, she wished herself back to those days, listening to Dolly Parton's 'Nine to Five', watching Bessie and Isolde dancing, their faces pink with pleasure underneath their powder.

She leaned across the seat and stuffed the remaining iced caramels into the glove compartment before reaching for her phone to message Scully.

> Hi S, FYI – outside train station waiting for the girls. Ellie

A sudden shrieking caught her attention. Giddy pockets of kids in uniform tumbled down the steps outside the station. Dropping the phone in her bag, she opened the door and sprinted up the steps.

She hurried through the sliding doors and positioned herself strategically in the centre of the concourse. Kids milled about everywhere. She was pushed back against the concourse wall to make way for a media crew lugging cameras and laptop cases.

On her toes, she spotted two schoolgirls walking side by side, studying a phone and glancing into the crowd, clearly looking for someone. Ellie had suggested Scully take her photo so the twins could identify her. She'd been dismayed to see the result – the shadows under her eyes and the swelling of a cold sore. Scully also sent his girls the registration number of her Škoda.

She jumped and waved to attract the two girls' attention. They separated from the flow, coming towards her cautiously.

'Ellie?'

'That's me.' She smiled.

It was startling to see just how identical they were, with their long dark hair, almond-shaped eyes and milky complexions.

'Your dad asked me to give you a lift home. You got the text?'

One of the girls nodded. 'I'm Maude.'

Ellie shook her hand.

'What's your car registration?' asked the child, not taking anything for granted.

Ellie tripped off her number. She was grateful the girls were wearing name tags, as were all the children on the trip. It would have proven impossible to tell the twins apart otherwise.

Two pairs of eyes looked down at their phones, verifying the registration information she had given them. They looked at one another, then at Ellie, remaining cautious.

'Did you enjoy the trip?'

Scully told her the outing was to Fota Safari Park.

'It was great,' said Maude. 'The penguins were cute.'

'The monkeys too,' said Scarlett.

They exited the sliding doors, towards the taxi. Ellie clicked open the car doors.

Scarlett looked her up and down. 'Jodie Gavigan puked into a see-through bag on the train.'

'Scarlett!' Maude was horrified. 'That's gross.' She looked at Ellie. 'Sorry.'

'No worries.' Ellie grinned.

'How do you know our dad?' Scarlett asked, climbing into the back after her sister.

'I don't really,' said Ellie, shutting the door. Getting into the front, and realising that had sounded odd, she added, 'I met your dad in Coleman Street garda station. We were helping gardaí with something.'

She turned on the engine and checked her mirrors.

'Was it about the man who's killing the brides?' asked Scarlett.

'Something like that.' Ellie didn't feel comfortable talking about murders with children.

'Dad won't talk about it either.'

Ellie leaned to open the glove compartment. 'Anyone for a sweet?'

A lull followed as the girls busied themselves with the packet of iced caramels.

The streetlights warmed up as Ellie weaved her way through town, heading for the Glanduff Road. The lights gave off an orange glow. The vehicles ahead were blurred and Ellie turned her fog lights on. Outside town, the lights grew fewer and they were soon driving on a wooded country road. Mist floated through the pine branches in the fading light. Ellie checked the girls. They seemed happy enough, chewing, chatting, and busy on their phones. She concentrated on her driving and the road markings.

'This is the first time we've taken a lift with a stranger,' Scarlett said after a kilometre or so.

'Not a stranger.' Maude was quick. 'Dad said a responsible person was picking us up.'

Ellie smiled. How responsible would Scully think her, she wondered, if he knew his girls were eating stolen sweets? She could make out the glow of an empty bus shelter ahead. It appeared to float above the road in the mist among dark pines.

'It's next turn right,' a voice from the back called out. 'Immediately after the bus stop.'

'I'm on it,' said Ellie, slowing. 'I have it here on Google maps.'

She indicated, taking a right turn on to a single-track road. The chatter in the back slowed and Ellie sensed unease as the car went down the bumpy track.

'You know our mum is sick?' said Scarlett.

'I do.'

Keeping her eyes on the boreen, Ellie thought back to all the times Scully had made mention of his wife, to how she'd thought he'd been sounding off about what a difficult woman she was. It had taken a while for her to gather that his wife was ill.

'She has motor neurone disease.'

'I'm sorry to hear that.'

Branches reached out to touch the car.

'You walk down this boreen every day?'

'Yes,' said Maude. 'Mum used to collect us . . . before.'

'I wish we lived in town,' said Scarlett, 'like our friends. But Dad could never be a townie.' She sighed. 'He likes fishing at the end of our lane. He's always talking about how he and Uncle Andrew used to fish when they were boys.'

Ellie swerved to avoid a pothole on the road. All three of them jumped as something fell and bounced across the windscreen.

'Oh shit!' Ellie exclaimed.

The back seat filled with giggles.

'A pine cone, Ellie. It happens all the time out here.'

Ellie looked in the rear-view mirror.

'I'm a townie now. I'd forgotten what country life is like . . . I can see some lights up ahead . . . is this it?'

'That's our house,' Maude confirmed.

Through swathes of mist, Ellie was just about able to make out a whitewashed dwelling in a clearing, and what looked like a number of buildings in a courtyard. Light came from the cottage windows. Between the cottage and outbuildings, a path disappeared into a copse of trees. Ellie drew up next to other cars parked in the front yard. A pale blue bubble-shaped Fiat and a white VW Polo.

'Aunty Lou's here,' said Scarlett.

Ellie left the engine running as she turned to talk to the twins.

'It was a pleasure to meet you, girls. We might see each other again.'

Two sets of large brown eyes blinked at her. Ellie noted a reluctance to leave the car.

'Thank you,' they answered together.

Ellie watched as they slump-walked towards the cottage. She reversed, intending to make a three-point turn, then braked sharply in response to a sound. She thought she must have skidded on something or even driven over a small animal.

There it was again.

A horrible sound.

A piercing, shrill sound.

Screams, coming from the cottage. In between the screams, a rumbling noise. And lights coming from a vehicle barrelling down the boreen, directly for her.

Ellie swung the car door open and propelled herself across the yard. She burst through the outer door, staring into the room from the inner door.

The scream stuck in her throat.

Half formed.

Frozen.

32

'Are you sleeping?' Johnny asked.

'I wish people would stop asking me that.' Ellie pulled at the cuff of her sleeve.

'You've gone very thin. Are you eating?'

'Something happened . . .'

Ellie glanced about the room to check for listening ears. The eyes and ears of prison visitors were trained on their own families.

'A few days back. It didn't make the news – they kept it under wraps.'

Johnny blinked.

'You know Cormac Scully, the reporter working on the murder cases, the one I'm in contact with?'

'The guy who says there's a copycat killer?'

Ellie nodded. 'He asked me to collect his daughters from a school trip and to drop them home to their place, out the Glanduff Road. They live there down by the river.'

'I know the place.' Johnny sat back.

'It was gloomy,' Ellie began. 'The kind of day where the mist doesn't lift. I had a feeling that afternoon.' She spoke just above a whisper. 'As I left the Glanduff Road, taking the boreen towards Scully's home, I grew more edgy. I've no doubt the place looks grand in daylight, but it's a bleak enough spot with darkness drawing in.'

Johnny drew his arms close and crossed them.

'I knew the kids were worried about their mother,' Ellie continued. 'The woman isn't well, and I could sense how apprehensive the girls were as they got out of my car. Almost like they didn't want to go in the house. I was about to drive away and leave the place when I heard screaming. It came from inside the cottage.'

Johnny's eyes grew large.

'I jumped out of the car and at the same time I could see Scully's Land Rover hurtling towards me. I made it into the cottage first – the girls were just standing there.'

Ellie shook her head, remembering.

'For God's sake, tell me what happened.'

'Scully came bursting through the doorway behind me and . . . it was awful. Simply awful. I don't know if I said, but his wife can't communicate, she has no speech. She was in her wheelchair. And someone had . . . someone had dressed her up – in a long white dress. The poor woman was sitting there with this long veil draped over her face, and a posy of dried blue flowers was on her lap.'

'Christ . . .' Johnny's jaw fell open.

'Christ, indeed.' Ellie nodded. 'Can you just imagine it? How I felt? How Scully felt? How his poor girls felt?'

'Is the woman . . . was she . . . alive?'

'Yes, she's alive. On sedatives. She isn't able to speak as I said but Scully says she was absolutely terrified. You should have seen the look in her eyes when he tore the veil off her. Like a hunted animal.'

Johnny leaned in. 'What was he thinking about, leaving her alone like that?'

'He didn't.'

Ellie checked around the room. 'That's the thing. There's this Polish woman who looks after Jill in the mornings. And her sister, Lou, comes to look after her in the afternoons. Lou's car was outside but Lou was nowhere around. So I sat with Jill and the girls while Scully got a shotgun and went outside to look. We could hear him calling out for ages. He eventually found his sister-in-law, bound and gagged in an outhouse.'

'Was the woman OK?'

'Physically, yes. She's traumatised too, of course. She'd gone to get logs for the stove and someone overpowered her. Someone in a balaclava. She'd been there quite a while before Scully found her.'

'And Scully's wife was alone with this . . . person all that time?'

'No one knows.' Ellie shuddered. 'The woman can barely communicate with her husband, not to mind answering questions from detectives. Scully reckons that whoever did this to his wife had contacted him earlier at a phone-in at the radio station. That this person – more than likely the Bride Collector – was trying to warn him off, possibly to scare him into abandoning coverage of the story. Or the opposite is also possible of course. That this person wants as much coverage as they can get. Who knows how these nutters think? Scully also thinks – and this is really horrific – that whoever it was had possibly been going into his home visiting his wife on nights that he'd go out fishing.'

'Christ. What a freakshow. What did the gardaí say?'

'They haven't managed to get anything forensically significant from the scene. It's traumatic for Scully and his family because they wanted Jill to stay at home as long as possible. But on the advice of the gardaí and her doctor, she's been moved into a nursing home for her own security. Of course, the situation isn't helped by tension already between Superintendent Begley and Scully.

193

I think those two have history. Begley is advising Scully to hang tough on any further reporting of the case.'

Johnny exhaled and leaned back. 'Jeez, your pal Scully is having a hard time of it, isn't he?'

Ellie nodded.

'You're right about there being tension between him and the gardaí,' Johnny added.

'I am?'

'I did a bit of asking around, and it seems that Scully went off the rails a bit in his late teens. He damaged church property. Some of the lads in here knew his younger brother. He also got into bother as a teenager. Scully lost his shit completely after his brother took his own life.'

Ellie felt a wave of sympathy for the reporter with the tough exterior. 'I didn't realise that he had died by suicide.'

'He'd been missing for days.' Johnny's tone was solemn. 'He'd broken into a church. They eventually found the guy in a confessional box. It wasn't pretty.'

Ellie shook her head and closed her eyes.

'How are Scully's kids?' asked Johnny.

'Upset,' said Ellie. 'I feel sorry for all the children while this is going on. They're all trying to make sense of it, the same as us adults. Liam and Ava – the other kids I bring to school – are adjusting to a new teacher too . . .'

'What is it? What's wrong?'

'I don't know, Johnny. There's something I'm not getting. If I thought hard enough or long enough something might come to me. Whatever or whoever it is that links all the cases together – I'm not seeing it, but I can sense that it's close.'

Johnny studied her. 'Is there something you're not telling me, Ellie?'

'What do you mean?' She was startled.

'I know you . . . I'm picking up that you're hiding something. It's not your job to figure any of this out.' He was sharp. 'That's the job of the gardaí. Your job is to keep yourself safe and out of harm's way. Who'll come and visit me if anything happens to you?'

'I'm not hiding anything, Johnny. And anyway nothing's going to happen to me.'

'I'm pretty sure that's what this guy, Scully, thought. You have to look out for yourself. Seriously. And I think your reporter friend may be right. I think there's a very real possibility there's more than one killer out there.'

Ellie looked at her brother in dismay.

'And for God's sake, get a good night's sleep.'

'I will.' That was easier said than done. Ellie was coming to the conclusion that the noises she was hearing in the attic were coming from inside her head.

Rain sluiced down the outside walls of the prison in grooves of moss and slime. A recent shower was moving off. Dodging a puddle on the return to the small housing estate and her car, Ellie retrieved her phone from her bag. She took it off Silent. It rang within seconds. Scully ringing on a Sunday? This had to be urgent.

'Ellie, you at home?'

'I should be around four thirty or so, why?'

'I have something to show you. I'd rather not say more just now.'

'OK. Call round. You want to bring the girls with you?'

'Thanks but no. Lou is here. See you in a while.'

33

Ellie cleared away last night's wine glass and a *Vogue* magazine that a fare had left behind, making way on the coffee table for Scully's laptop. She'd just finished putting her chilled groceries in the fridge when he'd tapped on her kitchen window.

Making himself at home on her settee, he held up a USB stick. 'A little something I came by.'

He opened up the laptop and stuck the USB stick in, patting a space on the settee beside him.

'The sound isn't great, shite in parts, so you're going to have to listen carefully.'

'What is it?' She sat down.

'It's a recording clip from the inside of 9 Arbutus Road on the night of March seventh.'

Ellie blinked. 'Where did you get it?'

'You have to ask?' Scully gave her a whimsical look. 'After what happened to my wife in her own home, my source has taken pity on us. He's taking a lot of risks for me.' He poked a finger at the screen. 'What I'm about to show you here is a recording from a miniature camera Dylan Coyle had set up in his home.'

Ellie breathed in sharply.

'Dylan emailed the file into Coleman Street in the last day

or so. He said the camera was taped above a picture rail in the hallway. It was set up for taking live feed and also to store foot age on a mobile phone. The idea was that Dylan could check in remotely and make Marina feel safe if she was in the house on her own.'

'How come the camera has only come to light now?' Ellie was puzzled.

'Dylan is saying he only just remembered it was there. It's a tiny gadget by all accounts, roughly double the size of playing dice – gardaí missed it in the search.'

'Maybe the guy is feeling guilty that he didn't check in on the feed when it was live – having too much fun on his stag?'

'Who knows?' Scully shrugged. 'That's Dylan's story anyway. Maybe the guy had even more cameras in the house. Maybe he was spying on Marina.'

'Play it.' Ellie gripped the seat cushion underneath.

'The sound quality isn't great, as I said.' Scully hit Play. 'Neither is the video, as you'll see.'

Ellie squinted at first, trying to make out exactly what she was looking at. 'Good job the guy's a lawyer,' she said. 'He's no spy.'

The camera appeared to be trained on a glass panel above a door. In the foreground, she could make out a crystal chandelier. Through the glass panel something was moving. Bare branched trees, it looked like, casting shadows from a streetlight.

A chiming sound.

'A doorbell?' Ellie turned to Scully.

'Listen,' he said.

Ellie squeezed the seat cushion.

Another chiming sound.

The sound of footsteps. And a scraping sound.

A door chain?

197

Ellie moved closer to the screen. The top of the door was moving. Slowly.

'*Oh.*' *A pause.* '*It's you.*'

Marina Willoughby's voice.

'*Just me. Listen, I get that you're a bit freaked out. Fancy some company?*'

A pause.

'*I'd hate to ruin your night.*'

'*It's your night really. And anyway, you're my friend.*'

'*Come in then. You sound like you've caught a cold—*'

Ellie watched on the laptop screen as the door closed.

'*I've brought a bottle.*'

Ellie tried to place the voice.

'*God, not more booze.*' *The sound of footsteps.* '*In here – the den is nice and warm.*'

'*Don't be such a party pooper, Mar.*'

'*Oh, stop. I've been listening to that all night. "It's your hen-night, Marina. No need to be so sensible, Marina. Little Miss Perfect." Blah, blah, blah . . .*'

The voice trails off.

Someone says something but the sound is faint.

'Can you turn it up?' asked Ellie.

'That's as good as it gets, I'm afraid,' said Scully.

'Play that bit again.'

Ellie closed her eyes and angled her ear.

'*It's a [muffled sound] night.*'

'*Jeez, all right. The look on your face . . .*'

Laughing sounds.

'*Why is everyone more concerned about tonight than I am? I give in. Hang on, I'll get a [muffled sound].*'

Scraping sounds. More activity.

A thudding sound.

Clicking sounds.

The sound of curtains being drawn.

'There you go—' Marina's voice again. She laughs. 'Don't drop the bloody thing. Here, you can't possibly get a grip with those gloves. I'll do it on the [muffled sound]. Give it here.'

'Sorry it's not Pouilly Fumé. I could only get a red.'

'I see you've put the side lamps on . . . and the furniture is pushed back against the wall. What are you up to?'

A pause.

Ellie shuddered. She swiped a look at Scully. His eyes were firmly on the screen.

'I thought that you might appreciate a last dance as a single woman. Why don't you put some music on?'

That voice. Ellie definitely knew it.

'Hold this.' Marina again. 'It'll have to be CD. I'm not allowed anywhere near Dylan's vinyl.'

Shuffling sounds.

Humming.

The sound of footsteps.

'Sade's "Smooth Operator" or Santana's "Evil Ways"?' Marina asks.

'Oh, "Smooth Operator", I think.'

Music.

'You're a good [muffled sound], Mar.'

'We still haven't decided what we're having for the first dance.'

'I thought it was Nora Jones, "Come Away With Me?"'

'[muffled sound] says he feels a dick prancing around to that.'

The sound of dancing and high-pitched laughing.

It was impossible for Ellie to make out a word.

'I'll fast forward.' Scully hit the keypad. 'There's nothing much until about . . . here.'

'Here's another glass – you're a proper night-owl.'

'Night ghoul, more like.' A pause. 'Too-wit, boo-hoo.'

More laughing.

'Whoops. I have to sit down. I feel a bit weird . . . quite weird in fact.'

'You want to go to bed?'

'Mind if we call it a night?'

''Course not. A bride needs her beauty sleep. C'mon, I'll walk you up. I'd love a proper look at that wedding dress.'

The sound of footsteps.

'You're a great friend, you know that? You always look out for me.'

'That's what friends are for. We had a good time tonight after all, didn't we?'

'We certainly did.'

Climbing footsteps.

Silence.

Scully turned to Ellie.

'That's it. Nothing else . . . until this, around fifty minutes later—'

Scully hit fast forward.

Ellie watched the screen.

The front door opened and it closed.

34

Ellie checked her complexion as she waited outside St Columba's. She pinched some colour into her cheeks. She'd lain awake much of the night before, dissecting the recording taken at Arbutus Road. She knew the killer's voice but she didn't know from where. She'd blinked up at the ceiling, hour after wakeful hour, trying to place it. Maybe it belonged to someone she'd met fleetingly, in the taxi perhaps, or some time ago.

The greater challenge was figuring out whether the voice was male or female. It could have belonged to a male with a high-pitched voice. Equally, there had been a breathiness – a more female quality – to the voice. Ellie had initially erred on the side of it being female, the gravelly tones explained by the killer having a cold or a sore throat, perhaps. Now, she didn't know. Scully had reserved his opinion, saying he was keeping an open mind.

Ellie tooted the horn. Liam was messing with the boys. Ava did her best to extricate him by pulling on his hood. It took a further toot or two to get Liam's attention.

'Sorry, Ellie, he wouldn't come—'

A breathless Ava clambered in, followed by her brother.

'Good day?' Ellie turned to face a tousled Liam.

'No homework, so yeah.'

'Seat belts on.' Ellie pulled out into the line of traffic.

'Liam got five gold stars from Miss Moran for his essay on aliens,' Ava piped up. 'It was pretty good, but there were lots of spelling mistakes.'

'The spelling will come,' said Ellie. 'I imagine the stars were for creative effort.'

'I suppose.' Ava mulled this over.

'Miss Moran isn't actually that bad,' said Liam. 'She gave us extra time at big lunch today.'

Miss Moran was proving herself an able dispenser of gold stars, which was doing much to improve Liam's demeanour. On more than one occasion lately, Ellie had to leave the car to prise the child from a huddle of boys exchanging game cards.

'She's still not as good as Imelda,' Ava objected. 'Miss Moran doesn't grow things in the garden, or put the chairs and tables against the wall so we can dance.'

'That's girl stuff.' Liam dismissed her. 'All that dancing was because she was getting married. Imelda just wanted to practise so she could show off at her wedding.'

Ellie's ears pricked up.

'Imelda said the first dance was important.' Ava leapt to the defence of her former teacher. 'The other boys liked dancing with her. I remember you danced with her too, Liam. Imelda said you were nearly as good as Ambrose.'

Ellie glanced in the rear-view mirror. 'This Ambrose is a boy in your class?'

'Ambrose was Imelda's dance teacher.'

'What's his surname, Ava?'

'I don't know.'

'And does this Ambrose work up at Mountain View community centre?'

'I think so. Why? What's wrong, Ellie?'

'Nothing's wrong, Ava.'

'But there is. I see it from your face.'

That child was far too observant.

'You're imagining it. Now, who'd like to stop for doughnuts?' She needed to send a text.

'Me!!!' shouted Liam.

Liam at least was easy to manage.

Scully responded in minutes. He agreed to meet her at Raftery's Rest, a viewpoint overlooking Kylebeggan, convenient to his wife's nursing home and only a kilometre or so from the Old Manse, Liam and Ava's home.

By the time Ellie had dropped the kids off and made her way to the viewpoint, Scully was hovering around outside Tom Horan's coffee van. Ellie tucked her hair tightly underneath an unflattering woollen hat and rubbed her gloved hands together as she marched through the biting cold towards him.

'Hi there. How are things with Jill today?'

Every time she thought of Scully's wife, she pictured Jill incapacitated, mute, unable to recount her ordeal to anyone. No one would ever know all that had happened to the woman that day in the cottage.

'Not good, Ellie. She's not in good shape at all.'

'I'm really sorry to hear that. I shouldn't have bothered you.'

'No, I'm glad you did.' He made a face somewhere between a smile and a wince. 'I want to catch this psycho.'

With his wife's condition worsening by the day, Scully had immersed himself in every detail of the ongoing murder investigation. If the intruder had thought the stunt in Scully's home was going to deter him, the intruder was mistaken. And if the intention had been to get even more attention from Scully, the reporter was only too happy to oblige. He was more determined than ever to follow up every lead.

'You said you had something for me?'

'Let me buy some drinks first.' Ellie fished her purse from her shoulder bag. 'You bought last time.'

They moved to join the queue. Tomás Horan ran a steady trade out of a refurbished caravan. Denis, Tomás's uncle, was hunkered down on a three-legged stool outside the caravan sporting a flat cap, with another at his feet collecting money. He was murdering a traditional Irish tune on a battered accordion.

'Christ above,' muttered Scully. 'I can't abide diddle-dee-eye shite. But the tourists lap it up.'

A coachload of Americans drifted about the car park. A rare sight these past few weeks, with reports of many tour operators cancelling their bookings. The tourists were taking photos and lobbing coins in Denis's hat.

Paying for the coffees, Ellie handed Scully a Styrofoam cup. They settled themselves on a low stone wall overlooking the town and valley below. Ellie breathed in deeply.

'So, you know I do a school run for a couple of kids up and down to St Columba's?'

'I do.'

'It's just something the kids were talking about in the car. It may be something, or it may be nothing.'

'Let's hear it.'

'OK then. Ava was saying how she missed the fun Imelda Gannon used to have with them in class. How she used to rearrange classroom furniture to dance around.'

'That's remarkable in some way?'

'Not particularly. That's not what I'm getting at.' Ellie hesitated,

204

all of a sudden unsure. Was she wasting Scully's valuable time? Perhaps she was making something out of nothing.

'It's just that Liam, Ava's brother, well . . . he was saying that Imelda was only interested in the dancing lark because she was practising for her wedding. It sounded like she was practising routines that she was being taught by her dance teacher. I guess to give a good account of herself when she hit the floor for the first dance.'

'The dreaded first dance.' Scully winced.

'I remembered something then,' Ellie continued. 'From the night I dropped Marina Willoughby home outside Arbutus Road.' She took a sip of scalding coffee. 'Her friends were trying to persuade her to go with them to Godiva's. They were egging her on, saying how she could show off all her "Strictly" moves. I guessed they were talking about *Strictly Come Dancing*.' She swiped a glance at Scully. 'Remember when you were talking to Dylan Coyle? According to him, Marina was taking lessons. Dylan had no interest. You heard it too on the recording . . .'

Scully's breath formed clouds as he breathed out. 'How taking dance lessons without your partner would be of any use, I don't know . . .'

Ellie turned to Scully. 'Marina Willoughby and Imelda Gannon could have been taking dancing lessons from the same guy. There can't be too many male dancing teachers here in Kylebeggan. It's hardly Broadway.'

'You're suggesting a dance teacher may have had something to do with the murders?'

'I think it's worth checking out.'

'All right . . . do you have a name for me?'

'Ambrose Casey.'

Scully set his coffee on the wall. 'Are you sure?'

'You know the guy?'

205

'I went to school with an Ambrose Casey. To be honest, if it's the same guy, I'm surprised he's still around the place. He didn't have a very nice time in Kylebeggan. I haven't laid eyes on him in years.'

'I think you have.'

'Nope.' Scully shook his head. 'I really don't think so.'

'If it's the same guy, you definitely have. Up at Mountain View community centre. That's where he teaches. He doubles as a care-taker and an odd-job man. He was mooching around the place when we were there. By the Coffee Station, up and down the stairs, and in the common area there in front of the pool. I defi-nitely saw him. He was wearing overalls and a baseball cap.'

'That's why you didn't want us to meet at the community centre today?'

'Exactly.'

Scully chewed this over. 'The Ambrose I knew was harmless. And even if it is the same guy, and even if he has some dance connection with Marina Willoughby and Imelda Gannon, there's no connection between him and Isolde Hanly. Certainly not in anything I've come across so far.'

'You're wrong about that too.' Ellie shook her head.

Scully blinked.

'I used to drive Isolde to Mountain View community centre – when we weren't travelling, that is. Isolde was keen on dance, ballroom dancing in particular. When she heard they were start-ing an afternoon tea dance, she was delighted. I must have driven Isolde there every week for three years at least.'

Scully gave a low whistle. 'OK, I'm beginning to see there might be something in this.'

'Of course, I may be adding things up wrongly here,' Ellie cau-tioned. 'Ambrose got on famously with the seniors at his tea dances.

Always polite and chatty. But I understand why people might call him harmless – he used to get a bit shy around me at times. I don't like to think he is involved in any of this, no more than you do. All I'm doing is looking at the evidence.'

'Detective at work,' said Scully, tracing his scar. 'Speaking of which, have you gone to Coleman Street with any of this?'

Ellie gave him a withering look.

'I don't exactly have much time for the gardaí.' She hesitated. 'My brother and I had some dealings with them when we were younger. Oh, it was nothing major,' she stressed, noting his surprise. 'However, he is doing a stretch for something he shouldn't be. I'm not going to go into all of that just now. Suffice to say, I really don't want detectives at my door, and I'd be grateful, Scully, if you didn't mention me in any of this.'

'If that's what you want. With your permission, I'll relay all of this to my contact in the first instance,' he said. 'Like you, I hope you're wrong about this guy.'

'Like I was wrong about Mervyn,' Ellie muttered under her breath.

Scully gave her a sideways glance. 'You don't still think your neighbour could have something to do with the murders?'

'All I know is the guy is very strange.'

'There's a lot of strange people out there, Ellie. It doesn't mean they're murderers.' Scully stood and tossed his empty cup into a nearby bin. 'Right then. I'll find out what I can.'

As Ellie waved him off, her eyes streamed in the cold. Her ears were also sore. Warming up in the Škoda, she answered a call on her phone. It was one of the girls from Klassy Kuts.

Ellie listened as the girl spoke. 'Yes. I've noticed that too,' she said, stuffing a stray lock of hair back into her hat. 'You're right. She does appear quite agitated lately and she *is* getting forgetful.

No, no, not at all, Róisin. I'll be there soon.' She started the engine and demisted the windscreen. She shivered. It may have been late March but spring felt a long way off.

35

There was nowhere to park outside Klassy Kuts, so Ellie parked down the street and made her way back to the salon. Klassy Kuts was in a Georgian building that hadn't seen a makeover since the seventies. Bells jingled as she opened the door.

A square-set woman in a check nylon housecoat looked up from her client. The woman spun around and directed her attention to the receptionist, whose head was buried in a *Bella* magazine.

'Jacinta, will you please get Doreen's purse for Ellie? If you bend down, you'll see it there, just under the till.'

The hairdresser turned to Ellie. 'Thanks so much for coming in.' She dropped her voice. 'As I said to you on the phone, I think Doreen may be beginning to forget a few things. Sure, we're all heading in the same direction, I guess.'

Ellie said nothing to confirm or deny her suspicions.

'You'll get that purse over to Autumn Grove straightaway, now won't you, Ellie? I don't want to be a feature on *Crimewatch*.'

'Straightaway, Róisin,' Ellie assured her, taking the metal-clasped purse from Jacinta.

When the salon had rung to report the purse had been left behind, Ellie had felt obliged to collect it. She hoped to find Doreen at home, alone, as she headed off in the Škoda to return it.

She pulled up outside Doreen's house and rang the doorbell. She glanced about the neat housing development as she waited. And rang again. There was a clink and the door opened a fraction, on a chain. Doreen squinted through the gap. 'Oh, it's yourself.' She appeared relieved. 'There's been all sorts calling lately.'

'Your purse, Doreen.' Ellie held it up. 'The salon rang me. They said you'd left it behind.'

Doreen took the chain off the hook and opened the door. 'Well, aren't you the best girleen? I'm so sorry to drag you all the way back here, Ellie. I hadn't even missed the blooming thing. You're a topper to drop it back. I could have sent my son for it.'

'He's here?' Ellie took a step back.

'Not at the moment.'

Doreen brightened, taking Ellie's reaction as an expression of interest. 'He's at work this afternoon.' She leaned in. 'Said he'd seen your good self, recently. Said he wanted to go over to you to say how sorry he was about Isolde. He missed you at the funeral. You were busy with a man.'

Ellie played innocent. 'I don't remember seeing him.'

Of course, she'd spotted him. She'd been with Scully when she'd seen him, staring across at her. He'd tried to get her attention, but she hadn't acknowledged him. She knew he'd want to commiserate with her about Isolde. But it wasn't convenient. At that point, she hadn't been ready to share with Scully that she had even known Isolde.

Doreen nodded, satisfied. 'I said the man was probably a client.' Her eyes twinkled. 'You do know my Ambrose has a soft spot for you, don't you?'

'You should be on *Blind Date*, Doreen.'

Doreen winked. 'I'll tell him you were asking for him.'

'Now don't you go bothering him.'

210

'Not at all, my dear. Since you took over the job of bringing me to the salon, he has more time to go about his business. He's your number-one fan, Ellie.'

Driving back to Botany Row, Ellie recalled how Ambrose would ask her help in demonstrating new sequences. He'd put out a hand. 'Slow, slow, quick, quick, slow,' he'd direct her. 'Slow, slow, quick, quick, slow,' drawing Ellie close towards him. She'd never once felt the merest frisson of attraction.

Ambrose was a big hit with seniors, however. Making them laugh, coming out with quips that were risqué but never offensive. When Bessie's dancing days came to an end, Wednesday after-noons were never quite the same again. Ellie's foster mother had a fall not long after Joe had died, and she went into a decline. Ellie remembered going to visit Bessie in a nursing home. The woman on the desk told Ellie that someone was already visiting, that this person regularly dropped by.

Ellie had hurried down the corridor to find Ambrose on a high-backed chair, next to Bessie's bed, reading Maeve Binchy's *Light a Penny Candle* aloud to her. Ellie had been happy that Ambrose was visiting. He was the kind of guy people stopped on the street to ask for directions, the kind of guy who offered a woman an opinion on a new outfit or a new winter coat. Ambrose advised on all sorts of things.

He'd also come to Myrtle Crescent. Over the years, Isolde had amassed an unmanageable collection of clothing and she wanted to clear out her wardrobe. The visit had left Ellie feeling slighted, smarting that Isolde had asked Ambrose, not her, to assist in the task of sorting and discarding unwanted clothes.

He'd spent a winter's afternoon in Isolde's bedroom going through her things as a manic wind rattled the window. Ellie had fumed in the drawing room below. After Ambrose had left with three large refuse bags full of designer clothing, Isolde explained to Ellie what the exercise had really been about.

'Ellie, have you never noticed how shabbily his poor mother is turned out? Those shiny nylon skirts she wears must be years old. I doubt they were ever fashionable.'

A mortal sin in Isolde's eyes.

'Ambrose and Doreen are proud,' Isolde had said. 'This way, they can feel they've done me a turn. I told Ambrose that if any items take his mother's fancy, she'd be doing me a favour by hanging on to them. She deserves a little, after all she's been through.'

'What has she been through?'

Isolde was a martyr for a sob story.

'You know, with her husband and all that.'

'I don't know.'

'He left the woman in dire financial straits.'

Nothing ever suggested Ambrose was anything other than decent. Unusual perhaps in that in his late thirties he lived with his mother, but Ambrose was the only family Doreen had. Ellie called to mind a conversation they'd once had on the dance floor.

'Isn't it weird, Ellie, how you and I enjoy the company of older people?' He'd twirled her around, pressing a hand into the small of her back. 'We're more alike than you know, you and I,' he'd said. 'A lot more than you realise.'

At home in Botany Row, Ellie found it impossible to relax. Maybe it was time to tackle the half-painted sitting room. She covered the floor with sheets of last week's newspaper. She had plenty as the delivery guy had made a mistake, dropping in one, then another a few hours later.

Prising open the tin of paint, she was dismayed to find a skin had formed on the top. She fished it out using a plastic take-away knife. She was no more than ten brush strokes in when she heard

212

a knocking. She tensed. Brush in hand, she went to the front door. She opened it a crack.

'Oh, it's you,' she said.

'It is indeed. May I come in?'

'Well, as you can see, I'm a little busy—'

'It'll only take a minute . . .'

She hesitated. 'Well . . . all right.'

Though it went against her every instinct, she nudged the door with her elbow and pushed it open.

36

Scully couldn't sleep. He hadn't slept the night before either. In fact, he couldn't remember the last time he had slept through the night. Lying alone, missing his wife, he stared at the ceiling, contemplating the unlikely possibility of Ambrose Casey being a predator, and the equally unlikely possibility the guy had trespassed into his home, terrorising Jill and the rest of his family. He lay there, trawling his memory for anything that stood out from their schooldays.

Staring at the flaking patches, something came to him, something unfurled from a long-forgotten recess. There had been talk. Whispers about Ambrose's whereabouts the day his father had died. But for the life of him, Scully couldn't remember the details. He sat up in the bed. He read his phone. He went downstairs to make a cup of tea. He went back upstairs and slept for an hour or two at most.

The following morning, driving the girls to school, the question of where exactly Ambrose had been that day was preying on his mind. He chewed his lip. He tried to think of who might know, who might remember that time from school, who might be willing to talk? Out of nowhere, it came to him.

He hadn't given this person a moment's thought in years. He

wondered if the guy was even working in the same place. Given the guy's limitations, he'd have been well-advised to stay where he was, putting his skills to use in comfortable surroundings.

Scully wasn't due at the paper until late morning. After dropping Maude and Scarlett, he checked with the nursing home for an update on his wife. There'd been no significant change.

It was a grey morning, poor in light, with low cloud suspended over the mountains as he drove out of town in the direction of Dromgeela Woods. Manes of water from melting snow scored paths down gullies in the Black Pins. Everything felt cold. Everything felt damp. Scully scrolled through his contacts, braced himself and dialled the offices of Coyle & Coyle. Clenching his jaw, he waited for the receptionist to put him through to Dylan.

'Scully, my friend, I believe you're looking for me.'

His tone was pleasant.

'Just a small thing, Dylan, and sorry to bother you again.' Scully was casual. 'You didn't say who Marina was taking dance lessons with?'

'Did I not?' Dylan sounded amused. 'It was Dainty Casey from Kylebeggan Comp. Remember him?'

Now that was a blast from the past.

'You were the one to give Ambrose that nickname, weren't you?' said Scully.

Dylan paused. 'Something I'm not proud of, I admit.' He sounded sheepish. 'Yes, I was the one who started that. I wasn't particularly enlightened at the time. But the guy was a bit light on his feet, wasn't he? Him, and that other lad he used to hang around with.'

'Darren Keating.'

'That's the lad. Like I said when you called in, Marina was a soft touch for the soft lads. I did agree to one dance lesson, to keep her happy. But I never got around to it.'

Dylan sounded sorry for himself.

'Ambrose was a bit odd,' Scully agreed. 'Didn't his old man die in an accident while we were in school?'

'I remember something like that.' Dylan cleared his throat. 'But I can't remember exactly. Why?'

'Ah, no particular reason. Listen, you take care of yourself. I'd better let you get back to your work. Cheers now.' Scully hung up before Dylan could ask any more questions.

A few kilometres beyond the Lackabawn turn-off, Scully caught sight of a well-kept Victorian lodge. Indicating, he drove in through pineapple-topped stone pillars, into the grounds of the nine-hundred-acre estate of Dunseally Castle. The grounds were open to the public, offering a number of looped walks. The main loop, Lady Louisa's Walk, offered a panoramic view of Lough Avulla and all its islands.

The approach to the castle was lined with trees and Scully's Land Rover rumbled throatily into a nearby car park bound by neat beech hedging. Outside, a south-westerly wind carried the scent of pine and a hint of new growth from the earth. Parking up, he spotted someone working the lawns in front of the castle. Someone on a ride-on mower with ear defenders.

Gravel crunched underfoot as Scully made a path towards the formal beds. It took some time before the man – sporting a base-ball cap and protective eye-gear as well as ear defenders – even noticed him. Stopping the motor, the guy jumped from the mower and headed towards him.

'Darren?' Scully asked as the guy drew up. With all the gear it was difficult to tell.

The guy pulled off his ear defenders. 'You're looking for Darren Keating?'

'That's right.'

The guy turned and pointed. 'You'll find him cutting rhododendron, up above. Either there, or in the woodshed chopping logs.'

'The woodshed?'

'Yeah. Up above, behind the east turret.'

'Cheers.'

Scully marched off in the general direction of the east turret 'up above'. As he rounded a crenellated turret, a jaunting car came towards him. Hurtling by, the pony tossed its head and snorted. Four passengers sat in the cab behind, rugs on their laps. The pony man tipped his cap. As the cart retreated, a nearby industrial sound interrupted trills of birdsong. There was a dull thudding, followed by a splintering sound. He was close. There was the woodshed, ahead in a clearing.

Moments later, he was standing in an open doorway, his nostrils filling with the scent of freshly cut wood. His eyes adjusted to the gloom. The man lunging with an axe at upturned logs was low-sized, just as Scully remembered. Darren's wiry hair was held back from his ruddy face with a ponytail. He almost looked bohemian. At school he'd looked dishevelled.

Mindful Darren was wielding an axe, Scully waited for him to stop. Darren squinted, set down the axe, then came towards him.

'Cormac? Cormac Scully?'

Scully clapped him on the shoulder. 'Long time no see, Darren. You're looking good.'

'Long time no see indeed. I've seen you on the box. I always knew you'd be famous.'

'Ah, I dunno about that.'

The odd appearance on the telly and people thought you had it made.

'You're not doing so bad yourself, Darren. Outdoors, here in this lovely place. Beats working in an office looking at a screen all day, I can tell you.'

Darren's ruddy cheeks inflated.

'An office is n-not for me. I'd go off my g-game cooped up. Mad-Bob Looby had that much right.'

Scully laughed. 'Mad-Bob had me pegged for a job in the county council, remember? A job in the council was the only way to go, in Looby's eyes.'

Darren gave a gap-toothed smile. Scully could see the guy was wondering what he was doing pitching up out of the blue like this. Talk of Mad-Bob Looby, their career-guidance teacher in school, led Scully nicely to his back story.

'Listen, Darren, I won't delay. I can see you're busy. Just to say there's talk of a class reunion and I wondered if you'd be interested? I tried to find you on Facebook but had no luck.'

Darren blinked. The very idea that he'd be on Facebook was laughable. He'd always been a shy and private person. And the notion that Scully'd be involved in organising a reunion was equally ridiculous. Luckily for Scully, Darren wasn't the sharpest tool in the shed.

'A-a reunion?'

His face was a picture of horror. After what his classmates had put him through, Scully couldn't blame the guy. He wouldn't want to see them again either.

'Yeah, I know . . . can't figure how I got roped into all of this. Not everyone's cup of tea, but I thought I should let you know.' Scully shrugged. 'There were some right assholes in school and that's the truth. Some good guys too, though. From what I remember you were mates with Ambrose Casey. Am I right?'

'Ambrose was a decent skin—'

Darren cast his eyes about as if he'd mislaid something. 'Where are they?' He scratched his head. A pepper cloud of sawdust sprinkled on to his shoulders.

Scully raised an eyebrow.

'My flask. My sandwiches,' said Darren. 'The hotel kitchen gives me a packed lunch. A perk of the job.' He pointed to the badge pinned to his chest with the Dunseally Estate insignia. *Darren Keating, Assistant Head Gardener.* Darren scratched his head again. 'I must have left them by the bathing huts.'

'Why don't I walk down there with you? I haven't been there in years. It's a magic spot.'

The two of them took the rough path through the trees towards the shores of the lough. Darren launched into a lesson about the tree species around about. Pointing out the sitka spruce, the Norway spruce, Scots pine, ash, beech, yew, birch and oak. Scully wondered how he was going to get the guy back on topic. As they approached the huts, Darren broke off, falling silent. He cast his gaze over the far side of the water.

'Ambrose wasn't ever the same. Not after what happened to his da.'

'Is that so?' Scully tried not to sound too interested.

'He could be a bit strange, you know . . .' Darren paused. 'Like he wasn't all there sometimes. Know what I mean?'

Scully kept a straight face. Now here was a case of the pot calling the kettle black.

'I met Ambrose that afternoon—' Darren darted Scully a look. 'Oh yeah?'

The gardener fidgeted with his hands. 'I was hiding out in the woods . . . there had been talk about a pair of ospreys in the area.' He twitched. He looked around him, nervous. 'After the explosion, all the birds rose up and scattered into the sky. If there had been osprey there, well, they never came back after that.'

Scully looked out over the water, imagining the scene. He said nothing.

'That's when I came across Ambrose.' Darren stopped his fidgeting. 'I asked him if he'd been looking for the osprey too, like me. He liked to birdwatch. But he didn't say.' He shrugged. 'I thought maybe he'd had one of those turns he sometimes had. He was wandering around on the path on his own. I thought he was shook up by the noise of the explosion. Neither of us knew at that point that it was his da's boat that had blown up. *The King of the Lake*. It was only when I walked him back to his ma's house and we saw the garda car outside that we knew something had happened. Something bad—'

'What did the gardaí say?' Scully's voice was soft.

'They asked Ambrose where he'd been.' Darren's brow furrowed. 'And his ma looked at me and said that Ambrose was with me all afternoon, wasn't that right? And I said yes, because somehow it seemed important to her. And I saw that she was very upset at whatever the gardaí were after telling her, and me – well, I just wanted to get out of their house and leave them all to it.'

Darren pulled at his hair, troubled by the memory.

They walked on in silence. Darren's mood lifted as soon as he spotted his lunch on a bench by the bathing huts. Unwrapping the parchment pack, he offered Scully an egg and watercress sandwich.

'I'd best get back to the office.' Scully turned it down. 'Not everyone can live the dream, you know.'

'I could put in a word for you with the hotel management.'

Scully patted the guy on the back. 'I'll get back to you on that.' He could think of worse jobs.

Darren stole a look at Scully from underneath his eyebrows. 'You didn't come the whole way out here just to ask me about the school reunion, did you?'

Scully considered the question.

'No,' he replied. 'I'd a bit of other business in the hotel too.'

'Aaah, I was thinking as much.' Satisfied, Darren bit into his sandwich.

'You take care now, Darren. Great to see you.'

Darren mumbled something and tipped his cap.

Returning to the car park, Scully mulled over what he had learned. While Ambrose Casey was the most unlikely candidate for a serial killer, Scully was finding him more and more interesting. Had the investigating team spoken to him? There was one way to find out. He pulled out his mobile.

'Busy at the moment here, pal,' came Tall Dark's gruff response.

'Call me when you get a chance? In the meantime, can you look into anything you may have on an Ambrose Casey?'

'I'll see what I can do.'

The line went dead.

37

Sitting into the Land Rover, Scully eyed an unappetising pear on the seat beside him. He was hungry and regretted not taking Darren up on the offer of the five-star hotel sandwich. Halfway through the pear, he dialled Ellie. No answer.

A squirrel darted up the trunk of a nearby tree. His eyes followed the animal. It stopped halfway up as if it were listening, and a moment later it disappeared into the canopy of leaves. Scully threw the pear core out the window, far into the undergrowth, and started up the engine. His mobile rang. Ellie returning his call? He glanced at the screen. The name on the phone confirmed it not to be the case.

'Hello?' he answered.

'Ambrose Casey, did you say?'

Tall Dark hadn't wasted any time.

'That's right. I wondered if the investigation team had spoken to him?'

'I saw that name all right, up on the whiteboard in the Incident Room. Tim Mullins and Thomas Mulcahy, two senior investigators from the Special Crimes Unit, have already paid your lad, Ambrose, a couple of visits.'

'Go on—'

'I wouldn't get overly excited, Scully. It didn't amount to much. It seems this lad is some kind of caretaker who also teaches dance. The detectives asked him if he could shed any light on the two young women who were murdered, considering he was teaching them how to hit the dance floor on their wedding days. Mullins asked the lad the same questions he put to the guy who runs the tanning salon. He asked if either of the young women had spoken of any worries or concerns.'

'Did they turn up anything?'

'I'm guessing not. There are no question marks against Ambrose Casey's name on the whiteboard. All the people Mullins has lined up for further interviewing have question marks against their names. Jen Healy, the bridesmaid, is up there. She still doesn't have an alibi for the night of Marina Willoughby's murder. And, of course, Begley has five big question marks of his own against Joseph Liston.'

'Can't say I'm surprised,' said Scully. 'I wouldn't be in a rush to rule Ambrose out just yet. There are a couple of things that suggest to me he could be a person of interest.'

'What exactly?' Tall Dark was brusque.

'I've just come from an old schoolmate of his who has more or less admitted to faking an alibi for him when his father was killed in an explosion on his boat years ago. *The King of the Lake*, remember that?'

'Yeah, it was news at the time.'

Tall Dark was breathing heavily, thinking. 'I could say that we'd had an anonymous tip-off to look into Ambrose Casey more closely. He lives with his mother, you said?'

Scully paused. 'Always a bad sign,' he said, knowing full-well Tall Dark lived at home with his ma.

'Fuck off, Scully. Doesn't mean that every bloke that lives with his mother is a serial killer.'

Scully chuckled. 'I'll be in touch.' He hung up. He rang Ellie's number once again, to put her mind at rest and to share the update. But once again, there was no answer. More than likely she was with a fare.

He checked to see if he'd missed any texts from her. The last text she'd sent him was a query about the other woman in her taxi the night Marina Willoughby had been murdered. Rose Moriarty. He'd been meaning to follow up on her.

> Hi S, been thinking. I've a feeling Rose
> Moriarty knows more about Jen Healy than
> she is letting on. I recall her saying she
> worked in the tourist office. Couldn't swear
> to it though. E

He checked the time. The tourist office wouldn't take him too far out of his way. Maybe this woman, Rose, did know something. Ellie had been chasing him for a while on this one. It was worth a quick chat, if she was willing to speak.

He ditched the Land Rover at the small car park behind *The Kylebeggan Echo* offices before a windswept walk took him to the purpose-built glass dome that was the local tourist office, two blocks away. A van with a satellite dish missed spraying water over his newly dry-cleaned coat as it swept by. Scully lowered his head. He didn't want anyone following on his tail.

Inside the dome were display stands showcasing Kylebeggan and the surrounding area. Shots of deer on the foothills of the Black Pins, shots of birds swooping over the still water of Lough Avulla. Facing him was a bank of desks in a semicircle, attended by staff in purple waistcoats. A quick enquiry pointed Scully in the direction of a café area selling snacks. He was informed that Rose Moriarty was on her break.

'Rose? Rose Moriarty – I wonder if I could have a word?'

He was glad he'd shaved and was looking officious. He held a pen and notepad in his hands. He sat down without waiting for her reply. 'It's about your last night out with Marina Willoughby.'

The colour drained from Rose's cheeks. She set aside her phone and her sandwich. 'I've said everything already . . .' She looked uncertain.

'Of course,' said Scully reassuringly. 'How are you holding up?'

'All right, I guess.'

'We understand it hasn't been a very nice time for you and Jen Healy,' he said soothingly. 'But questions have to be asked, unfortunately.'

Rose's chest heaved under her waistcoat. 'It's horrible.' She looked off into the distance. 'People in the street with their sneaky sideways looks. Reporters pitching up to Jen's shop with bogus requests, taking sneaky photographs . . . broadcasting vans slowing down outside her shop.' She pulled at her cuff. I'm getting away lightly by comparison.'

Scully looked at his notepad as if he were checking something. 'The difference is you have an alibi for the night Marina died. Jen does not.'

Rose picked small bits off her napkin and rolled them into a ball, almost as if she hadn't heard him. She looked miserable. 'Everyone's asking if she's sure she banged the front door shut that night. One of you people said it was a shame she'd never get to wear her bridesmaid dresses. What kind of way is that to talk to anyone?'

The woman clearly felt her friend was being wronged. Scully shrugged as if agreeing with her.

Rose looked into the distance again. 'Jesus, Jen didn't even like her bridesmaid dresses.'

'That so?'

'I remember Marina joking, saying her wedding dress looked better on Jen.' Rose's eyes brimmed with tears. 'Poor Marina.'

Scully needed to keep her focused. 'Pity Jen doesn't have an alibi for later that night.'

'I don't see why she needs one.' Rose scrunched up her face as she lined up the paper balls. 'Jen wouldn't hurt anyone. Kill anyone. That's just ridiculous.'

'An alibi is an alibi.'

'She has a bloody alibi!!' Rose exploded.

Scully sat back.

A look of horror spread across Rose's face. 'Oh Christ, I didn't mean . . . Look, forget I said anything. You're going to get me into trouble.'

'Was Jen seeing someone she shouldn't have been?' Scully asked softly.

'I can't say.' She squashed the remainder of her napkin into a single ball. 'I shouldn't have said anything at all. You'll have to ask Jen.'

Scully flipped his notepad shut and moved to stand.

Rose got up as well, touching the table to balance herself. 'What's your name, detective?'

'I never said I was a detective.'

Her hands fluttered to her throat. She looked even more horrified.

'But I thought . . .'

Scully didn't give a shit what Rose thought. He turned on his heel and made for the door. He'd been disingenuous, of course he had. The principles he'd operated by had changed the day someone had trespassed into his home and threatened his wife and family. Any moral high ground was now the preserve of others.

38

Holding the paintbrush like a weapon, she could feel droplets of paint sliding down her wrist. She watched as her visitor's eyes darted and swivelled over her small sitting room, taking it all in. It was his first time inside Ellie's home and he did little to conceal his curiosity. She set the paintbrush aside and folded her arms, challenging him.

'Yes, well, ahem' – he cleared his throat – 'I can see I'm interrupting. The reason I'm here is to invite you to my place. I was thinking it was time I did some entertaining of my own, and that it would be most pleasant to have your company. I was thinking next Saturday night?'

Ellie opened her mouth, searching for an excuse. Seeing she was about to decline his invitation, he cut in quickly.

'We only ever seem to talk in passing, and I thought it might be nice to catch up properly. Have a chat, you know – a bit of wine, a little music, maybe even some dancing.' He wiggled his hips.

Ellie gave a polite smile. 'That's very kind of you but I work Saturday nights.'

'Of course . . .' He smacked his forehead in sudden irritation.

Ellie stepped away.

Just as quickly his expression softened. 'Sorry, I didn't think.

You know there's no reason we couldn't do it on a Friday night instead, if that suits?'

'Friday nights are tricky too. The weekend's my busiest time of the week.'

A darkness crossed his face. 'There's such a thing as working too much, you know. All work and no play makes Jack a dull boy, as my old dear says.' He attempted a smile. 'Or Jill in your case.' He leaned towards her. 'Have a think about it.' His breath smelled stale. 'You and I could have some fun.'

Ellie felt trickles of paint hardening against her skin. 'I'd better crack on.' She was business-like. 'These walls won't paint themselves.'

He perked up. 'I could help you. I'm handy enough with a brush—'

'I'll manage. Thank you.'

'You're sure?' He blinked.

'I am.'

She edged past him to open the door with her free hand.

'Right then.' He turned. 'You know where I am if you change your mind.' He stepped into the street.

'I do.' She closed the door and pressed her back firmly against it.

She let out her breath. Had she known it was him, she'd never have answered the door. She needed to get one of those peepholes fitted. She inched up on tiptoes and stole a glance through the fanlight in the door.

Jesus.

Two bulging eyes stared right back at her. He was still there. There was a knock.

'Yes?' she said sharply, opening the door a crack.

'I forgot to ask.' He smiled apologetically. 'I wondered if you could keep an eye out for whoever is messing with my nameplate? I've asked Pauline to do the same. If I don't find the culprit, I'll have to install a camera.'

'If I spot anything, I'll be sure to let you know,' she said.

She shut the door. The thought of Mervyn spying on her with a camera made her shiver. In the past, as Isolde's younger companion, she'd become adept at deflecting unwanted attention. It was one story on a cruise ship where she could walk away, but no easy matter with someone living next door.

Swabbing paint from her arms, she went back to the job of decorating, her thoughts returning to Isolde. She pressed the brush hard into the uneven wall, thinking back to the time she'd bought Isolde a mobile phone as a gift. It had never made its way out of the box. Isolde had regarded mobile phones as invasive, especially when visitors interrupted engaging conversations to answer a call.

The irony was that Isolde heartily enjoyed a phone conversation. She could spend whole afternoons on the landline in the conservatory, drinking tea from her silver teapot, or could while an evening away with gin and cucumber cocktails, and reminisce about her husband.

In Ellie's last few months at Myrtle Crescent, Isolde had grown increasingly frail. The routines that had marked her life had started to fall by the wayside. Visits to the library, tea dances and visits to the hairdresser had all but stopped. And after she'd been fired, Ellie worried even more about Isolde's care.

Considering her diminishing contact with the outside world, Ellie wondered if Isolde might have been better off in a nursing home after all. Although she'd always balked at the idea. There wasn't a lot Ellie could have done about any of it. Freddy was the one with power of attorney.

Ellie knew not to mention nursing homes in Isolde's company. Whenever anyone moved to Lisnashee, Isolde would speak about them as if they had died.

'Gertie Hackett was a terror for dropping her cards, God be good to her,' Isolde once remarked to Ellie.

Gertie Hackett had been Isolde's bridge partner.

'Gertie's not dead, you know,' Ellie had scolded.

'True,' said Isolde, 'but she might as well be.'

Nursing homes were for old people. Isolde was never going to be that kind of old. She would drop down dead and be done with things. She was not going to wither away with different bits falling off her every other day.

'Not like your poor dear foster mother,' she said to Ellie, 'strapped to a bed, peg-fed, with her mind completely gone. There's no way anyone is sending me to Lisnashee. All those chairs pushed up against the wall, with everyone dribbling and staring at one another, half mad. That is *not* happening to me.' Isolde had no idea then that what was going to befall her would be even worse. At least Bessie had the blessing of a medicalised departure from the world.

The wind had picked up by the time Ellie had finished painting and she headed upstairs for bed. As she placed her phone on the beside locker she noticed that the battery was dead. It explained her lack of 'interruptions' from that 'vexatious gadget' as Isolde might have said.

In bed and with the phone charging, Ellie swiped and scrolled, reading through the messages. She'd missed a number of calls from Scully but it was too late to call him back. She'd leave it until the morning. She read a few more pages of *Rebecca*. Though her eyes glided over the words and she turned the pages, she absorbed nothing. She put the book aside.

Despite listening to a meditation podcast, her mind kept pulling her down into dark worry holes. She wondered what Isolde's last moments had been like for her. Knowing that sleep was nowhere near, she set her feet on the chilly floorboards and opened the door to the landing. A warm cup of something might be in order. She stopped. There were banging noises coming from the back of the house. At this hour? Removing a pile of freshly laundered towels from the stool, she stood up and peered through the rooflight into the back.

Mervyn's yard was lit up like a spaceship. Her neighbour had clearly bought every last string of fairy lights in town. They swung around this way and that as he ran around working to make them secure. Winter hadn't gone and yet Mervyn seemed determined a party was going ahead.

Downstairs, Ellie set a pan of milk on the hob and took a few steps into the sitting room, switching on a lamp to survey the results of her painting. A few patches thinner than others needed a touching up. Not bad, considering she wasn't a professional. The gurgle and bubble of milk sounded on the hob. She bent down to remove a piece of newspaper sticking to her foot.

She stared at the paper. At an entry in the Classifieds. At the 'Buy and Sell' section.

> For sale. Designer wedding dress, white lace.
> Mandarin neck. Ankle length with small train.
> Never worn. Size 8. Open to all reasonable offers.

There was a mobile phone number. What had drawn Ellie's attention was not the ad itself, but what was drawn around it. A large circle in what looked like a pink fluorescent pen, accompanied by a message in large capital letters.

YOUR SIZE, ELLIE?
INTERESTED?

Ellie stood there staring, her nostrils filling with the stench of burning milk.

39

'Ellie?'

'Yes?' she answered.

'Did I wake you?'

She felt like she'd hardly slept. 'No.'

Why did people with kids assume they were the only ones to get up early?

'I've been trying to get you.'

'Do you want to call over? The place is like a bomb site, just to warn you.'

'Sounds like home. I'll be over shortly.'

Ellie set to, opening the kitchen window a fraction. The smell of burnt milk lingered from the night before. It had taken her a while to scrub the hob clean. She tidied the remains of a fruit and yogurt breakfast. She rinsed the bowl and spoon and put the kettle on. The cafetière was single serving size but if she made the coffee strong enough, she could split it between two cups and add boiling water. She moved the brushes that were steeping in white spirits, along with the tin of paint, to the windowsill behind the sink.

She didn't have scheduled taxi runs until later in the day so was dressed simply in jeans and a blue cotton T-shirt. Casting a critical eye in the mirror above the mantelpiece, she thought she looked pale.

She went upstairs in search of a warmer colour and changed into a coral T-shirt, tying her purple and orange scarf around her neck. Even with the change, she looked peaky. She applied some blusher, a coating of mascara and a slick of lip gloss. By the time she heard the door, she felt presentable.

'The wind out there would take your face off.' Scully stepped hurriedly in. 'Oh, I like the smell of paint, or the smell of progress, as Jill used to say.' A shadow pulled his smile away.

'How's she doing?'

'We take each day as it comes.' He blew on his hands.

'And the girls?'

'Their aunt Lou is keeping a close eye.' He attempted to free a bit of newspaper that stuck to his sole. Ellie's eyes darted to the mantelpiece where she'd left the message from the night before.

'That didn't last long.' Scully pointed to the plant withering on the windowsill.

She pulled a face, and directed him to the settee before reaching for the message. 'This is something I spotted last night. I'd put old newspaper down to protect the floor.'

She handed him the torn piece of paper. 'I get my papers delivered,' she explained. 'I'd thought the delivery guy had made a mistake – I got two copies last week, one an hour or so after the other.'

Scully examined the scrap of paper. 'Mmm . . .' he said, his expression dark. He set the paper down on the coffee table and looked around the small room, taking some time to consider.

'Are you going to Coleman Street with this?' he asked.

She'd been awake most of the night, wondering what to do. She didn't want any garda attention. 'I don't think so. It's only a note. Like you said when your home was invaded . . . why give this psycho any more oxygen?'

'You sure, Ellie?'

'I am for now. Listen, if there's anything else, I'll go straight to the gardaí.' She scratched at a spot of paint on her hand. 'You said on the phone that you'd been trying to get me?'

'I did . . .' He drew a breath, seeming reluctant to move on. 'The investigation seems to be widening.'

Ellie perched on the armrest.

'The Serious Crime Squad is going to interview Darren Keating about our friend, Ambrose. And of course Sean Begley is none too pleased that the focus is shifting from his preferred perpetrator, Joseph Liston.'

'Who's Darren Keating?'

'A schoolmate of Ambrose Casey's. I think I've landed poor Darren in it. The fella's a bit of a God-help-us and he won't thank me for sending the law to him.'

'You didn't let on to the gardaí that I'd been talking to you?'

'I've only been dealing with my source. And he's feeding your suggestions into the investigation as anonymous tips.'

'You know I was only going on a hunch?'

What if her suspicions were wrong and all her meddling landed an innocent man in trouble?

'I know that.' Scully ran a hand through the thatch of wind-thrashed hair. 'To be honest, I can't imagine Ambrose Casey overpowering anyone. Unless the guy has hit the gym, done protein shakes and taken testosterone. The picture I have in my head of this person, of this sick fucker who came into my home, and whoever's responsible for this' – he pointed at the note – 'let's just say it's not consistent with Ambrose's character, or certainly not the Ambrose Casey I went to school with.'

Scully gave a crooked smile. 'There are problems with all our suspects, Ellie. I'm aware that, like everyone else, I'm subject to confirmation bias.'

'What do you mean by that?' Ellie angled her head.

'I'd dismissed what I thought was a madcap theory from Begley, but I've been thinking again about this guy Joseph Liston.'

From his expression, Scully had clearly found it a painful exercise.

'Begley's suspect of choice seems so obviously based on a vendetta, but maybe I was wrong to dismiss Liston just because I think Begley is a prick.'

Ellie didn't say so, but she'd also thought Scully had been far too quick to dismiss Mervyn as a suspect. Especially with his persistent interest in Ellie and anything she might glean in the taxi.

'And where are things with Jen Healy?'

'That was my other piece of news. I spoke to her friend, Rose Moriarty, like you suggested.'

Ellie straightened. At last. It had taken Scully long enough to get round to it.

'She blurted out something she didn't mean to. It seems Jen does have an alibi but it might be one that's compromising.'

Ellie widened her eyes. 'How did you get her to disclose that?'

'She didn't mean to.' He got to his feet. 'The Serious Crime Squad is going to be busy. They're following up on Darren Keating, they're obtaining search warrants for a number of places and they're off to give Jen Healy another visit.'

'I knew there was something about that woman,' said Ellie, walking Scully to the door.

He opened up to an icy blast of wind. 'Batten down the hatches, Ellie. There are trees down out my way. It's going to get nastier before the week is out.'

'Apologies.' Ellie suddenly remembered. 'I had intended to make you a coffee.'

'No worries.' He blew on his hands and rubbed them together. 'And listen, if you change your mind about letting the gardaí know about that little message, or anything else like it crops up, just give me a bell.'

'I will.'

Scully put his head into the wind and marched off, turning briefly to look behind as he headed down the row of houses.

Ellie looked to her left. Standing silently at the door adjacent was Mervyn, a cloth in hand. He squinted as he smiled, all the while rubbing a cloth steadily over the brass goblin door knocker. She nodded and retreated indoors.

That afternoon she had a number of fares from the train station. Journalists were descending in greater numbers. As the fevered, febrile atmosphere grew more intense, so too did her need for release.

This time when she walked past a shop assistant in a news-agent's, she held his gaze, daring him to challenge her on her bulging Barbour pockets. She even lingered in the doorway as she grappled with an umbrella. When a cautionary tip on the shoulder didn't happen, she stepped into the rain and wind, adrenaline pumping, returning to the Škoda.

That evening, Ellie broke with her midweek routine. She took out the half bottle of wine that was in the fridge. She'd had enough of lying awake, thinking about murders, agonising about Isolde, worrying about Johnny, worrying about her safety, wondering if the noises in the attic were real or imagined. Later, she pulled the bedclothes over her head, trying to block the shrieking of the wind in the telephone wires outside. It wasn't long before she fell into a groggy sleep.

The alarm on her phone woke her at seven. She was surprised to find she'd slept through the night. Reaching out to turn it off, she looked up at the angled ceiling as the wind squalled and whooped outside.

She longed for spring sunshine, the blaze of rhododendrons on the Black Pins. She couldn't remember a winter as long. Her cheeks felt cold, along with the tip of her nose.

As she lay blinking, she became aware of a gentle movement. Her gaze drifted from the ceiling to the top of the curtain rail, down to the bottom of the curtains. They were fluttering.

She pushed herself up on the side of the bed and swung her feet out on the floor. That was strange. She could also feel a chill. A definite draught, coming through the gap below the bedroom door.

She stood, bare-legged in her T-shirt, and slowly turned the door handle. The bedroom door creaked open. She stepped on to the landing. She felt it then. She looked up. The hatch to the attic. It had been moved. It was a quarter of the way open. The breeze from above blew softly through her hair.

40

Ellie had just dropped Liam and Ava to St Columba's when her phone rang. It was Scully. She hadn't felt like breakfast and she felt a bit light-headed. Scully wasted no time.

'Detectives have found something –'

Ellie held her breath.

'– a backpack containing overalls and a baseball cap. Also a make-up purse with lipsticks, blusher, nail polish, that sort of thing. A couple of pairs of ladies' white nylons and a hairbrush. There's also some jewellery boxes from McAuliffe's in Cork. They think it's part of what they're calling a murder kit.'

'A murder kit?'

'The boxes were in a fancy bag, complete with a receipt for purchase.'

Her hand went to her throat. 'Ring boxes?'

'Looks that way. According to my information, Detective Mullins from the Serious Crime Squad is off on a jaunt to Cork to check it all out. With the receipt, they can tell the date and time of purchase. There's bound to be CCTV in a jeweller's. They may even have the person on camera.'

'Do you know where it was found?'

'My source wasn't too keen to tell me. He's convinced that Superintendent Begley is on to him. He may take a bit of coaxing.'

'Who'd you put money on it belonging to?'

Scully gave a dry laugh. 'I've plenty of vices, Ellie, but betting isn't one of them. I'd say there's more than one possibility.' He sighed. 'Anyhow, what do I know, really? This is the first time I've worked on anything like this.'

Ellie thought a moment. 'Do you know if the investigation is re-interviewing their suspects?'

'They're looking at lots of stuff. Tall—' Scully started again. 'My source tells me the lab is looking at the toxicology reports again. This time in conjunction with medicines they'd lifted from someone's house. There'll be DNA tests on the hairbrush from the murder kit. And the technical bureau is looking at mobile phone activity at particular masts around the times of the murders.' Scully paused. 'Listen, there's still a load of stuff that doesn't add up, Ellie. Not yet anyway. Part of why I wanted to speak to you was to ask if you could shed light on why someone like Ambrose Casey might have wanted the women dead? Can you think of a reason? Anything at all?'

'I wish I could,' said Ellie softly. 'But I'm not seeing any at the moment.'

As her brother said, she'd always fancied herself as a bit of a detective. But she could think of no earthly reason why Ambrose would want the women dead.

'Well, if you do think of anything, you have my number. I'd better crack on and write my piece before the other media get wind.'

'Good luck with that.'

'Thanks. It's tricky.'

'The investigation seems to be moving pretty quickly now.'

'It is, and I need to keep up.'

Ellie was busy with fares for the rest of the morning, and by the time she headed out again after lunch, any promise of blue sky had closed in. It had darkened over the Black Pins. She was on her way to fill the car up with petrol when her phone pinged. A text from Doreen. She smiled. It was all in capitals as usual:

> HELLO ELLIE, I WENT A BIT FAR ON MY
> WALK AND HAD A BIT OF A WEAKNESS. I AM
> RESTING ON A BENCH AT THE ENTRANCE TO
> THE OLD SALLY WILLOW GARDEN CENTRE.
> CAN YOU GET ME? DON'T TELL MY SON.
> HE'LL BE ANGRY. DOREEN XXX

The Sally Willow garden centre was roughly six hundred metres from Autumn Grove. Doreen's outward journey would have been easy, mostly downhill. But Ellie could see how the journey back with a frame would have seemed daunting. As had happened with Isolde, Doreen's behaviour was becoming less predictable. Nothing startling at the outset, just an odd tell-tale sign of a cognitive decline.

Ellie scanned back over her reply, making sure it was clear:

> Doreen, stay there. Traffic's heavy but I'm on
> my way. I may be ten minutes but I'm coming.
> Call me if you feel any worse. Ellie xxx

She checked the time. Once she'd collected Doreen, she'd half a mind to swing by the medical centre for a quick assessment before bringing her home. There was probably enough time to do that and collect Liam and Ava from St Columba's.

The Sally Willow had been shut for a number of years and the place had since fallen into disrepair. Beyond the gated entrance, now overgrown with shrubs, rows of broken glasshouses could be spotted from the road. Ellie had been happy to read in *The Kylebeggan Echo* that a late spring reopening was planned under new ownership. Isolde used to enjoy going to the tearooms there, and walking along the many bays, deciding on what bedding plants to buy for Myrtle Crescent.

At the turn-off for Autumn Grove, the traffic dwindled to one or two vehicles coming Ellie's way. The small retirement village nestled on a gentle hillside beyond the garden centre. Passing a disused water fountain, Ellie rounded a bend. The garden centre was coming into view. Poor Doreen. The dash read 4 degrees Celsius. It would be chilly enough sitting on a bench. Ellie squinted. She saw a vehicle with its rear end poking out from the entrance.

An ambulance.

She should have driven faster. Wait . . . no, actually. She let out her breath. It was a large white van. Not an ambulance. Skidding in off the road, Ellie drew up alongside the vehicle and came to a halt outside the chained-up gates of the garden centre.

Slipping her phone into her jacket pocket, she jumped from the car and ran around to the other side of the vehicle, which was blocking her view of the bench. The bench sat empty. There was no one there. On tiptoes, Ellie edged close to the van and peered up to look inside the passenger window. No one there either.

A clunking sound came from the back of the vehicle and a rear door swung slowly open. Ellie moved towards the door. Two feet appeared underneath. Someone had hopped out of the back of the van.

'Oh, Ellie, it's you . . .'

Ambrose Casey stood there in overalls, a haunted expression on his face.

'What are you doing here?' he asked.

'Your mother – is she all right? Doreen texted me—'

'She called me too. And no, Ellie, I don't think she is. She's in the back. Come and see for yourself.'

41

Scully had just paid for diesel and was striding across the petrol station forecourt back to the Land Rover, sandwich in hand, when he noticed something. In dust and storm debris on his back door, some joker had scrawled, *MY OTHER CARS A PORCH*. He scuffed the illiterate message with his sleeve just as his mobile rang in his pocket.

It was Tall Dark.

'Hang on a sec there, bud.' Scully searched for his keys. He didn't want to talk in the open.

'Fire away,' he said, back inside the car.

'You wanted to know the results from toxicology.'

Tall Dark sounded as if he were ringing from the ocean floor.

'I'm finding it hard to hear. Where are you, pal?'

'The laundrette.'

Scully imagined the improbable sight of Tall Dark as a character in the homoerotic film *My Beautiful Laundrette*.

'Ma's washing machine is broken. I'm waiting on a load.' He sounded miserable.

'Can you speak up?'

'You have no idea the fifty shades of shite I'd be in if Begley knew I was talking to you.'

Hanging around the laundrette was obviously testing the sergeant's patience.

'Only this morning he was banging on about the 2005 Garda Siochána Act. "We know all about Clause 62, don't we, boys?" he goes, and I'd swear he eyeballed me.'

Clause 62 prohibited rank-and-file gardaí from leaking to the media.

'Is your mouth next to the speaker?'

Tall Dark snorted. 'Hear me now?'

'That's better. Those pay-as-you-go yokes can be dodgy. You were saying something about toxicology?'

'I'll read from a report I have here. Just a sec, hang on . . . some fella's about to come in . . . no, it looks like he's moving on.'

Scully got his notebook and his pencil ready. He wedged the phone between his ear and his shoulder. 'OK, shoot.'

'Here goes –' Tall Dark heaved a breath – 'and I quote: In the cases of victims Imelda Gannon and Marina Willoughby, the toxicology results support a cause and manner of death resulting from a fatal mix of alcohol, tramadol and ami– amitrip— ah feck it, something unpronounceable.'

'Did you take a screenshot of the report?'

'Why?'

'Wouldn't it be easier to ping me over the screenshot?'

Scully knew he was pushing his luck.

'I'm not having that kind of link between this phone and yours.' Tall Dark was curt. 'The technical bureau are on the ball, I'll give them that. For all I know, Begley's already on to me, and he certainly has it in for you. I'll spell that word. OK?'

Scully readied his pencil.

'A-M-I-T-R-I-P-T-Y-L-I-N-E.'

'Amitriptyline,' confirmed Scully.

'Let's call it the A-word. The report goes on . . . blah, blah, a fatal mix of tramadol and the . . . A-word . . . toxicity. Both these cases report the tissue and fluid distribution of tramadol, the A-word and their metabolites in an acutely fatal ingestion . . . blah, blah . . . there's some more stuff –' Tall Dark paused – 'here in a comments section. It says that searches by Detective Tim Mullins and his team at the home of Ambrose Casey at Autumn Grove produced sample bottles of both the A-word and tramadol.'

'Is there a report there for Isolde Hanly?'

'I have it somewhere. From memory there's not a whole lot in it.'

Scully waited.

'Got it. OK, there's mention of two drugs found in Isolde Hanly's system. I'll spell them out. B-E-N-Z-O-D-I-A-Z-E-P-I-N-E. I'm guessing that's benzo. And L-Y-R-I-C-A. There's a narrative as well that goes on to say, and I quote: All medications were present at therapeutic levels. The cause of death was suffocation.'

Scully chewed on his pencil. 'That supports what we already knew about Isolde Hanly.'

'I also have the names of other drugs that were found at Casey's home. There's a list along with a description. I don't expect you want that, do you? I've already given you the toxicology report. I don't imagine they're relevant.'

'I might as well have them. Fire away.' Tall Dark might not be the best judge of what was relevant or not.

Silence.

Scully wondered if the call had dropped.

'I used non-biological.'

'Pardon?' said Scully.

'Yeah. The whites went into a separate load.'

It dawned on Scully. 'I take it you have company?'

'That's right.'

'Want to call me back?'

'Just a minute . . .' There followed an exchange and low laughter. 'You still there?'

'I'm still here,' said Scully.

'Sorry about that. Some young one in collecting her washing.'

'Ah . . . love in the laundrette.'

Tall Dark muttered under his breath. 'Lisdoonvarna is a bit of craic, at least.'

The sergeant went looking for love at the West Clare match-making festival, did he?

'Back to that list,' Tall Dark was gruff, realising his indiscretion. 'The drugs found at the Casey house in Autumn Grove included the anti-anxiety drug Xanax. Also the muscle relaxant B-E-N-Z-O-D-I-A-Z-E-P-I-N-E, the painkiller L-Y-R-I-C-A, the antidepressant M-I-R-T-A-Z-A-P-I-N-E and a drug used for mood conditions called Q-U-E-T-I-A-P-I-N-E.'

'Quite the little pharmacy.' Scully whistled, scribbling down the names. 'You mentioned the garda technical bureau earlier. Are there any reports about Casey's phone?'

'No, but I did overhear something.'

'Go ahead.'

'I was having a bit of soup back in the canteen after freezing my balls off outside Imelda Gannon's in Friary Lane. I heard Mullins' sidekicks at the table next to mine. According to them, the technical guys found nothing between Casey's phone and the mast at Pottershill, or indeed any of the masts close to the murder scenes. Casey's phone was placed at the house in Autumn Grove on each occasion.'

Scully was still having a hard time picturing Ambrose as a murderer. 'Any criminal knows not to bring a mobile to the scene of a crime.'

'You'd be surprised, Scully. There are some right gobdaws out there. Anyhow, pal, you'll be delighted to know my wash is finally done and I'm out of here. If I hear anything more I'll be in contact.'

'Take it easy.'

Tall Dark cleared his throat. 'How's Jill? I've been meaning to ask.'

Scully stared through the windscreen as a young mother opened a car door and lifted a toddler into a car seat.

'The staff are good,' he replied. 'She's safe.'

A pause.

'You're not the only one who'd love to get his hands on that fucker, Scully.' Tall Dark cleared his throat again, as if in some difficulty. 'I'm very fond of Jill, as you know.'

'I know that, pal.'

It was time for Scully to head back to *The Kylebeggan Echo*, to hunker down and do some research. On the way, he rang Ellie. There was no answer.

His eyes glazed over at the pharmacological data spewed up by his Internet search. He was no Walter White but from what he understood, benzodiazepine was a muscle relaxant and was also a drug used to treat insomnia. Lyrica appeared to be a painkiller. Both had been present in Isolde Hanly's body at therapeutic levels, meaning not enough to kill, only to sedate.

He went through the list, next researching mirtazapine. It seemed to be used mainly as an antidepressant for geriatric patients. And quetiapine was used to treat aggressive behaviour in those with dementia, but could also be prescribed as an anti-anxiety medication.

The combination of tramadol and amitriptyline proved the most interesting area of his research. Scully felt he could be on to something. His eyes were dry and gritty.

He'd heard of tramadol before. It may have been one of the early drugs prescribed for Jill. He knew it was a strong pain medication, prescription only. It sounded like it wasn't a clever idea to mix amitriptyline with tramadol. Given the number of accidental deaths he was reading about, it seemed a very bad idea indeed. Unless of course someone had decided to check into the departure lounge.

Scully got up from his desk and headed to the office kitchen. He needed to stretch his legs. It was quiet at the paper this morning. Shona was looking morosely at her screen. She'd had a fight with her boyfriend. Doyler was flicking bits of paper into the waste bin. Gerry Bradshaw was holed up in his office looking at videos on how to improve his golf swing.

Looking around the office, there was little to indicate that a major murder investigation was under way in the town. Scully was about to change all that. He returned to his desk with a mug of tea and hit the keyboard. A bit later he sat back to read over his piece:

BRIDE COLLECTOR ARREST IMMINENT?

by Cormac Scully, Crime Correspondent

The net is closing in on whoever killed Isolde Hanly, Imelda Gannon and Marina Willoughby, the three women who were murdered in their homes and laid out in their wedding dresses.

The Kylebeggan Echo can reveal exclusively that, having considered a number of suspects, detectives have whittled down the list of chief suspects to one individual. Detectives are now following a particular line of enquiry and are currently working on forensic and toxicology evidence.

Speculation is rife about the identity of the killer in these apparently motiveless crimes. The individual in question is already known to the gardaí and was questioned in relation to another incident a number of years ago.

In the case of one of the murder victims, an item of a personal nature was removed from the murder scene. Detectives believe it was taken as a trophy. To date, that item has not yet been recovered.

While Scully would have loved to include some of the details Tall Dark had given him, that would risk exposing the sergeant. His musings were interrupted by Doyler heaving himself up from behind his desk.

'I'm off to Buckley's,' he announced. 'Anyone feeling eleven-o'clockish?'

'You're always feeling eleven-o'clockish,' said Shona peevishly.

'A bacon roll it is, for me,' Scully piped up. 'No tomato sauce.' He pulled out his wallet.

'There's some funds left in the kitty.' Doyler held up his hand. 'As for you, Shona, you're not getting a thing.'

'I'm on a diet.' Shona pulled a face. 'I'm a bit on the chubby side, apparently.'

Doyler headed to the bakery as Scully settled back to scan his article again. He had concerns. Something was holding him back. As he sat there, uncertain, his mobile pinged. It was a text from Tall Dark.

> Detectives reported back from Cork.
> Jewellery purchases confirmed. CCTV sighting
> confirmed. Other purchases of interest also.
> Getting all set up here for an arrest. More
> shortly. Keep your phone on.

It was all the confirmation Scully needed. He hit Send.

Doyler's eyes narrowed as he lumbered over to Scully's desk

on his return from Buckley's. He offered up a paper carrier bag and cracked a knowing smile. 'You're looking mighty happy with yourself there, my man. About to lay an egg?'

'Looking forward to my bacon roll is all,' said Scully. 'The fastest way to a man's heart, as you well know.'

'Enough of your sweet talk, Scully,' said Doyler, handing over the bag. 'You're getting me all confused.'

All through his radio slot, Scully kept an eye on his phone. But there was nothing coming in from Tall Dark. Not yet, anyway. As he left the offices of Skellig FM, he put in another call to Ellie to bring her up to speed. Her phone continued to ring out and he thought about leaving her a voicemail, just as she picked up.

'Ah, there you are – eventually,' he said, making for his Land Rover.

'Who is this?' a male voice answered.

'Who is this?' Scully countered. 'This is Ellie's phone, right?'

'My name is Jim O'Connell. I'm the new owner at the Sally Willow garden centre. I've just pulled up here and saw the phone lying on the ground, ringing away. I'm having some difficulty getting my truck in – there's a taxi blocking my gates.'

42

Metal grooves dug into Ellie's back and shoulder blades, digging deeper every time the van hit a bump on the road. She was finding it hard to swallow with a gag in her mouth. Steel cuffs dug into her wrists and lower back, and some of her fingers were already numb.

The back of her neck and her head hurt as she raised it up. Ambrose's thin blond hair lapped into the hood of his military-style camouflage jacket. She could see his fingers tapping away on the wheel in time with the traditional tune 'She Moved Through the Fair'.

'This is right up there with the best wedding songs.' He looked over his shoulder. It was the first time he'd spoken to Ellie inside the van. 'Beautiful, isn't it?'

When she'd leaned into the back of the van, looking for Doreen, he'd grabbed her wrists behind her back and slipped on the handcuffs. Ellie had been pushed face-down into the van. Hopping in behind her, Ambrose yanked her scarf around her neck, making a gag. He'd rolled Ellie on to her back, secured her feet together, and turned her so her feet faced the front of the van. It had all happened in seconds. Doreen hadn't stirred, lying curled up in her coat.

Jumping out and slamming the back doors shut, Ambrose had leapt into the front and started up the van. Ellie felt the van swing around and speed downhill, away from the direction of Autumn Grove.

'Sorry about that. I hope I didn't hurt you back there.'

Ellie cast her eyes about the white metallic cabin, about the scratched ridges of the side panels, craning her head back to see film-covered back-door windows. Light came through the windscreen and front windows only.

'You're slighter than I remember. I'll need to get a good look at you shortly.' He glanced back. 'Still a size eight, I hope?'

She turned her head to the side.

'Doreen,' she whispered.

Nothing.

As Ellie examined the bundle next to her more closely, she saw she wasn't in fact looking at Doreen, or anyone else for that matter. Underneath the coat were bundles of something – cushions, perhaps, and alongside, made to look like a head, was something stuffed into a hat of Doreen's. The coat had once belonged to Isolde.

'I always liked you, Ellie.' Ambrose's eyes were on the road. 'You and Isolde. I used to look forward to you coming to my tea dances.'

Lifting her head and listening for noises, Ellie tried to figure where they were, where they might be going.

'I know you were upset at her funeral. I apologise that I never got to commiserate with you but I had to get back to work before the service ended. You accept my apology?'

Lined up against the side of the van, Ellie saw boxes of cleaning supplies. *Bleach*, said one. *Liquid Soap*, said another. *Latex Gloves*, said another.

She set her head back.

'Maybe you can't hear me.' Ambrose turned the music down a notch.

'I saw you up at Mountain View community centre. Very chummy over coffee with Cormac Scully. I was going to go over to you and offer my condolences at that point, but . . . you looked away from me.' He sighed. 'I was hurt, I don't mind telling you that, Ellie. You clearly didn't want to talk to me.' He shook his head. 'But you accept my condolences now, don't you?'

He turned around and looked at her, his fair eyebrows pulled together in a frown.

Ellie raised her head so that he could see. She nodded.

He smiled and turned back to face the road.

'At Isolde's funeral, I got to thinking quite a bit. It's where I perfected my plans.' His hands caressed the wheel. 'I sat in the pew between Mother and Ursula. Of course, you know Ursula – Mother's posh friend with the guesthouse in Pottershill, next door to Isolde. I'll never live in a fuck-you house like that in Pottershill, or Arbutus Road, or anywhere. I'm more a creative person than a businessman. Anyway, Ursula and Mother nattered across me as if I wasn't there. You can imagine them, can't you, Ellie?' He chuckled. 'Mother was always in awe of Isolde 'cause of all her visitors – politicians, writers and such-like. Mother thought she was some kind of celebrity.' He glanced over his shoulder. 'Compared to people like us, I suppose she was.'

Ellie pushed against the gag with her tongue, testing it for signs of movement. She closed her eyes and tried to keep her breathing steady.

'Mother knew about Isolde's death before it even reached the news. She heard about it from Ursula. How Freddy had run like a scalded cat out his front door, into the road, knocking over a wheelie bin.' Ambrose chuckled again. 'Ursula had been putting out her own bin.'

Ellie could see a pedestrian road sign showing an old couple crossing. She recognised the one. They were heading towards the centre of town on Darglin Drive.

'Freddy looked like he'd seen a ghost, Ursula said. He'd found Isolde laid out on the bed, and he refused to go back in until the gardaí arrived. She nipped in home to get him some whiskey. That Freddy is far too good-looking for his own good, she used to say.'

Ambrose twisted around.

'I'm not upsetting you by telling you this, am I? You know what? From now on I won't say any more about Isolde. It's just that you were always such a good listener, Ellie. All my ladies were good listeners.'

He turned back.

'There was a lot more media at Imelda and Marina's funerals. They put photographs on their coffins that didn't do them justice. I don't like to brag, but Marina looked radiant by the time I'd finished with her. Imelda too. I'm kind of sorry I didn't take any photographs of my own. But you live and learn, eh?' Reaching for something on the seat beside him, he held up a camera. He raised his chin to the mirror. 'And you, Ellie, you're my fairest lady of them all.'

Ellie flexed her fingers, trying to get some feeling, as she searched for the lock on the cuffs.

'Dylan Coyle put on a great show. Up top with his parents. All his old rugby mates patting him on the back. I have to say, though, Imelda's funeral was the saddest. Those nine-year-old kiddies in a guard of honour, their faces full of snot and tears. That would melt anyone's heart.'

Ellie heard the indicator. As the van turned, she slid across the floor into the boxes of cleaning agents.

'Careful back there,' said Ambrose sharply, as if she'd somehow deliberately rolled against the boxes.

She saw the back of Ambrose's head shake. 'In fairness to Scully, he put together a nice article on Imelda . . . even I watered up. The guy is wasted in *The Kylebeggan Echo*. He used to read his stuff aloud in school back in the day. Coyle and that Kirby prick used to act the maggot, flicking rolled-up bits of rubber at the back of his head.'

He stroked the wheel. 'I really have to wonder what Scully is still doing in this town? Do you know what he's up to, Ellie?' Ambrose turned around. 'Well, do you?'

Ellie raised her head and shook it from side to side.

'Uh-oh.' He raised his finger and wagged it. 'I don't know whether to believe you, Ellie. You two have been doing quite a bit of poking around.'

He put on the same music again. 'See that woman out there.' Ambrose pointed through the windscreen. 'Silly me, of course you can't. Well, Ellie, I can tell you that woman's hair is scraped back into a ponytail, the kind that women are told not to wear while jogging in the dark. It may not be dark just yet, but attackers can always easily overpower a woman wearing a ponytail.'

He fell silent, appearing to think about this for a moment or two.

'Scully has a nose on him, you know. Like a bloodhound. Funny how people look different on camera. He's no oil painting. But to give the guy his due, he scrubs up well. I've seen him a good few times on the telly. *My* community centre was on the telly with the bold Cormac Scully strolling out the doors. I remember the camera panned to the mountains behind. And who was that now coming out next, I said to myself? Why, you, Ellie. *My* Ellie. *My* Ellie Gillespie.'

Ambrose checked the rear-view mirror.

'Don't those out-of-town reporters make Kylebeggan sound like some picturesque backwater, being preyed upon by a ghoulish killer?' He snorted. 'Jumped-up hacks haven't got a clue. Not like Scully. Now he knows this place. Knows who to talk to and how to get them to talk. So, you see, Ellie, I had to teach him a lesson. His wife was a great listener these past few weeks, but I see she's gone to a nursing home now. Pity. I'm sorry my final visit to Jill wasn't so special, but nothing but the best for you, Ellie. What I've got for you is very special.'

43

Surely someone would have spotted her taxi, parked up outside the abandoned garden centre? Ellie prayed it would arouse someone's curiosity. Liam and Ava would be standing outside the school gates by now, wondering where on earth she was. She'd never been late before, she'd never not turned up.

She couldn't feel her phone when she squeezed her arms against her sides. She was pretty sure she'd slipped it into one of her jacket pockets before launching out of the car. Maybe it had fallen out of her pocket, or maybe Ambrose had rolled over it, destroying it. The stopping and starting was making her feel nauseous, but she couldn't be sick. She'd choke with the gag on.

'Would you look at this guy. Hasn't a clue where he's going. Fucking out-of-town reporter, judging by the rental sticker.' Ambrose spoke into the mirror. 'Pardon my language, Ellie. I don't like to be uncouth in front of a woman.'

The hum of traffic came from outside. There was the occasional toot, and she'd heard a man call in salute to a passer-by.

'Speaking of uncouth,' Ambrose continued. 'I googled Joseph Liston. There's a lot of chatter around the town about that guy, but nothing in the media. I found an old photo of him on the Internet, standing by his minibus. You know what, Ellie? It's an insult that anyone would credit a horrible low-life scumbag with my work. The word is that he did, in fact, rape those women. He looks seedy. No chin and a right pair of bug-eyes behind those heavy glasses. Although, every cloud as they say –'

He busied himself at the dash.

'It's nice to get a break from the detectives' questions . . . now, time for some more music, I think.' He ran his fingers through his hair, checking himself in the mirror. He licked his fingers and flattened down his eyebrows. 'I know I'm scruffy in this khaki coat. Wait until you see what I'm wearing underneath.'

Ellie's head smacked off the floor as the van hit a pothole on the road.

'All right back there? I love a good mystery tour, don't you?'

He hummed to the music.

'Rehearsing stuff is all well and good, Ellie. But when gardaí turn up at work in front of people' – he shook his head – 'and then they come over to Autumn Grove and Mother lets them in . . .'

He tutted.

'One long volley of questions. Worse than Mother. They flipped between the women, Ellie. It wasn't an easy job keeping track who they were talking about. Superintendent Begley came by with some guy from the Special Crime Squad, Detective Tim Mullins. The guy stank of cabbage. Like, *really* bad. I hate cabbage. Do you like cabbage, Ellie?'

Ellie shook her head, thinking it best to agree.

'"Where were you the night of March seventh?" Mullins asks. "Here at home," says I. "Here, in Autumn Grove, in *sheltered housing*?" he goes, implying I'm in some way compromised. "Where were you the night of February fourteenth?" he asks. So, I tell him. "Really, Ambrose, you're telling me you spent the fourteenth of

February, Valentine's night, at home with your mother?"' Ambrose paused. 'What a cunt.'

He wiped the rear-view mirror with a screen wipe.

'"And when you say you were in Autumn Grove on January twenty-first, did you spend the *whole* of that night at home?" goes Mullins. So, I tell the guy I got a call from the alarm company – one of the sensors at the community centre had been activated by the wind. These days I have to wait until all the women have vacated the changing room before I go in to check, all because that young one accused me of lurking in a toilet cubicle trying to watch her. "What time did you get home?" Begley joins in. "Around nine thirty," says I. It was bin night and Brendan, the warden, puts out the bins for assisted houses at that time, I said.'

He swigged from a bottle on the seat beside him.

'Tricky stuff, Ellie. Have you ever been interviewed by gardaí?' He looked over his shoulder.

Nod or shake her head?

She shook her head from side to side.

'They pretend like they're your friend.' Ambrose's eyes were back on the road. '"When your mother was interviewed by the Serious Crime Squad on a previous occasion, she said you were at home on the nights of the fourteenth of February and the seventh of March," goes Begley to me. "Did you nip out on an errand on those nights, like you did on the night of January twenty-first?" He grins at me like a dead hare, suggesting we were in on something together.' Ambrose shuddered. 'That guy gives me the creeps.'

He checked his side-view mirrors.

'Mother wanted me to run her to St Malachy's to light some candles after they left. She reckons she can achieve global nuclear disarmament by lighting her holy candles. "I hope they catch the bastard," she said.' Ambrose tutted. 'Sometimes Mother's

259

language is deplorable. There's nothing worse than a woman with a potty mouth.'

With the noise and bakery smells wafting in from outside, Ellie guessed they were on Main Street. Everyone in and out of Buckley's and Kenneally's Food Emporium getting their last-minute purchases before the shops shut for the day. She felt the prickle of tears.

Ambrose raised his chin. 'It's great to have this time with you.' He smiled into the mirror. 'Remind me I have to nip back after we're done, to bring Mother for her evening medical appointment. It's time she got a repeat prescription. Last time, I was a hundred milligrams short of the ideal dosage. Not a total disaster, I'll grant you, but combining different pills to get the same effects is risky, and asking a pharmacist for advice is out of the question. I have to use the Internet.'

The red glow from the traffic lights disappeared and part of the inside wall of the van turned green. Ellie raised her head. From the signage of an old tobacconist's shop behind, she recognised it as the last set of traffic lights before the road headed out towards Dunseally Castle.

'It's all a learning curve.' Ambrose moved down through the gears with a gloved hand. 'Put the finery on before or after? The ideal time is probably in the last few seconds between life and death when, amazingly, corpses do feel that fraction lighter. You wouldn't think it, Ellie, but it's true. And there's no point in doing all that prep and having an accident and pretty gowns ruined with vomit and leakage. Not to worry – that's my problem, something for me to look out for, Ellie.'

He tapped the steering wheel.

'Mother says she's worried about me. She wants me to take a course of iron. We have some in the top left cupboard above the microwave. She's not taking them 'cause she thinks she has haemochromatosis, like Sheila in number six. Poor woman has enough real conditions to contend with without any phantom ones.' He chuckled. 'Over the years her ailments have proven pretty useful. The woman isn't that demanding, as you know. She has her outings – the hairdresser, visits from Sheila in number six, chats on the phone with Ursula in Pottershill. *Winning Streak* on a Saturday with a glass or two of wine. And if she's behaving, I'll buy her a scratch card during the week.'

Ellie could make out rhododendron bushes on the slopes ahead.

'It's only because you've been so kind to Mother that I'm taking you to my special place, Ellie. I didn't take my other ladies there.'

As the van climbed, a box sitting on top of the bleach supplies fell on to her. She smelled blood in her nose. Ambrose shifted the carrycase to the side, keeping his eyes on the road.

Ellie read the label:

Callinder & Dick
Wedding Couture

'I'm afraid I haven't been very nice to Mother, lately. It's stress, I think. And I can't afford to get stressed. Much as I love her, there are days that even she can be trying. I'm sure you've found that too. We have a lot in common, don't we? Isn't it crazy we haven't got together before now?'

Lying on the cold floor, Ellie felt damp all over. She was shivering. Liam and Ava's parents would know there was something amiss by now. As would staff at St Columba's. But what action would they take? No one had any reason to suspect she'd been abducted.

'Take for example the day that carrycase arrived for me,' said Ambrose. 'That one in the back.' He glanced over his shoulder. 'Mother was in her armchair, knitting that awful matinée jacket for Sheila's latest grandchild, when she told me she'd put a parcel on my bed. As soon as I went to my room, I knew. I knew she'd been poking around.' He tutted. 'My collection had been in a neat row under the lip of the windowsill and out of the sun, arranged according to contents. Fingernails, hairs, eyelashes, bits of discarded plasters. It's amazing what people leave behind in changing rooms. And stuff from when I was a kid – robins' legs and various *objets trouvés*. I knew she'd been through the drawers in my desk, the one second from the bottom, where I kept my wedding magazines. And the bottom drawer where I kept my photos. The ones of the women in the changing rooms.'

Ambrose sighed. 'It actually hurt me more than it hurt her. But I'd told her, actions have consequences. Anyway, bloody Sheila had already waited months for that stupid matinée jacket. A few more weeks wasn't going to bloody kill her.'

Ellie wiggled her toes inside her ankle boots, trying to keep her circulation going.

'Mother knows what happens when I get stressed. The first time it happened, my hand felt like it was on fire. It looked like a margherita pizza.'

Feathery branches of pine reached into the road. They'd have passed the entrance to Dunseally Castle by now, Ellie reckoned. They must be heading high into the Black Pins. To the rough terrain of gorse-clad mounds and jaggy outcrops. It was late afternoon on an early April weekday. The place would be quiet.

'The doctor asked me how it happened. Sure, I had no idea. I couldn't remember what I'd been doing that day, or the day before. Mother laughed, as if it were somehow funny. The doctors didn't laugh. And the technician who scanned my head joked that he hoped they'd find my brain in there. You know me, Ellie, I played along just to be polite but, jeez, he wasn't a funny guy at all. In fact, I'd say it was his only gag. I spat into his coffee before I left the room.'

Branches scraped against one side of the van as Ambrose swerved closer to the verge.

'They said in the hospital that memories can fail to stick. Imagine spending the bones of ten years training to be a doctor and that's the best explanation they could come up with.' His tone was indignant. 'My brain looked normal, so they said. Which was something, I suppose – Big Jack was always telling *me* I was the weirdo.'

He shook his head.

'On the way back, Mother and Meena talked about what was happening on *Coronation Street*. At home, Meena gave an extra happy cheerio and drove away pretty sharpish. When we went inside, the ironing board was up against the television with a broken screen. Big Jack had come home between his boat tours and found me ironing. He'd reached for the iron and branded the back of my hand. He stayed away for a week after that, went to Cheltenham for the races with his pal, Mikey Maguire. It was quiet that week, I remember. Partly because the TV was broken but mainly because the mad bastard was away.'

Ellie watched as Ambrose switched the wipers on. Left, right. Left, right. They swished over the drizzle on the windscreen.

'Big Jack thought he was a businessman.' Ambrose scoffed. '"Be an entrepreneur," he'd say, or "entreprenoor", as he called it. Just how my father's lake tour was different to any others, I'll never know. I guess I had the sense to know where such a question would land me. Thrown up against kitchen cupboards, like Mother. Oh, he'd stand you a pint, help anyone out, and he ran a spotless boat. If it was a laugh and a bit of craic you were after, Big Jack's *King of the Lake* pleasure cruise was the only cruise to take. He was a gent, so everyone told me. They should have tried living with the mad bastard.'

Ambrose tapped his temple.

'So, Ellie, that's when I started to have my little turns – as Mother puts it. So she knows. She *knows* she shouldn't stress me. Doctor Kingston told her, way back, I had an anxiety disorder. The medications might take a bit of fine-tuning, he said. Fine-tune away, I said. Now, every morning I remind her to take her medication, and she tells me to take my amitriptyline.'

He dropped down another gear as the engine struggled.

Ellie rarely drove out this far. Most of her regular fares were closer to the town. She felt her head sliding towards the rear doors. She'd rather fall out through those doors and on to the road than face whatever Ambrose had planned. A bundle of tied newspapers slid from one end of the van floor down towards her.

'Oops,' said Ambrose in the mirror. 'There goes my newspapers. I've been keeping those. You know, I've half a mind to dig up Big Jack and show him all the coverage. Show him what I've been up to. Maybe when we're done, I'll head up to the graveyard and do just that. I forgot my shovel with all the excitement. I have to go home for Mother anyway. I could dig him up and show the mad dead bastard exactly what I did. Ask him if he's happy now. Made my mark, so I did.'

This time Ellie couldn't stop the tears. As the van bumped over the rough road zigzagging up the hillside, she wondered if in years to come they'd find her bones. Before she had a chance to think about it any more, the van swung in off the road.

'Here we are. Bride's Point, where the First Earl of Dunseally proposed to his lovely bride, Margaret Erskine. Only a few people know that.'

Ambrose's teeth were white in the grey afternoon light.

'You and me, Ellie, we're going further in. To somewhere no one knows.'

He turned around, grabbed something and sprayed it into his mouth. Fine particles of mint vapour wafted around the van.

44

Tall Dark sounded unusually breathless. 'First chance I've had to call you, pal. It's all kicking off here today.'

Scully could hear outside noises and church bells.

'As well as preparing for an arrest, we've had reports of suspicious activity up at the Sally Willow garden centre. We've just sent a car up to check out an abandoned taxi.'

'I know all about it.'

Scully had advised the owner of the garden centre to contact Coleman Street straightaway. 'I think it's Ellie Gillespie's taxi. She's been helping me out with some research. I don't have a good feeling about this. I hope she's all right.'

'I hear you, pal.' Tall Dark's voice dropped to just above a whisper. 'But to be honest, all the focus is on the big arrest. Begley can hardly contain himself, despite it not being Joseph Liston.'

'So, it *is* Ambrose Casey?'

'Looks that way.'

Scully hopped into the Land Rover, placing the flowers he'd bought for Jill on the passenger seat.

Tall Dark filled him in.

'What detectives think is part of a murder kit – the white stockings, lipstick, nail varnish and women's make-up was found in Casey's work locker up at Mountain View community centre. It's also where they found receipts from McAuliffe's Jeweller's in Cork. Our further enquiries confirm that Casey purchased two nine-carat-gold wedding rings from there.'

'Do they have the guy on CCTV?'

'That they do, my friend. The weddings rings found on the bodies of Imelda Gannon and Marina Willoughby are a match for the two nine-carat rings bought. CCTV places Ambrose in the jeweller's buying them. Something else as well . . .'

'Go on.'

'Casey can be seen on McAuliffe's CCTV making another purchase. That of two antique silver reul sixpence coins. Imelda Gannon and Marina Willoughby were found with coins like that in their shoes.'

'It's enough for an arrest?'

'There's more. Remember, I told you they'd found a hairbrush in the murder kit?'

'I do.'

'Forensics did DNA analysis. The hair on the brush matches that of Marina Willoughby.'

'I see.' It sounded like Coleman Street and the Special Crime Squad had their man.

'And if that's not enough, they found traces of Ambrose Casey's DNA in Myrtle Crescent, in the home of Isolde Hanly.'

Scully started the engine. 'What's happening now?'

Above the throaty engine, Tall Dark was barely audible. 'Begley and a crew of arresting officers were over at Mountain View earlier, intending to arrest Casey. But he's taken the afternoon off, according to the receptionist. They're not sure where he is.'

'Where is Begley now?'

'Heading over to the Casey family home in Autumn Grove, as

we speak. I thought you might want to be there. First on the scene, as it were.'

'Pal, if I wasn't already married, I would kiss you.'

Tall Dark dismissed him with a snorting noise.

Scully waited for a gap in traffic, swung out in the middle of Main Street and reversed again, making a turn to change direction. Jill's nursing home was accommodating about visiting time and he rang Lou to ask her to hang on with the girls until he got home.

He headed out of town in the steady flow of early evening traffic until he reached the signpost for Autumn Grove. Catching sight of the weather-beaten sign for the Sally Willow garden centre, he slowed. Ellie's taxi was still there. As he drove by, two crows landed on the Škoda's rooftop. They pecked at the roof and bent their heads to look inside.

Scully spotted a large wooden billboard signposting Autumn Grove, advertising the development of one- and two-bedroomed units for assisted living. Tall Dark had given him the exact address of the Casey home.

Rather than alert Begley to his presence, Scully ditched the Land Rover by the picket fence of Autumn Grove's community garden. Beyond the fence, a few white-haired men bearing trowels were moving around.

Scully ambled along the footpath, scanning for unmarked garda cars. Detectives would do their best not to alert Ambrose to their presence, the same way that Scully tried not to draw attention. He'd thought better about bringing Paudie, his sound guy, along. Scully wanted this scoop but had no desire to jeopardise any arrest.

Along the path benches were placed at regular intervals and Scully passed an elderly man, sitting reading a paper.

'Soft day, thank God,' said the man, without looking up.

'It is,' said Scully, keeping his head down. He gave a sideways squint down the avenue, marked units 1–7. Disabled stickers were stuck on the windscreens of the cars parked there. Scully slowed his step, affected a limp and hunched his shoulders. The next avenue, where Doreen Casey lived with her son, was busier. Scully spotted at least three Hyundai cars, all occupied.

Shuffling to the nearest bench with line of sight to 14 Autumn Grove, he sat down gingerly, took out a notebook and turned the pages as if it were a paperback. Every now and then, from underneath his eyelashes he checked for movement. He listened for traffic. He waited.

45

'Sorry about this, Ellie.'

She shivered at the side of the white van in the deserted mountain layby. Ambrose fumbled in a backpack. He was on the ground, on his hunkers. At his feet was a patterned canvas chill bag along with the Callinder & Dick carrycase.

'I did what I could earlier . . . now, where is it?'

With a gasp of satisfaction, he straightened up. In his hand, he held what looked to Ellie like a dog lead. He came towards her, clipping the lead on to her cuffs. He'd already moved the handcuffs to her front.

'What a view,' he said, turning to admire the dramatic craggy outcrops that fell away to a band of trees below. Lough Avulla stretched across the valley floor. 'They may call Kerry "The Kingdom"' – he waved an expansive arm about – 'but this – all this is *my* kingdom.'

He turned to Ellie. 'I'll take off the scarf if you promise not to call out. Not that anyone would hear you all the way up here. But there's no need for drama. What do you think?'

Ellie nodded. She flinched as Ambrose slipped behind her, undoing the gag. Above them, a bird swooped and shrieked. 'There we go . . . it's no fun, talking to myself.'

'Please, Ambrose,' she croaked. 'You're scaring me.'

'No need to be scared.' He pulled something from his pocket, giving her a kindly look. 'You're going to have to trust me, a bit like at the tea dances when you'd follow my lead, remember?'

Before she knew it, he'd pulled something over her eyes and had settled it over her ears.

'What's happening?' Her voice was panicked.

She heard him gather up the baggage.

'Careful,' he said, and she felt herself pulled by the lead. 'I'm bringing you to my secret place.'

'Please, Ambrose . . . no.' She stumbled.

'Lift your feet. There's one or two rocks . . . there – well done. See, you can do it.'

She heard the contents of his backpack shift about as he moved.

'OK, Ellie. The going's a bit softer here . . . wait up a sec, you just need to take one giant step, just about . . . now.' She could hear the gurgle of running water. 'You don't want to get those feet wet . . .'

Underneath her, the stones were slippery.

'Jesus.' She righted herself. They were journeying down scree or shingle. 'I'm sorry I ignored you, Ambrose. I didn't mean any offence.'

'Colder than I expected today,' he said. She could hear his laboured breathing. 'Not nearly as cold as the night in Marina's garden, when I waited for you and the other two ladies in the taxi to head off.'

She went over on her ankle.

'Lift those feet up.' His breath was hot against her cheek. 'You're OK, don't worry. I'm guiding you.'

She felt the tug of the lead.

'Marina had told me she'd no intention of going to a nightclub on her hen night. I knew she'd be back home around midnight.'

Bog water seeped through Ellie's ankle boots.

'I knew where she'd put everything.' Ambrose was breathing heavily. 'Her gown was in its carrycase, like she said.

'I don't know what this is all about' – Ellie stumbled – 'I'm sorry if I did something to offend you . . . please . . . please take me back.'

'Marina said she could handle Dylan. Dear sweet Marina. When I'd finished with her, do you know what I thought, Ellie?'

The pull on the lead grew stronger.

'I thought how Marina wouldn't be forced to handle that guy ever again. She was free. Looking down on her, she looked so peaceful, elegant as always. So still and so serene.' He sighed. 'It was perfect. The ring I'd bought her fitted perfectly too. She was already wearing something old – earrings that had belonged to her mother. And when it was done, I got on to the bed, the side where Dylan slept, and sang to her. I stroked her hand, her hair, her face.'

'Help!' The cry came from the deepest part of her that she could find. 'Help!' cried Ellie.

Ambrose tutted. 'I thought we said no drama? There's no one up here, Ellie. It's you, me and the birds. Shriek, if you want. Did you know the shriek of a human sounds just like that of a mountain hare?'

Maybe someone had noticed his van driving erratically at the garden centre. Maybe someone had reported it. The thought that nobody knew Ellie was missing was too much to bear.

Somewhere ahead, Ambrose muttered. She tried to make it out. 'Spare the rod and ruin the child, Doreen,' he murmured. His tone was cruel and mocking. 'Pee Wee Casey wets the bed. Good for nothing, Pee Wee Casey.'

'Where are we going?' Something told her it was important to keep him engaged.

Her arm was grabbed, hard. His breath was at her ear. 'Down here. That's right . . . lean on me. One step, two . . . you're doing great. There, a few more and . . . that's it, we're here.'

She heard him exhale, long and slow.

'Where?'

She heard the sound of a zipper opening.

'Not yet, Ellie.'

A rustling sound.

'Darren and I used to come here, back in the day.' His breath came in excited bursts. 'Here, step on this.' Ellie could feel the heat of him, hear him breathe, smell his scent. He was standing in front of her. He put his hands on her hips. She gave a sharp intake of breath. He ran them down the length of her thighs, down her calves. He was at her feet, undoing her ankle boots. 'Step out,' he said. He pulled off a sock. 'Other one . . . good.' His breath was ragged. 'Love those trousers.' Her skin prickled as he dragged them down.

She would do it now. Kick him full-force in the face, knock him over.

'I wouldn't do that, Ellie.' She felt a grip on her ankle. Something cold rested against her skin. She heard the sudden snip of scissors. In seconds, she was in her knickers, her bare skin exposed to the mountain air. She clasped her arms in front of her. She could hear him breathing. Feel him watching.

'What are you doing?'

No answer.

'Ambrose?'

He cupped the heel of her foot. Something silky shimmied up her leg. He cupped the other heel. Ellie followed his instructions as he dressed her in stockings, a long sleeveless dress and some shoes.

'Why?' Ellie felt her voice crack. 'Why are you doing this?'

273

'Just a minute.'

She felt something slide into her hair at the crown.

'I was right. Strapless suits you.'

He took off the blindfold and Ellie blinked. They were in a hollow, stony place. Above them, a ledge dripped with moisture. She saw the path they'd taken through tufts of gorse and heather. She looked to the travel rug underneath her feet. Behind was a military-style canopy pegged out with a groundsheet, and two camp chairs either side of a fold-out table. A small rusted iron cross was staked in the ground a few metres away. Ambrose had attached the lead to the cross by tying a knot around it.

'What's this all about, Ambrose?' Using his name so much might endear her to him.

His expression darkened.

'Don't stare at me like that, Ellie. Like I'm some mental case.' Unzipping his jacket, he draped it over a rock. 'It's not like I want to slice you up with some fava beans and a glass of Chianti. Like I said to Imelda, I'm not your man from *Silence of the Lambs.*' He pointed to a camping chair. 'Sit.' His skin looked pale against the black tuxedo. 'Lovely, trusting Imelda.' He sighed.

Ellie ducked under the canopy and sat.

'When Imelda opened the door that night in that wanker's rugby jersey' – he unzipped the canvas chill bag – 'I knew it would be easy to get off. She pretended like she didn't care Harry was away on Valentine's night.' He put two small bottles on the table, one of wine and another of diet cola. 'I asked if she'd like to prac- tise. Because she'd missed a lesson with her injured leg.' He set out two plastic goblets. 'We started with a waltz, then a jive. I had to put on "Eye of the Tiger", Harry's choice for the first dance. We spun round on our toes, under each other's arms and back in on the return.' His fair eyelashes blinked steadily. 'You remember that from the tea dances, don't you, Ellie? When you spin out one way, you have to come home again.'

A plop of water dripped from the canopy on to her bare shoulder.

He looked above him at the darkening sky. 'I'd brought wine with me that night. A red, Imelda liked, and one for me. This time, I'd prepared. I'd popped the pills from the blister pack, crushed them and poured the resulting powder into the bottle at home. I used five pills. Mother's always good for a prescription. Poor woman's practically a junkie.

'We sat there side by side against the wall, listening to Adele. Her stuff was boxed up ready to go to the new house.' He smiled. 'We were like a couple in those mortgage ads on the TV. Young, in love, in their first home, having wine and larking about with paintbrushes. Adele was still playing when Imelda's head lolled off to the side. I spent a good while sitting there, stroking her hair, cradling her.'

'Why?' Ellie had to keep him talking. She had to slow things down. 'I don't understand why, Ambrose.'

He put two cartons on the table. She spotted *Kenneally's Food Emporium* on the labels.

'When you're up close, you notice things,' he said. 'Those injuries Imelda had . . . they were not from hockey, no matter what she said. And all those cheery explanations, just like Mother. I saved Imelda. I saved kids from being born into that.'

On the mountain road below, Ellie spotted what looked like headlights crawling upwards in the gloom. 'But what about Marina?'

'I saved her too.' He set out paper napkins, decorated with pictures of wedding bells. 'The cut of Dylan, blubbing away in the church after the carry-on at his stag. It's enlightening what you hear by the showers at the pool. Dylan thought he was a big man paying some poor prostitute double for what he did to her.' He opened the cartons, placing plastic knives and forks on either side of each. He looked up and winked. 'Sorry, Ellie. It's not General Tso's chicken. I had to improvise.'

She felt cold inside and out.

'I knew Marina from way back,' Ambrose explained. 'By the time she came to me for lessons, her confidence was shot. Dylan had told her she had to change her name. He's the kind of guy who'll raise his kids to mock the shy ones, to cheat. He'll raise entitled pricks like him. *I* was the one Marina shared her hopes with. *I* was the one who gave her undivided attention. She liked tradition. Just like Mother. Like Imelda, too, and I gave her the traditional ceremony she deserved, just like in the wedding rhyme of Mother's. "Something old, something new, something borrowed, something blue, and a silver coin in her shoe."'

Ellie could hear the purr of a vehicle coming closer.

'I listened to my ladies' plans, all their hopes, their worries for the future. They trusted me. They shared their lives with me. I knew their secrets. I knew where all their precious things were kept.'

She would call out again if it came close.

Ambrose twisted the cap on the small red wine bottle. 'I didn't want my ladies to have lives like Mother. You wouldn't think it to look at her but she's only seventy-one. I was a very small kid when that mad bastard pushed her. I remember staring at a pool of blood slowly seeping out from underneath her blue maternity dress at the bottom of the stairs. I didn't really understand what had happened. Mother said there wouldn't be another baby after all and I remember we put the baby clothes into bags for the Oxfam shop. Meena Clancy from next door was in floods helping her to dismantle the baby cot. You'd swear it was Meena who'd lost the baby. For weeks all the neighbours could talk about was Mother's accident.'

He poured the richly coloured wine into Ellie's goblet.

'Weird how I can't remember the day Big Jack was killed on the boat.' He opened the cola. 'Anyhow, why on earth are we talking about him? That man ruined enough of my life. I'm not letting him ruin our special day.'

He filled his goblet with cola. The vehicle had disappeared. Ellie looked over her shoulder, listening out for any engine sounds.

'You keep looking back at that cross.' Ambrose smiled. 'Did I tell you it's the spot where the Earl of Dunseally buried the heart of his wife when she died?'

No one was coming for Ellie. No one knew she was here.

'I've more to do, Ellie. There are more fiancées out there. More guys who tormented me in school. Those women need to be rescued.' He paused. 'I must admit to a bit of a mischievous side.' A smile spread slowly across his face. 'It was quite a thing to see Coyle and Kirby suffer after all this time. I remember every single one of them. Everyone who poked me in the back, called me names, day in, day out, never a moment's peace. Coyle, Kirby, Shrek Fitzpatrick and Diarmuid Mulqueen – all taking the piss. It went on for years. But I waited, Ellie. I waited until my name faded from their consciousness, my face from all their memories, until I became invisible.'

'I'm not like Marina. I'm not Imelda,' Ellie pleaded. 'You don't need to save me from anyone.'

'Oh, I know that, Ellie.' He winked. 'I've been saving you all for myself.' He raised his goblet. 'A toast to us.'

Johnny would spend the rest of his life wondering what had happened to her.

'You're not having wine?' Her voice trembled.

'I never drink and drive.' He checked his watch. 'I'll have to get back soon for Mother. Come now, Ellie, drink up. I'll do the photographs when I get back.'

She looked down at the handcuffs.

'Here, let me help you,' he said, raising the wine to her lips. Ellie spat and spluttered. Ambrose tutted. 'Look what you've done to those lovely white shoes.'

Pinching her nose, he held her head back. He waited. When she opened her mouth to breathe, he tipped the dark red wine down her throat.

46

Cold pierced through Scully as he looked up from his phone. Daffodils tossed their heads in a border outside Doreen Casey's bungalow. Not one of the Hyundai cars had budged in the hour or so that he'd been waiting on the bench. He was about to get up to stretch his legs when he picked up the sound of a vehicle approaching. Two Tesco delivery vans had driven into Autumn Grove in the past forty minutes. He dropped his head, keeping watch underneath his eyelashes.

Cresting the hill, a vehicle grumbled into view. Across the road, a couple making slow progress with walking frames stopped to wave. The unmarked white van indicated, slowed and turned into 8–15 Autumn Grove. Scully held his breath as a man in a dark suit hopped out.

The air suddenly filled with the sound of car doors opening and running feet. Scully launched himself from the bench and hurried across the road. The man in the black suit turned to see the source of the commotion.

Gardaí in uniform formed a shield, closing in behind him. The man turned, his knees dipped and he made as if to run. The door to Doreen Casey's house opened. Two people appeared in the doorway. The man in the suit froze. He looked to his

279

right, to his left, as Scully closely followed the advance towards number 14.

Superintendent Sean Begley helped Doreen Casey out of the house by the elbow. The man in the suit edged towards her, checking on gardaí closing in behind. No one had spotted Scully. He waited by a cherry blossom, close to where the white van had parked, close enough to hear.

A man in plain clothes approached Ambrose. 'I'm Detective Tim Mullins,' he said. 'And this here is Garda Sergeant Lally.' A uniformed garda approached Ambrose from the other side. 'Ambrose Casey, we are here to arrest you under Section 30 of Offences Against the State Act.'

Superintendent Sean Begley and Doreen Casey looked on.

'You are not obliged to say anything unless you wish to do so, but whatever you say will be taken down in writing and may be given in evidence.'

'*No!!*'

Doreen Casey was shaking her head. '*No, no, no . . .*'

'It's all right, Mother.' Ambrose raised his hand. 'I'll handle this.'

'Are you OK, Mrs Casey?' Superintendent Sean Begley sounded kindly. 'Is there someone we should contact?'

Doreen Casey pulled her shoulders back, clutching at the high neck of her polo jumper. 'I'm fine.'

'Lads,' said Begley, looking at no one in particular, 'one of you might swap with me.' He tilted his head towards the house and made his way to Ambrose. 'You've led us a right merry dance.' He lowered his voice. 'When we get you to Coleman Street, you're going to confess to all you've done. Maybe we can leave your mother out of it.' His eyes moved up and down the street. 'I've been trying to get my old dear into Autumn Grove. It's a nice set-up.' He shook his head. 'If your mother is found to be aiding and abetting a crime, I'm afraid it's Garvenstown women's prison for her.'

'Leave Mother out of this, if you don't mind,' said Ambrose calmly.

Doors started to open across the street. Scully turned to see people looking out. The neighbours might be good for a quote or two. Turning back, something caught his eye. He had a split-second flashback to Ellie in Lorrigan's Mill, a brightly coloured orange and purple silk scarf around her neck. Alarmingly similar to the orange and purple fabric his eye had caught, trailing under a door at the back of Ambrose's van.

'Superintendent!' he shouted. He advanced towards the arresting party.

Stepping away from Ambrose, Begley came towards him, his cheeks flushed.

'A woman's life's in danger!'

Slipping through the wall of gardaí, Scully pointed to the scarf poking out of Ambrose's van. He explained that it looked the same as one belonging to taxi driver Ellie Gillespie. The woman whose taxi was abandoned a few hundred metres away. A woman who was missing.

'Did you say Ellie Gillespie?'

Doreen Casey had overheard. Her hand was at her throat. She teetered towards her son. 'Ambrose, what have you done? Where is Ellie?'

Ambrose put his hands up and shook his head.

Doreen made down the path towards the van, her hip dipping as she went. Inspecting the scarf, she waddled back across the grass towards her son. Begley hung back. Ambrose listened as his mother touched his elbow, her expression grave. Scully couldn't make out a word of what she said. Ambrose pursed his lips and looked off into the distance. Doreen tugged his sleeve, then clasped her hands in supplication. 'Please, son.' Scully heard her say. 'That girl is a godsend to me . . .'

'It's no good, Mother,' said Ambrose.

'Where is she, son?'

Ambrose scanned the human shield that had formed around him, considering his response. Scully drew closer.

'It's too late now.'

'That's as maybe, Ambrose. Tell us anyway,' Begley said. 'You see what this is doing to your mother.'

Ambrose kicked the ground and looked away.

'Bride's Point,' he said. 'Where there used to be a bird hide.' He spoke in a monotone. 'Where the Earl of Dunseally buried Margaret Erskine's heart.'

'Right, Ambrose. I know roughly where you are.' Begley took him by the arm. 'You can show us exactly.'

'I'll be back shortly, Mother,' called Ambrose over his shoulder.

Scully was quick. 'I can help,' he said. 'I've done lots of climbs round there over the years.' The area around Bride's Point was known for overhangs and tricky rockfaces.

He took Begley's grunt for approval.

'Bride's Point,' shouted Begley to the gardaí as he bundled Ambrose into a car. 'And call an ambulance,' he said to Detective Mullins. Mullins didn't take the order kindly.

Squalls of rain swirled around the search party. Below them, balls of mist were dotted across the valley, and over Lough Avulla was a floating layer of vapour. It was hard to tell what direction the wind was coming from. Ambrose had taken the lead, with Superintendent Begley following. Begley was having a hard time keeping his footing on the slippery heather and shale, and couldn't keep up with Ambrose. Scully had been forced to trail along behind, and noted the distance between Ambrose and the superintendent getting greater. Between Scully and the superintendent clomped two green-jacketed paramedics wearing high-visibility armbands.

Scully had changed into an old pair of hiking boots in the back of the Land Rover and, despite the cover of a waterproof fishing jacket, he felt damp seep through to his bones. Watching the slow-moving Begley round a gorse-clad boulder, he had to face the reality that this was not a search-and-rescue operation but a retrieval.

A flap of wings came from somewhere nearby, followed by the cry of a bird. The cry was carried off by the wind. He heard a cry again. He looked to the sky above him. A human cry. It was Begley bellowing into the wind. Scully picked up the pace, breaking past the paramedics, scratching his hands on the thorny gorse. Rounding the boulder, his worst fears were confirmed.

Begley's hands were clasped and they pumped up and down on Ellie's chest. Her face and hands were as white as the wedding dress she lay in. Ambrose watched as the paramedics kicked aside a bloodied shoe and joined in. The sound of loosening shale and low chatter signalled the arrival of the rest of the search party. Scully looked to Ambrose, rage building. But Ambrose wasn't there. He couldn't see him anywhere. Where had that sick fucker gone?

He sidled towards the hollow's edge and peered over the side. Ambrose was scrambling his way through scrub towards a ledge below. Scully felt a surge of adrenaline. Ambrose was nimble, making speed, but Scully would be faster. He hopped from rock to rock, avoiding grykes and gullies. He blinked away rain on his lashes. He was closing in. Ambrose slipped around an outcrop, out of view. Scully righted himself on slippery rock as he looked for Ambrose past the outcrop. He jumped across a gully, coming to rest on a ledge. He squinted. Where had Ambrose gone?

He scanned around. No sign of that khaki-coloured jacket. And then he saw something. A couple of metres away. He'd nearly missed it, there, just a metre or so from the top of his leather boots. A hand. Scully immediately found himself on his belly, instinct kicking in. Ambrose was hanging on to the ledge, nothing but a sheer rockface below.

Scully grabbed Ambrose's wrist. He heard activity behind. He saw the pink of Ambrose's thumbnail. The milky white half-crescent at the base above the cuticle. The clipped nails. The soft, white skin over the bumps and ridges of the knuckles. A silent current of cold air drifted by. There was a bristling in the scrub behind him, the clomp of advancing strides and heavy foot-steps. Ambrose's wrist was wet. Scully loosened his grip. He stared at Ambrose's wrist moving, wrinkle by slippery wrinkle. The foot-steps were closer now. A large moth flew by. A bird called loudly. It sounded like a corncrake. A cry and a dull thud followed.

Scully stayed there on his belly as a row of feet lined up beside him. Together, they stared on to the rocks a long way below. At the body of Ambrose Casey.

47

For much of that week, the rain stayed the far side of the Black Pins and out at sea. It looked like the weather was about to turn. Towards the bottom end of Botany Row, opposite the convent wall, Pauline Brennan was in her housecoat. She cleaned her out-side windows with vinegar spray and crumpled-up old newspaper. Every now and then she stopped wiping and peered in through a window of the house next door.

When the front door opened, she stepped back, startled. 'I didn't expect to see anyone.' She gripped the neck of the vin-egar spray, squeezing tightly. 'Not after what happened,' she said, her eyes dark rounds of curiosity. 'It's been so quiet round here lately.'

'Morning, Pauline, or should I say good afternoon? I believe it's promised dry today. I sense a touch of spring in the air.'

Pauline was taken aback at the cheery greeting. 'Are you sure you should be here?'

'And where would you expect me to be?'

'With all I read in the papers and saw on the news, I kind of expected you might have spent a few more days in hospital, get-ting over your ordeal.'

'Pauline,' whispered Ellie, 'will I let you in on a little secret?'

Pauline's eyes widened.

'I got out of that place as quickly as I could, because once I was out of danger, all I had was a steady stream of detectives asking me bloody questions.'

'Oh.' Pauline shoved the ball of newspaper into a pocket. 'Right enough. You need some peace. I understand. I must say, we're all enjoying getting the town back to ourselves.'

Ellie had slept remarkably well on her first night home. And if there had been any scratching or scraping sounds from the attic or the yard next door, she hadn't noticed.

'You have your place sparkling, Pauline. You're putting the rest of us to shame.'

'Not so sure himself would agree.' Pauline nodded in the direction of Mervyn's door.

'It's been quiet there too,' said Ellie. 'He must be away.'

Pauline sprayed the glass above her door. 'I was thinking the same. I haven't seen him in days.'

Ellie stepped off the pavement, crossing the cobbles to her taxi. The gardaí had returned the car to Botany Row, having checked it over. Settling into the Škoda, she switched on the national news. There had been a mass shooting on a university campus in the USA. Kylebeggan had slipped from the headlines.

She waved to Pauline as she passed by. By the time she arrived at Kenneally's Food Emporium, Scully had started on a bowl of soup. He stood and put out his arms as she approached.

'Great to see you, Ellie.' He kissed her on both cheeks. 'Hats off to you, you're one tough cookie.'

Ellie pulled a face. 'I didn't feel that tough on that mountain. I thought my time had come.'

Scully squeezed her shoulder. 'It was close, but you made it.'

'Thanks to the paramedics and the ER team, from what I hear.'

She paused. 'And to you, of course. They told me it was you who spotted my scarf.'

'And they say we men notice nothing.' Scully grinned. He pointed to the table. 'You all right to sit outside? It's just about warm enough. I thought some sunshine would do you good.'

'This is perfect.' Setting her bag on the ground, Ellie moved towards the table and looked about her. 'All very jolly.' A striped awning covered the patio, which was bounded from pedestrians by tubs, planted with what she thought might be hyacinth and dianthus. In hospital, she'd flicked through some gardening magazines with a view to improving the outdoor space at Botany Row.

'Snow's gone.' Scully pointed to the mountain peaks visible over the buildings in Main Street.

'Nearly,' said Ellie, spotting some lingering patches in a corrie. 'How are things with you?'

For a moment she thought he hadn't heard her. She saw something in his eyes and realised he wasn't going to answer. She let the moment pass.

Scully attracted the attention of a waiter, and Ellie ordered a sparkling water along with a crabmeat salad with homemade brown bread.

'Congratulations on your scoop. Your name's all over the media. You're up in lights.'

'Ah, these things tend to be short-lived.' Scully shrugged off the compliment. 'But the attention hasn't hurt.' He lowered his voice. 'All down to my very obliging contact, of course.'

Ellie glanced about. Tables about them were filling up with lunch-time trade.

'He maintained his cover?'

'Just about.' Scully nodded. 'The guy really went out on a limb for me.' He buttered a corner of bread. 'He hopes he's in the clear, especially now that Begley thinks it was one of the Dublin detectives who was the leak. The superintendent's doing his level best to diminish the contributions of the Serious Crime Squad to the investigation.'

'Excuse me, honey . . .'

An elderly man with elaborate camera equipment around his neck approached their table. He smiled at Ellie.

'Can I interrupt you lovebirds to get you to take a photo of me and my wife?'

He pointed to a woman looking at a tourist guide, sitting at a table close by.

'Oh we're not—'

'Let me.' Scully got to his feet.

While he obliged as photographer, Ellie responded to some of her texts. Her regular fares had sent well-wishes.

Back at the table, Scully proceeded to fill her in on happenings in Coleman Street. She drew close as he spoke, breaking off when the waiter returned with her order.

'From what you told the gardaí, Ellie,' he said, 'it sounds like that sick fucker, Ambrose, figured himself for a good Samaritan.'

'That was certainly part of it.' She moved her fork around but didn't eat.

'Listen, Ellie, I get if you don't want to talk about things. You've had a terrible time.'

'No, that's all right.' Ellie shook her head. 'In a way, it helps me get things straight in my head. Ambrose told me he foresaw a life of pain for his victims. He said he was rescuing them from a miserable fate. At the same time, he admitted to enjoying getting revenge on those who'd tormented him in school.'

'Casey had a hard time, and that's a fact.' Scully looked up from his bowl. 'A childhood lasts for ever, but it doesn't turn you into a killer. I'm no psychologist, psychiatrist or whatever – but it sounds like Casey had a case of something called White Knight Syndrome. I've been doing a bit of reading about it. It's also called Hero Syndrome, where someone has a compulsive need to rescue others from their problems.'

'Ambrose was physically and mentally abused by his father too,' Ellie added.

'So are lots of people. It's not an excuse. A killer is a killer.' Scully was firm. He paused a moment, waiting for Ellie to swallow. 'I know Ambrose confessed to killing Imelda and Marina. But he didn't say anything about Isolde, is that right?'

'Not about her murder, no. He said he wouldn't talk about Isolde, out of respect for me.'

'A proper hero.' Scully smiled wryly. 'We know he was on medication. Amitriptyline to control an anxiety disorder. He got blackouts when he was stressed. Memory blocks, periods of amnesia, according to his mother.'

'That poor woman. I feel so sorry for her. Poor Doreen.'

Scully rubbed his chin. 'Ambrose was called out to a suspected break-in at the community centre the night Isolde was killed. The investigation team listened to the recording of the calls between the alarm company and Casey, and by all accounts the guy sounded very agitated. Maybe that agitation triggered something else that night. Maybe he left Mountain View and headed from there to Myrtle Crescent.'

'Maybe.' Ellie placed some crab on a small square of bread. 'You'll be wrapping up on this story now.' It dawned on her that her meetings with Scully were coming to a close.

'There's a few bits and pieces yet to do. The garda press liaison office has been on to me. They want *The Kylebeggan Echo* to cover a statement they're going to issue, and Begley's all over me like a rash, keen to shape the narrative, to minimise credit to the Serious Crime Squad. The crafty bollocks somehow figures himself as the brains behind the breakthrough.'

An elderly man at a table next to them lowered his newspaper and gave Scully a disapproving look. Scully didn't notice.

'There are still a few things that don't sit right with me, Ellie. Remember I'd been saying how, on the face of it, all three women were killed and laid out according to the same ritual. But that there were subtle differences.'

'I remember.' Ellie tilted her head in anticipation of an explanation.

Scully dabbed his mouth. 'There was also the way the victims' clothes were treated,' he continued. 'The clothes Marina had been wearing were folded into a pile on a chest of drawers. Imelda's were folded and placed on a cardboard box.' Scully ran a finger over his scar. 'According to Freddy Hanly, Isolde had been wearing a long nightdress. But that was not at the crime scene. Which leaves us with a question. If Ambrose took the nightdress as a trophy, where is it?'

'I'm assuming detectives checked in Autumn Grove?' said Ellie.

'Several times. No sign.' Scully smacked his lips together. 'In my view, Ellie, while the signatures of all three killings appeared to be the same, they were not identical.' He shrugged. 'I said it way back at the beginning of the investigation, and I've come back to my original conclusion. The Kylebeggan murders were not the work of one person. Ambrose Casey killed Imelda Gannon and Marina Willoughby, just as he admitted to you. But someone else killed Isolde Hanly.'

Scully was interrupted by his phone. His expression darkened. 'I'm on my way—' He jumped from his seat, snatching a glance at Ellie. 'It's the nursing home.' He took out his wallet. 'Not good news.'

'Go, I'll get this,' said Ellie. 'Be with your wife and leave all this for now.'

Ellie had known at the outset that Scully was good. Of course someone else had killed Isolde. Anyone with half a brain could tell that. That afternoon as she lined her Škoda up against the pavement beside the convent walls, she looked across at Mervyn's house. It remained quiet, with no signs of life coming from inside.

48

The back of the house was nicely sheltered from any breeze. Though no *Homes & Gardens* retreat, the place had spruced up nicely. Ellie's purchase of two stripy deckchairs from B&Q had been an extravagance. She only needed one, but two looked more convivial. She draped three strings of solar fairy lights around the breeze-block walls, and repurposed a mosaic-topped plant stand she'd salvaged from a skip to be a side table. It would do for wine and olives on a balmy night.

She stripped the plastic sleeve from the barbecue tray. She'd bought the largest one she could find. She set it on the plant stand. The instructions for lighting seemed straightforward. She lit a match and set it to the coals.

In the kitchen, she snipped the links between the sausages, tipping them into a plastic container. A smoky smell wafted in from outside. She headed up the stairs, making for the chest of drawers. It was there, in a bottom drawer. Behind the underwear, shoved in at the back. Downstairs, she listened for any sounds at the back door. All was quiet. Nothing but a steady dripping of the kitchen tap.

Tongues of flame danced and shimmied above the barbecue mesh. She placed the bundle on the fire. Flames licked the sides of the parcel, as dark plumes of smoke billowed up from the home-made pyre. Wafer-like confetti drifted up into the afternoon air.

Ellie reached for some sausages and popped them on to the smouldering mesh. The aroma of cooking pork began to fill the air. Sinking back into a deckchair, she took a breath, settled herself, closed her eyes and allowed the knot between her shoulders to ease.

Hermano appeared on the wall behind, the promise of food luring him from his hiding place. He hopped down and she picked him up to snuggle him on to her lap, but the cat wouldn't settle. He sniffed the air and studied the barbecue. She set him on the ground.

On her feet, she grabbed a tea towel, picked up the foil tray from the mosaic stand and tipped the contents over. Hermano sniffed, reversed and slowly picked his way around the offering, circling the meal as she poured herself a glass of wine.

Ellie stood over the animal, watching him paw and eat – unfazed that his meal was covered in burnt cotton shavings. And afterwards he set to, preening, grooming his face, his flanks, his paws.

She went back to her chair. When the cat had finished his preening, he jumped on to Ellie's lap and settled in for a snooze. Stroking his back, she also closed her eyes. She must have dozed off as she was startled by the sound of footsteps in the yard next door.

'Hey, Ellie – great to see you home from hospital. Fancy some company?'

It was Mervyn, standing on something and looking over the wall.

Hermano's ears pricked up.

'Now that you're home, maybe we can talk about getting the slates on the roof seen to?' he said. 'I think some birds have found their way in and could be nesting in the crawl space.'

'Mervyn, would you mind doing me a favour?' She didn't bother looking round.

'Of course,' he said, excitedly.

'Don't take this the wrong way. But would you mind clearing off and giving me some space? I've had quite a time of it.'

It wasn't every day you burned the nightclothes of a woman you'd killed. Without a working fireplace, the barbecue had been a crude solution. She closed her eyes once more, stroked the purring cat and cast her mind back to the night of January twenty-first.

The night she'd murdered Isolde Hanly.

49

The incline to Myrtle Crescent was ideal for hill sprints. To the casual passer-by, that's what Ellie was doing on the night of January twenty-first. Dressed in black leggings, a dark hooded running top and running shoes, she'd tucked her ponytail under a black baseball cap.

Unlike other runners, Ellie wasn't wearing a high-vis vest or a high-vis armband. Unlike them, she had no desire to be seen. She'd prepared as well as she could, making several practice trips in recent weeks.

Having been sacked as Isolde's companion, Ellie had kept watch on her friend from a distance. In her running gear, she'd checked on comings and goings at 7 Myrtle Crescent. She'd seen Freddy and Regina moving into Isolde's house, and she'd built up a picture of their movements.

On Tuesdays, Regina left 7 Myrtle Crescent to attend a weekly Weightwatchers' class. She liked smart clothes. Expensive clothes. She liked high shoes. Designer shoes. She liked to look well.

Every Tuesday, approximately six or seven minutes after his wife took off, Freddy would appear at the front door of number 7. He'd crane out, to the left and right, before scurrying to his car.

Ellie had no idea where Freddy Hanly went. But when she got her own transport, she quickly figured it out. One night soon after she'd bought the Škoda, she followed Freddy driving his VW Scirocco. She gave herself the cover of two or more vehicles between them.

Skirting town, she followed Freddy as far as the entrance to a disused forestry track on the edge of Dromgeela Woods and she pulled into a passing place on the other side of the road with line of sight to the track. She killed the engine and the lights.

Freddy emerged from his car and got into another car alongside. A Mini Cooper with an L-plate. Ellie slunk down in her seat, started her car and drove three hundred metres along the road before finding somewhere to turn.

On her way back, she passed the two cars and noted that the windows of the Mini Cooper were all steamed up. She smiled. It confirmed what Isolde had always said. What anyone with an ounce of sense could see. What anyone apart from Regina Hanly suspected. Freddy Hanly had a roving eye.

On the night of January twenty-first, Ellie parked her car in darkness at the playing fields behind the Myrtle Crescent houses. The hurlers had finished training for the night. The floodlights were switched off and Kylebeggan Gaels GAA clubhouse lay in darkness.

She made her way on to the playing fields by easing herself through a gap in a hedge. An owl hooted somewhere in the distance. She was careful of her footing as she picked her way across the hurl-pocked field towards the lights at the back of Myrtle Crescent.

She reached the stone wall that provided the boundary between the playing fields and the tradesmen's lane at the rear of the crescent. Clearing the wall, she stopped to adjust her backpack. It had loosened as she'd pushed herself through the hedge.

Following the unlit lane downhill, she came out on to the street just below the crescent of houses. Joining the path, she began to sprint up and down. Down and up. She carried on until the familiar VW Scirocco passed her by, just as she'd anticipated. When Freddy's tail-lights disappeared, she stopped to catch her breath. Her chest felt tight.

It wasn't Weightwatchers' night, as she'd planned. It was better. Something unexpected had happened and a better opportunity had presented itself. Monitoring the house the previous evening, Ellie watched as Freddy waved his wife off.

'*Bon voyage*, babes,' he called from the steps.

Regina was humping a sizeable suitcase into the boot of a waiting taxi.

'Missing you already,' he called out.

Regina turned to blow him a kiss before getting into the taxi. She was holding on to a floppy hat and multi-coloured straw bag. It was close to perfect. Ellie would have even more time, should complications arise.

On the night of January twenty-first, using housekeys she'd held on to, Ellie opened the door to 7 Myrtle Crescent for the first time since she'd left more than a year earlier.

Inside, she shut the door behind her. She stood, listening for the grandfather clock in the hallway. Nothing. No one had even bothered to wind it. She stood listening to the house settle itself in the darkness. Could she really go through with this?

She'd done things in the past that ordinary people would shrink away from. Ordinary people with ordinary lives and ordinary childhoods. Unlike the childhoods she and Johnny had. This last while, Ellie realised it was about that. About her childhood, about promises she'd made, about promises she didn't keep.

Her eyes adjusted to the gloom. The lamps on the sideboard

were unlit, the only light in the hall was coming from the kitchen beyond. A flower vase sat on the sideboard, empty. There was no smell of the lavender furniture polish Isolde liked.

She set a tentative foot on the stairs, bracing for the creak of the bottom step. Creak it did. With a gloved hand on the banister, she treaded softly to the upstairs landing, wrinkling her nose at the sickly smell of cologne lingering in the stairwell. Dust marks outlined spaces along the stairwell wall where work by Irish artists had hung.

Ellie paused outside Isolde's room. Taking a breath, she turned the handle. From the doorway, surveying the husk of the woman she once knew, a conversation they'd once had in this room played back in her head. The words were as clear to her now as they'd been that day.

Isolde had been cupping a mug of chicken soup that Ellie had made.

'I've had a good life, you know. I've been blessed.'

'You're not for the knacker's yard quite yet,' Ellie joked.

'I feel something in my water.'

'Antibiotics will sort that.' She'd been suffering repeated kidney infections.

'I'm serious.' Isolde pulled a face. 'I want to go out with a bang. Something like a heart attack.' She sipped from the mug. 'Or knocked over by a bus.'

'That's not very likely, is it?' Ellie was quick. Isolde hated public transport.

'But I don't want to die by inches. "Fastened to a dying animal" as Yeats would have it. If that day comes, I want you to come on one last trip with me, Ellie. To Switzerland.'

Ellie shook her head. 'That's not legal.'

Isolde managed a knowing smile. 'Since when did *legal* bother you, my dear?'

'Still . . .' Ellie shrugged.

'All right then.' Isolde sat up straight. 'This is what you do. You give me sleeping pills and put a pillow over my head.'

Ellie said nothing.

'Don't look at me like that, Ellie. I'm serious. Those are my wishes. And while I'm at it, I want to be laid out in my wedding gown. In the same dress that I married Clement Hanly in. I want it like the day I got married. According to the rhyme, "Something old, something new, something borrowed, something blue."' Her head turned to the silver frame on the chest of drawers. 'I miss that man. God was cruel to take him from me. Not that I really believe in God, as you know.'

'When the day comes, I'll make sure the undertaker gets your instructions,' Ellie humoured her.

Isolde went back to her soup. 'Now, I'll tell you where everything is. Don't forget to bury me with my wedding ring. I don't care how they get it on.' She grimaced, looking at her swollen hands. 'I want to be buried with that ring. Don't forget.'

'I won't forget.'

Isolde was staring into her mug as if she'd seen something she didn't recognise. Her eyes darted to Ellie.

'You won't let me go into a home, will you?' Her voice trembled. 'You know I couldn't bear that, don't you?'

'I'll do what I can to honour your wishes,' Ellie assured her. 'But I'm not family, as you well know.'

'I love you like a daughter, Ellie. You know that, don't you?'

'I do,' said Ellie gently.

'Clement Hanly was a fine man. As was his brother, Dominic, if easily led. Small wonder that Freddy turned out just like him.' Isolde never voiced disquiet about Regina directly.

She locked Ellie with a stare. 'Promise me, when the time

comes, you won't let me die an undignified death. That you won't let it all drag out. I want you to put a pillow over my head. I don't want to linger on for weeks and months. I don't want to suffer. Promise me that. And if you do, I won't bring it up again – as long as you just promise me.'

'I promise you I won't let you suffer,' Ellie said. 'Now hurry and finish your soup. Ursula is coming in from next door to see your new wallpaper, remember?'

It puzzled Ellie why Regina had not put Isolde into a care home after she'd been fired. She hadn't figured Regina as the caring kind. And then it dawned on her. She was pocketing a carer's allowance and Isolde's pension.

On the night of January twenty-first, as Ellie stood looking down at the pathetic creature in the bed, at the uncombed hair, the skeletal frame, Ellie knew that what she was about to do was humane.

She'd brought what was needed in the backpack. Stockings. Something new. A book of Keats' poetry. It was borrowed from the library. Flowers. Blue – Isolde's favourite. Isolde's gown was something old. It was under the bed in a suitcase, just as Isolde had told her, months before. Freddy would find Isolde's body on his return from his assignation with his young friend.

When it was all over, Ellie was distraught. She threw up in the fields behind the house. But as time went by she had to admit she also felt relief. She had not kept her promise to her mother. She had not kept the family together. She had not prevented what had happened to baby Owen. But she had kept her promise to her dearest friend, Isolde Hanly.

After Isolde's funeral, Ellie found an uneasy peace. But when news came of a young woman found in similar circumstances, she was appalled. And later, when she learned what had happened to

Marina Willoughby, the woman who'd taken a ride home in her taxi, Ellie was horrified. Why was someone killing brides-to-be? Posing their bodies in the same way that Ellie had laid out Isolde?

Meeting Scully was a stroke of luck. With his source inside the gardaí, she'd been able to keep abreast of the investigation while following up on suspicions of her own. In the beginning, she'd gone along with the notion that the killer was Joseph Liston. Then, she'd suspected the grooms-to-be. She'd had her doubts about Mervyn too. But her strongest suspicions of all she'd reserved for Jen Healy. Ellie had even resorted to her own surveillance, impatient for Scully to follow up. Passing Blooming Vales at every opportunity, she'd noted the frequent presence of broadcasting vans nearby. Ellie hadn't been the only one with an interest in the bridesmaid.

Her drive-by surveillance yielded nothing. However, in her haste to get to the Sally Willow the day of her abduction, she'd taken a shortcut through the town at Brannock Square, witnessing something strange. She'd spotted a woman handing over a flower arrangement to another woman at the door of Coyle & Coyle Solicitors.

As the woman delivering the flowers had walked down the steps towards the pavement, a man had emerged from the doorway, calling out. Both figures chatted briefly on the pavement. Jen Healy and the smartly suited man. From a distance, Ellie had found the exchange curious. Jen had touched the man on the elbow, and as she'd turned to go, the man had patted her on the hip. Jen had looked over her shoulder with something of a coquettish glance before she sashayed off.

Pointing a key at a nearby car, the man got in and pulled out into the queue of traffic. Ellie had seen the distinctive shape of not one but two children's car seats in the rear of his car.

50

Lou had taken Maude and Scarlett swimming. The council had installed diving boards on Lough Avulla for the summer. It was the big news story on the front page of this week's paper, and was the first story Scully had written for *The Kylebeggan Echo* in weeks. It was also his first story that hadn't been about the Kylebeggan murders.

'I have some news for you,' he said to Jill. 'Interesting news, in fact. I've been offered three jobs, no less. Imagine that.'

The foreign news crews had departed. The national media had gone back to Dublin, and the southern editor for RTÉ had moved on to a story about a fishing crew that had disappeared off the south-west coast.

The roads were free of broadcasting vans, and the scrum had cleared from outside Coleman Street garda station. Scully's coverage of the investigation had not gone unnoticed. He'd heard on the grapevine that RTÉ had been impressed. However, the offer that came in was from a British broadcaster. They'd seen his television appearances and heard his reports on Skellig FM. They wanted to offer him a contract. A contract that would see him based in the United Kingdom.

Another offer had come in from a fledgling independent TV company based in Dublin. They offered Scully a contract as crime correspondent. They were enthusiastic about him joining their team.

The third offer came from an unlikely quarter. He was offered the job of editor of *The Kylebeggan Echo*. Gerry Bradshaw had finally had enough. This offer came with the blessing of the board, along with Mayor Halligan and Superintendent Sean Begley. Of course, it wasn't as lucrative as either of the other two jobs.

Halligan had swung by his desk the day before. 'A great opportunity, Scully,' he said, spittle settling in a corner of his mouth.

'You think?' They didn't know about his other offers.

'It mightn't come around again.'

'Better have me inside the tent pissing out than outside the tent pissing in, is that it?'

'I wouldn't go putting it like that. I have the welfare of the town at heart.'

Superintendent Sean Begley had swung by too. 'Taking the job?' he asked.

Scully shrugged.

'I'm pretty sure you had one of those Dublin detectives feeding you on the case.'

Scully had smiled, neither confirming nor denying his suspicions.

Tall Dark had taken himself off on holiday. He'd always wanted to go to Nashville. Maybe the sergeant wouldn't need to look for love at Lisdoonvarna matchmaking festival this year.

'We got our man with solid police work,' Begley had said. 'All things considered, you didn't make a bad fist of covering things.' He twiddled with a ring on his wedding finger. 'I'm very sorry about your wife, Scully.'

'You'll know my decision soon,' he had said.

303

As he sat on the grass in the cemetery, swatting away the flies, he talked through the pros and cons of his job offers with his wife. He arched his head back, allowing the June sun to warm his skin.

'Don't you worry about a thing, Jill. Me and the girls will be fine. We're all going to be just fine.'

51

'I'm so sorry for everything I put you through, my dear.'

Ellie had put Doreen's walking frame in the boot and was getting in behind the wheel.

'What happened was none of your fault, Doreen. I don't blame you in the slightest.'

'You've a heart of gold, Ellie. I was thrilled to get your phone call. Not everyone's been so kind. But it is all my fault. His upbringing. I should have left his father. That man was cruel to him. No matter how hard he tried to please, he'd never give him any credit. Any time my boy did anything, Big Jack would ask him whose idea it was, who was he copying now. In his eyes, Ambrose could do no right.'

Ellie headed out of Autumn Grove, passing the newly opened Sally Willow garden centre. It felt longer than six weeks since her abduction. It had been five weeks since Ambrose's funeral.

'He was a good son to me, Ellie. Until towards the end.'

Doreen wrung her hands. Her skin had the look of an age-blown apple and her usually blue-grey hair had a couple of centimetres of white at the roots.

'I should have noticed, Ellie. I knew things were going wrong. He'd started to act very strangely. Things were going missing. My pop socks were disappearing. And all these parcels were coming to the house. I'd never checked up on him before but I was worried. I remember one night, we were watching one of those news conferences and Superintendent Begley said they were following a definite line of enquiry, and Detective Mullins contradicted him, saying all lines of enquiry were open. I clocked Ambrose smirking at that and I asked him why. He didn't answer, but when he made my tea, he left the teabag in and when he scooped it out to put it on the saucer, he dropped it on my hand. He said it was an accident even though we both knew it wasn't.'

The sun was high in the sky when they pulled into Limekiln Road, pulling up at Klassy Kuts. Doreen turned to Ellie. 'You've been very kind to me, my dear. But there's no need any more. Brendan, the warden, can always drop me to the hairdresser. He's already offered to drive me to the bingo at the day centre, and to my medical appointments.'

'I'd like to continue to bring you to Klassy Kuts, Doreen. If that suits.'

Doreen was still smiling when she shuffled through the jingling door.

Ellie took her time in her journey out of the valley. With the windows down, she breathed deeply as the scent of wildflowers and rain-washed leaves blew in. She heard the pew and trill of a wood warbler somewhere overhead. Spring had been exceptionally late. The odd patch of bluebells here and there clung on to dying heads. Most had lost their flowers.

Climbing up the slopes to the foothills of the Black Pins were swathes of rhododendron in full purple bloom. Dense thickets of richly coloured flowers covered brackish ground between tall, ancient oaks. Conservationists were warning of native species being strangled by the shrub. How could the most insidious of nature's pests be so beautiful, Ellie wondered.

Bluebell Lodge had taken down the *Vacancies* sign since she last passed by. The cycle bay at the front of Clashbeg Rectory was packed with bikes in slots. With long June evenings stretching out against the sky, Ellie too had started cycling.

She'd bought a second-hand tourer and cycled on the backroads out towards Dunseally Castle. She'd joined a hill-walking club. She could still travel, maybe not to fancy, expensive hotels or on luxury cruises, but there was much to see in Kerry. She'd started to think about a hostelling trek, in the Pyrenees maybe, or the Picos de Europa, when Johnny got out of prison.

Today, there was a bounce in her step as she sailed past the row of prison visitors' tables to where Johnny waited, his eyes crinkling with humour.

'Well, look at you, all windswept and interesting. Who's been getting fit then?'

'I'm trying to get out a bit more.'

'So I see. Things settling down at last in Kylebeggan?' His tone sobered.

'The tourist trade is slowly creeping back, if that's what you mean.'

'You're busy with the taxi, I suppose?'

'It's ticking along. I have some more runs with school kids too.'

'My my, you're turning into a regular Mary Poppins.' He grinned.

'I hardly think so.' Ellie made a face. 'It's more like a favour really, helping someone out.'

Johnny cocked his head. 'Cormac Scully?'

'That's right. His wife passed away and I help out with lifts for the girls when needed.'

'Poor guy. He did a reasonable job of covering things, considering.'

'Considering what?'

'I've heard enough from lads in here to know how hard it must be to get any bad news out.'

'You heard right. The place is full of secrets.' Ellie nodded. 'But enough about that for now. I've got some news. Good news.'

Johnny rubbed his hands together in exaggerated glee.

'I've got the name of a good solicitor. She's only starting out but already she has a reputation for being dogged, thorough and frankly doing whatever it takes for her clients. I've been talking to her about you. Her name is Brona Sullivan.'

Ellie went through the main points of discussion she'd had with Brona. Johnny followed every word, hardly blinking. He raised his chin to look up at a high window. A bird had landed on the bars outside.

'Things are looking up,' he said when she stood to leave.

'Keep the faith,' said Ellie, pushing back her chair.

'One more thing, before you go.'

Ellie stopped.

'Kylebeggan's full of secrets, like you said.'

'I did.'

He studied her. 'You haven't been keeping any from me, have you, Ellie? These past few months I always felt you were?'

She thought a moment. All the other visitors had left the room. The prison guard was waiting.

'You gave me a piece of advice once, Johnny. A good few years ago. It's stayed with me, and now I'm going to offer it back to you.'

'Please do.'

Johnny was amused.

'Never ask a question unless you're very sure you want the answer,' Ellie said.

'Good advice.' Johnny nodded sagely.

Ellie smiled.

'I thought so too,' she said.

Acknowledgements

Thank you, reader, for picking up my book. Without you the voices in my head would never make their way onto paper and the only audience for my stories would be the cat – and she's more interested in videos of birds.

Kerry is home to many of Ireland's finest writers. Though not a native of the 'kingdom', I have been fortunate to holiday there and drew on the inspirational landscape and its people as a setting for this thriller. I trust the fictional goings-on in the *even more* fictional town of Kylebeggan will prove an engaging read.

Heartfelt thanks to my agent Jo Bell for her encouragement, writer therapy sessions, and sunny guidance. Thanks also to the wider creative team at Bell Lomax Moreton.

Thank you to my editor, Krystyna Green, for helping me to shape this novel to be the best it could be. Thank you to The Brewster Project for creating a stand-out cover. Thanks to Rebecca Sheppard and to Mari Roberts (who knew the forensic art of copy-editing could stretch to the finer points of dressing and undressing dead bodies?) and to all at Little, Brown.

Thank you to the hard-working publicity team of Elaine Egan, Siobhan Tierney and all at Hachette Ireland, along with Mark Walsh at Plunkett PR.

Half-sleuth, half-seanchaí, I love creating stories. However, a writer cannot live on words alone, and the support of my lovely friends and family means everything to me. Much gratitude to my early readers, Sarah O'Donoghue and Joanna O'Donoghue. Thanks also to my sons, Jamie and Alasdair – always guaranteed to make me laugh.

I very much appreciate the support I've received from other writers, be that a review, advice or shout-outs on social media. Particular thanks to the crime-writing community. We all need a tribe.

Thanks to the libraries that stock my books, to the bloggers and to the festival organisers, and to all the booksellers who have helped to keep us sane throughout the long months of the Covid-19 pandemic. Frontline workers of the book world, one and all!

A big, squeezy hug to all those who support my writing on social media, and to those who post reviews on Goodreads, Amazon, Netgalley and other book reviewing sites.

And finally, thanks to Neil as always – purveyor of the finest breakfasts known to humankind. First reader, first editor, first responder. Always my first.